Praise for *I Could Live Here Forever*

"Aching and tender . . . Halperin's radiant second novel walks the fine line between the longing for couplehood and the torture of codependency. . . . Halperin writes from a millennial point of view, probing themes of social anxiety and intense trepidation about the future. But Halperin's take on love sets her apart: As misguided as Leah's feelings for Charlie may seem, they are pure and hopeful—about as untainted by cynicism as it is possible to be."

—Leigh Haber, *The New York Times Book Review*

"A compelling new version of the addiction novel . . . *I Could Live Here Forever* brings readers deep into the world of addicts and those who love them. . . . Like addiction, and codependence, and internalized misogyny, *I Could Live Here Forever* is a wrenching story that's been lived and told before. Halperin does us a service by sharing her version of it, entertaining, warning, and educating us with her all-too-accurate novel."   —Meredith Maran, *The Washington Post*

"This novel is so good and follows closely on the heels of Hanna Halperin's prior novel (which I also loved), *Something Wild*. There's just something about Halperin's writing style and how she captures difficult, troubled characters."   —Zibby Owens, *Good Morning America*

"Somewhere between *Fatal Attraction* and what narrator Leah Kempler calls 'some beautiful love story' sits *I Could Live Here Forever*, Hanna Halperin's smoldering, troubling, and indelible second novel, following *Something Wild*. Although fraught love is a commonplace subject in fiction, Halperin's sophomore effort has staked out fresh territory with a relationship that feels sui generis."

—*Shelf Awareness* (starred review)

"*I Could Live Here Forever* fearlessly delves into powerlessness in the face of addiction. . . . Halperin keenly captures the obsessive nature of [Leah and Charlie's] relationship. . . . Halperin skillfully builds a story that carries us along on the couple's journey, creating very human characters that we come to care about either despite or because of their flaws, and she keeps us turning pages to see how the story will unfold. You will find yourself wondering, will love win out, or the unnerving sense of foreboding prove true?"   —*The Martha's Vineyard Times*

"I was intensely moved by *I Could Live Here Forever*—I read it in one day and finished sobbing, feeling that I and the author and her beautifully rendered characters had all been through something profound together. Leah's relationship with Charlie is drawn with unsparing, unpretty candor that is constantly undercut by moments of dazzling tenderness—this book acts as a kind of vivid, devastating answer to the often heard question 'How could you stay with a person like that?' Halperin's desire and ability to so deeply consider the lives in her book became as affecting to me as the story itself, creating the sort of author-reader intimacy rarely found but always prized. I will remember and reread this gorgeous, emotionally intelligent, truly beautiful book often."   —Megan Nolan, author of *Acts of Desperation*

"A superb, uncynical novel about the innocence of unsustainable love—a wonderfully haunting and memorable book."
      —Joan Silber, award-winning author of *Secrets of Happiness*

"A gripping novel about a couple's troubled love story."   —*Cup of Jo*

"Brutal, beautiful, unputdownable, *I Could Live Here Forever* is a dark romance that reads almost like a thriller and captures the emotional complexity of life in the twenty-first century. I loved it."
      —Joanna Rakoff, bestselling author of
      My Salinger Year and *A Fortunate Age*

"I was immediately gripped by Hanna Halperin's stunning novel *I Could Live Here Forever*. With a frank assuredness reminiscent of Sally Rooney and Emma Cline, Halperin balances a close lens over both the anxiety and hopefulness of the millennial viewpoint, bringing so much that has come to define the generation—the opioid crisis, economic and occupational precarity, the uncanny intensity of intimacy expressed on a smartphone—into stark relief. I felt so much heartbreak and fear and frustration for Leah and Charlie, whose love affair was as irresistible to me as it seemed to the characters themselves. This is a book that will stay with readers and make them feel alive."

—Liv Stratman, author of *Cheat Day*

"With an attention to intimate detail that is both unflinching and compassionate, Hanna Halperin conjures full, complex characters who challenged my understanding of the relationship between love and harm. I devoured this in a day."

—Naomi Krupitsky, *New York Times* bestselling author of *The Family*

"A rich, deep, star-crossed love story both heartbreaking and beautiful to read." —*Booklist*

"A stark, beautiful novel about the risk and intoxication of obsessive love and a young woman's need to be needed. Hanna Halperin makes you feel her heroine's hunger in every action and hesitation. Even as I feared for Leah, Halperin's writing made it impossible to look away. You won't be able to put this book down."

—Alyssa Songsiridej, author of *Little Rabbit*

"Staggering . . . The characters are real and vulnerable. . . . Many readers will feel they can identify with this portrait of self-discovery, messy emotions, and challenging relationships. Fans of Halperin's first novel will also enjoy this offering." —*Library Journal*

"*I Could Live Here Forever* is a gripping novel about the ways we try to be the best versions of ourselves and pull each other back from collapse. With careful prose, lush descriptions, and skilled character insight, Hanna Halperin gives readers a stunning story that changes the way we see the people around us."

—Ethan Joella, author of *A Little Hope*

"*I Could Live Here Forever*, Halperin's second book (after *Something Wild*) is about a woman's relationship with an addict, fraught with compassion and codependence, and her enduring search for love."

—*PureWow*

"While Leah's self-destructive relationship with Charlie is the dark heart of the narrative, it is Leah's gradual self-discovery of her own worth that breathes like a fresh new life. This, in the end, is a relationship well worth reading about." —*New York Journal of Books*

"Halperin humanizes the tragedy of drug addiction through Charlie, who is sweet and kind and loving and also irreparably damaged. Wistful, honest, and heartbreaking." —*Kirkus Reviews*

"A doomed love affair frames this perceptive sophomore outing from Halperin. . . . The 'buzzing electric hum' between the couple feels vital, as does the pull of exasperating and enchanting Charlie on Leah. By the end, even the most grizzled reader might turn into a hopeless romantic." —*Publishers Weekly*

PENGUIN BOOKS

I COULD LIVE HERE FOREVER

Hanna Halperin is the author of the novel *Something Wild*, a finalist for the National Jewish Book Award for Debut Fiction, winner of the Edward Lewis Wallant Award, and longlisted for the VCU Cabell First Novelist Award. Her stories have been published in the *Kenyon Review*, *n+1*, *New Ohio Review*, and *Joyland*. She has taught fiction workshops at GrubStreet in Boston and worked as a domestic violence counselor.

Penguin Readers Guide available online at penguinrandomhouse.com

ALSO BY HANNA HALPERIN

Something Wild

I Could Live Here Forever

HANNA HALPERIN

Penguin Books

PENGUIN BOOKS
An imprint of Penguin Random House LLC
penguinrandomhouse.com

First published in the United States of America by Viking,
an imprint of Penguin Random House LLC, 2023
Published in Penguin Books 2024

Grateful acknowledgment is made for permission to reprint lyrics from "Perfect Day."
Words and music by Lou Reed. Copyright © 1972 Oakfield Avenue Music Ltd.
Copyright renewed. All rights administered by Sony Music Publishing (US) LLC,
424 Church Street, Suite 1200, Nashville, TN 37219. International copyright
secured. All rights reserved. Reprinted by permission of Hal Leonard LLC.

ISBN 9780593492093 (paperback)

THE LIBRARY OF CONGRESS HAS CATALOGED THE HARDCOVER EDITION AS FOLLOWS:
Names: Halperin, Hanna, author.
Title: I could live here forever : a novel / Hanna Halperin.
Description: New York : Viking, [2023]
Identifiers: LCCN 2022017093 (print) | LCCN 2022017094 (ebook) |
    ISBN 9780593492079 (hardcover) | ISBN 9780593492086 (ebook)
Subjects: LCGFT: Novels.
Classification: LCC PS3608.A54865 I52 2023 (print) | LCC PS3608.A54865 (ebook) |
    DDC 813/.6—dc23/eng/20220415
LC record available at https://lccn.loc.gov/2022017093
LC ebook record available at https://lccn.loc.gov/2022017094

Printed in the United States of America
1st Printing

BOOK DESIGN BY LUCIA BERNARD

For G, with love

Just a perfect day
You made me forget myself
I thought I was someone else
Someone good

"Perfect Day"
Lou Reed

I Could Live

Here Forever

1.

CHARLIE WAS SOFT-SPOKEN, BUT WHEN HE SANG, HE COULD transform his voice to sound like anyone—Tom Waits, Frank Sinatra, David Bowie. The first time I heard him sing, I couldn't believe that something so loud and powerful was coming from him. We met in Madison, Wisconsin, while I was getting my MFA in fiction writing. I was twenty-five years old. Charlie was thirty-one. He had studied creative writing, too, as an undergrad, but when I met him he was working in construction. He was tall and boyish-looking. He had the most beautiful face I'd ever seen.

We met waiting on the same checkout line at the grocery store. I noticed him before he noticed me. As soon as we looked at each other, it seemed obvious what was going to happen. First he complimented my cereal choice—Raisin Bran—and then he asked if I'd ever tried Raisin Bran Crunch. I shook my head no. I could feel how insanely I was blushing, and I was mortified at how easily I gave myself away.

He smiled a little and held up the purple-and-blue box in his basket.

I pretended not to notice the way the woman behind the register was smirking at us, like she was watching the opening scene of a romantic comedy. I agreed to meet him the next night. Our first date was in mid-October at a pub called the Weary Traveler.

I got there first. The pub was warm and dimly lit, and pretty full for a Thursday night. It was all dark wood inside, except for the tin ceiling, copper and embossed. The walls were covered with weird art, simple paintings of random people, and there were built-in shelves lined with old books and board games.

The waitress sat me at a table facing the door. When he walked in, he was wearing a T-shirt and no coat even though it was freezing outside. His hands were stuffed inside his pockets, his shoulders hunched, like he was cold. When he spotted me, he looked surprised to see me sitting there waiting for him. He raised his eyebrows and lifted one hand from his pocket to wave.

I got shy when I saw him. He was so much better-looking than me. It seemed uneven. I was wearing jeans and my favorite black sweater, my hair down.

"Sorry I'm late," he said, sliding into the seat across from me. "I see you got started." He nodded to my rum and Coke.

"I hope that's okay." I'd already drunk half of it.

"Of course. I should have texted saying I was running behind. I ended up cooking dinner for my mom, and the traffic coming from the other side of town was worse than I expected."

"That's nice of you," I said. "That you cooked dinner for your mom."

"I like to do it when I have the time. Do you cook?"

"Not really."

"I didn't really start till a few years ago. Nothing too fancy. I make a pretty decent quesadilla." He smiled then, and his whole face opened up—bright and sweet. His smile made him look like a kid.

I don't remember much of what we talked about that night, except that he made me laugh a lot, and I could tell he was observant.

He spent a long time picking out a certain IPA on the menu but once it arrived he barely touched it. I worried this meant he wasn't having a good time, but he didn't seem in a rush, and he wasn't doing the thing that some people did—glancing around to see who else might walk in. He didn't pull out his phone once.

At some point during the evening he told me that his father had left his mother before he was born, but when Charlie was a teenager, he'd looked his father up on the internet and confronted him at his place of work—a pharmacy in Janesville, Wisconsin. When his father realized who Charlie was, Charlie leaned over the pharmacy counter and said, "Don't worry, Dad, I'm not here to kill you." Then he'd clapped his father on the shoulder and walked out. He reached over and clapped my shoulder, to show me how he'd done it. It was the first time he touched me. I could feel where his hand had just been, reverberating on my shoulder, even after he'd pulled it away.

"Wow," I said. "What was it like to see him?"

"One of his ears was really fucked up. It was kind of shriveled and pinched and there was this piece of dead skin growing out of it. I might have stayed longer but I couldn't stand looking at his ear. Do you think that's weird?" he asked me. "That what I remember most is his ear?"

"I don't think it's weird," I said. "I feel like it's usually those small things that you're not expecting that hit you the hardest."

He nodded vehemently. "That's exactly it. The details."

Then I told him that I hadn't seen my mom since I was thirteen.

He sat back in his seat and looked at me, as if seeing me for the first time. "Is that why you write?"

It was startling, to be looked at like that. I felt like I could tell him anything, but I held back. I was already scared that I might never see him again. Nobody had ever asked me that question.

I shrugged. "I'm sure it has something to do with it."

He didn't try to kiss me at the end of the night, and at the time I took that to mean he didn't like me. But he called me the next day. When I saw his name on my phone, I panicked and almost didn't answer. I figured it must be an accident.

"I know I'm supposed to make you wait three days," he said when I picked up, and the softness of his voice, his slightly monotone rasp, was so sexy to me that I could feel my whole body warm, as if a switch had been turned on. "So that you'll think I'm busy," he continued, "and maybe not that into you. But I'm more straightforward than that."

"Oh," I said. "Well, thanks."

"Are you free tonight?"

I told him I was busy—which was a lie—but free the night after.

"Great," he said. "So what do you have going on? Another date?"

"No. I'm hanging out with my friends."

"Must be nice, having friends to hang out with."

I couldn't tell if he was joking, but I laughed.

"On Saturday can I pick you up at eight?"

"Sure," I said.

I was confused. I didn't know things could be so easy. I didn't know why he liked me. I also couldn't fathom why he thought I had dates lined up. I hung up the phone and masturbated.

When he called back, not even an hour later, I was still lying on my bed thinking about him.

"Hi," I said.

"I started to write you a text but it was getting really long, so I thought it would be better to call."

I grew tense. "Okay."

"I was wondering if you'd be up for hanging out at my place tomorrow." He paused. "I know it's a weird thing to ask since we just met, and I didn't want you to think I was creepily trying to lure you over or anything. The thing is, I'm a little tight on money at the moment and I don't love spending ten dollars on a beer at a bar when it's pretty much the same amount to have a six-pack at home, you know? But, all of that to say, if you don't feel comfortable, I totally understand, given that we've only known each other for, like, twenty-four hours."

I sat up in bed. "Right. That's fine. I feel comfortable."

"How about I give you my address? So you can text it to your friends or look it up, just so you know I am who I say I am."

He told me his address and I wrote it down on the inside cover of a book.

"My last name is Nelson, by the way."

"Mine is Kempler," I told him. "Are you going to look me up, too?"

"Should I?" he asked, and I could hear him smiling. "If I google you, am I going to find your mug shot or something?"

I laughed. "No."

"Leah Kempler," he said thoughtfully, as if testing out the sound of my name.

"Yeah?"

"Your voice is cute on the phone."

I was sweating, even though I was alone in the room. "So is yours."

The next night, I was ready and waiting for him by seven-thirty. He didn't show up at eight like he said, but he texted saying he was running late. When he finally did call to say he was outside, it was after nine. I glanced at myself once more in the mirror. I was wearing my good jeans and another sweater—navy, ribbed, with a mock turtleneck. This time my hair was up, for some variation. When I got into his car, it reeked of cigarettes. After thinking about him a lot for the past two days, I had forgotten what he looked like. Like studying something up close for too long, my memory of him had become blurry. But, sliding into the passenger seat, I was stunned all over again. He was beautiful. A mix between Johnny Depp and Jake Gyllenhaal. This time he was wearing a multi-colored pullover fleece, like a dad.

"Hello," I said.

"How's it going?" His voice was even softer and less animated than it had been on the phone. Neither one of us knew what to say after that, and we made small talk; the kind that made me feel uninteresting. We didn't laugh or seem to have anything in common this time. The drive was longer than I expected it to be, and at some point I realized that we were leaving the city and driving into the suburbs. When we pulled up to a large, split-level house with stone siding, a two-car garage attached, and a nice lawn out front, I was confused. "You live here?"

He nodded.

"By yourself?"

"I live with my mom and stepdad."

I let the information settle. When he had invited me over, I'd assumed he lived alone. And he was pretty old.

"They're asleep," he said softly, when he led me inside. "We can go to the den."

All the lights were off, but I could see that the house was very neat. There was no clutter. It smelled clean, too—like fresh laundry and lemon soap. The state of the house was in such opposition to the inside of Charlie's car—with the stench of cigarettes, the layer of trash and empty soda cans and paper bags on the floor—that it was hard to connect the two spaces to the same person.

I followed him through a hallway and down three carpeted steps to a separate wing. The room he brought me to, the den, was brown—brown carpeting, brown wallpaper, brown, lumpy furniture. There was a flat-screen TV and video game consoles sprawled in front of it. On the far side of the room was a mini-fridge and a sink and a table with a few stools. "Make yourself at home," Charlie said. "Do you want soda or something? Water? To be honest, I don't really drink that much."

It occurred to me then to be nervous. I hadn't been, up until that moment. The room itself was creepy, and I didn't know where I was. Nobody knew where I was. I hadn't texted Charlie's address to my friends like he'd suggested. I hadn't wanted anyone to tell me not to go.

The only thing that made me feel slightly comforted was that I could feel the presence of the sleeping parents in some other part of the house.

I considered asking Charlie to drive me home, but I felt bad doing that. The drive had been a good thirty-five minutes. I figured the best thing to do was stay for a little while and then ask to be taken home in an hour or two. "I'll have some water." I smiled politely. "Thanks."

He brought a glass of water and a can of A&W root beer from the fridge back to the couch where I had sat down.

"Want to watch something?" he asked.

"Okay."

He turned on the TV. Underneath my fear, I was disappointed. This all seemed boring. Especially after the date we'd had two nights before. Laughing, sharing stories. And the way he'd called me the next day; how self-assured he'd sounded on the phone. I didn't want him to be just some guy who lived with his parents who invited me over to watch TV. I wondered, sadly, if we were two losers on a bad date. He was too handsome to be a loser, though.

"You're really quiet tonight," he said, turning to me.

"I guess I'm nervous."

"Why are you nervous?" He looked offended, or maybe, I thought, he was disappointed by me. My quietness. I wasn't sure how things had become so strange so quickly between us.

"I don't know," I admitted. "It's just the beginning of getting to know each other, so . . ."

He seemed to consider this. "Sometimes I don't always know how to, like . . ." He paused. "I get worried about overstepping my bounds."

"What do you mean?"

"Well, on our first date I really wanted to kiss you."

"You did?"

"Of course."

"Well." I shrugged. "You should have."

When I looked at him, a softness had come back into his eyes. He wasn't disappointed with me, I realized; he was nervous, too.

"I'm going to try something."

He kissed me then, and as soon as we were touching, I wasn't scared anymore. I was no longer shy. We pulled each other closer. His hair and his clothes smelled like cigarettes. When he pulled off his fleece his hair stood straight up with static and I smoothed it down. Underneath he had on a plain white T-shirt, like the one he'd been wearing on our first date. He was so thin I could feel each of his ribs. He kissed softly, almost a little sleepily, like he wasn't in a hurry. His lips were soft, and he tasted fresh and sour at the same time—like tobacco and toothpaste and coffee and kind of cool, like air. I'd never felt that way kissing anyone before. I desperately didn't want it to end.

When I took my sweater off he pulled back for a moment and looked at me, his eyes moving from my eyes, down to my chest and hips. He smiled a little. "I thought there was something interesting going on underneath those sweaters of yours."

I'd never felt so gorgeous in my life.

I woke up the next morning on the couch, which Charlie had pulled out into a sofa bed, him curled around me. We hadn't had sex. We'd gotten naked and kissed. Touched each other a decent amount. Talked for a long time, and then fallen asleep together, in the same position we were waking up in now. Later in life, I'd come to think of this as not so different than fucking, but at the time, our restraint moved me. It was the kind of night you had with someone you liked—someone you wanted to see again.

When I opened my eyes, the room looked less menacing. There were sliding doors looking out onto a perfectly mowed backyard with lawn furniture. Sunlight poured into the room. Charlie's arm, which had been crushed under my body for hours now, was olive-toned, almost gold, the hair on his skin fine and black. I turned over so I was facing him. He nestled his head against my breasts, tightening his arms around me. "I could live here forever," he said, his voice morning-soft.

His words touched me somewhere deep and tender—almost painful—but all I said was, "I should get back soon. I'm meeting a friend at ten."

For several moments he didn't respond. Then he looked up and met my gaze. His eyes were pale blue and filled with light, his pupils massive. His eyelashes were thick and dark and longer than mine.

I brushed the back of my hand over his cheek and jaw. His face was rough with stubble that had been just a faint shadow the night before.

"Leah?" he said.

"Yes?"

"Can I see you again? Soon?"

I nodded. "Of course."

"I might be downtown later for work. I'll let you know."

We got dressed and I followed him through the house. In the kitchen, a woman was standing at the sink washing dishes. She was young-looking—she couldn't have been older than early fifties—

and she was beautiful, with thick honey-blond banana curls pulled up into a ponytail. She was dressed in exercise clothing—a pink top and black spandex leggings—a headband in her hair.

I saw the resemblance between them right away—the wide-set eyes, the sweet, almost youthful smile. "Rise and shine," she said, and it was her voice that really got to me. The warmth in it, almost like she was singing.

"Mom, this is Leah," Charlie said.

"It's so nice to meet you, Leah. I'm Faye." She walked over to us. She was smiling like I'd never seen anyone smile before, and I realized that I, too, was grinning, like a fool. Up close I saw that her eyes were blue like Charlie's.

"I'm about to drive Leah home," Charlie said. "Can I borrow the credit card for gas?"

Faye winked at me and then handed Charlie a credit card from her purse. "Gas, Charlie—nothing more."

As we put on our shoes Faye followed us over to the entrance. "Tonight's BLT night in our house. Leah, if you want to join us we'd love to have you."

"Oh," I said. "Thank you." I glanced at Charlie, but I couldn't read his face. "I probably can't tonight, but maybe another time." The truth was, BLT night in their lemon-scented family room sounded nice to me, but I didn't want to push anything.

"Anytime, sweetheart."

When we got in the car, Charlie rolled down his window and lit a cigarette. "Do you mind?" he asked.

"That's fine."

"Last night when I drove you to my house was probably the longest time I've ever been in my car without smoking."

"Really?"

He nodded. "I didn't know how you felt about it. I didn't want to scare you off."

"Well, I can smell it all over you, so you're not exactly hiding anything."

"Right."

Out the window we were passing miles of cornfields, golden and rippling in the pale early light. Charlie was wearing the fleece he'd had on the night before, and he'd also put on glasses—round and wire-framed. His hair was messy and soft-looking. I swallowed; I felt so much for him in that moment. I stopped myself from saying so or reaching over and touching him.

"You probably have a lot of questions about me," Charlie said then, glancing at me.

"What do you mean?"

"Things that you want to know. Things that don't make sense about me."

"I guess so," I said. I didn't ask him anything, though, and he didn't say anything more. We drove the rest of the way back to Madison in comfortable quiet. Once he was done with his cigarette, he drove with his left hand on the steering wheel and his right resting gently on my leg.

He came over the next evening. When I let him inside I couldn't wait for him to touch me again, but we sat on my living room rug—him against one wall, me against another, miles apart. He was wearing a long-sleeve waffle-knit shirt and jeans, gray moccasins. I was sensitive to his scent now—tobacco and soap and something woodsy. It was faint but unmistakable.

I asked him about his stepdad.

"They got married when I was twelve," he told me. "Paul has two sons. Tyler and Chad. They're as douchey as their names sound," he said, smiling. "My mom and I moved in with them to the house when I was, like, ten, I think. Before that, we lived downtown, on Fish Hatchery towards Park Street. Ty and Chad used to fuck with me growing up. I was smaller than they were and not as good-looking."

"That can't be true," I said.

"They were huge. On the football team and everything."

"I can't imagine they were better-looking than you. You're . . ." I trailed off.

He shook his head bashfully. "Stop."

"You're perfect-looking." I was blushing.

"They used to tell me I looked like a girl. That my eyelashes were too long. I looked like I was wearing mascara or something." He shrugged. "And I'm too skinny. I know I need to bulk up."

"No, you don't," I said. "I don't think so."

He smiled at me. "I keep thinking about last night. I'll be doing something totally random, like peeling an orange or brushing my teeth, and I'll remember a detail. It's starting to become a problem."

"I know," I said. "Me, too."

"You're stunning, Leah."

When I didn't respond, he said, "I bet you're usually the prettiest girl in the room, and you have no idea."

I didn't say anything. Deep down I knew that I was pretty, but it seemed embarrassing to admit this, because I knew there was something ugly about me, too. My prettiness wasn't straightforward or consistent and it was something I felt more when I was by myself. I was never the prettiest girl in the room, and never would be. I wondered if he was lying to me or if it was possible that he saw me how I saw myself in my most private, most generous moments.

"I have to go meet up with my colleague," he said then, standing up. "Will you be around in a few hours?"

"You have to go now?" I asked.

"Yeah, but it shouldn't take very long. Can I come back?"

"All right," I said. "I'll be up."

When he came back later, he was high. I wanted to sit on the living room floor again and keep talking like we had been. But talking to him now was like talking to a different person. "How was your meeting?" I asked.

"It was good. We had to figure out some scheduling shit. Hey, have you ever seen those YouTube videos of dogs imitating sirens?" He did an impersonation of a dog howling and then burst out laughing in a little-boy way that embarrassed me.

"I haven't," I said.

"You have to watch. They're so good."

"They don't sound all that interesting."

"They're hilarious." Then he pulled me into the bedroom.

We undressed, and when he didn't say anything about how I looked, I wondered if he'd realized that I wasn't as attractive as he'd convinced himself. I started to feel humiliated, being naked in front of him.

He was just as attractive as the night before. Rail-thin, dark hair on his concave chest—dark hair all over, really. It wasn't just that Charlie was sexy. His face was beautiful in this almost painful way. It was hard for me to look at him and not stare. There was the definition of his cheekbones, his lips—soft and plump and rose-colored, the shadow of his facial hair softening his jawbone. He had a few perfectly placed beauty marks—one above the swell of his upper lip, two faint dots on his left cheek. His hair was a rich autumnal brown, silky and messy, like he'd just rolled out of bed. He was handsome and pretty at the same time.

"What about a condom?" I asked, as he positioned himself on top of me.

"Are you on the pill?"

"Yeah, but . . ."

"I get checked pretty regularly for STDs and I haven't had sex with anyone for a long time. It's up to you, though. But I don't have a condom with me."

I didn't have a condom, either.

"It's fine," I said.

The sex wasn't very good. The night before, kissing him had felt like an escape into some other perfect reality. But this just felt like having sex with a stranger. We didn't exchange a word or make any eye contact. Finally, he shuddered against me and dropped his face into my neck.

Afterward, I rolled away from him and thought about Robbie, from back home. How well Robbie knew my body, how sometimes we used to fall asleep—not naked and clinging on to each other, but fully clothed in big T-shirts and pajama pants—holding hands. How, somehow, that was even more intimate.

Beside me, Charlie was asleep. I regretted not using a condom. I didn't know why I did things like that, as though lack of protection might make us closer, or bonded. I didn't feel close with him. I felt as if I barely knew him at all.

2.

BEFORE MOVING TO MADISON I'D BEEN LIVING IN BOSTON, where I'd lived my whole life, including college. I'd been working a desk job that my stepmother, Monica, had gotten me at her law firm. It hadn't been going very well. I'd worked desk jobs before but I wasn't organized or detail-oriented—two things I had claimed to be during the interview. In my other jobs, I got away with a lot, but at the law firm, fuckups weren't tolerated and it wasn't as easy to scroll the internet or read a book during work hours. Things between Monica and me were getting tense, and they hadn't been good to begin with.

I had always liked to write. My stories were often about mother-less daughters or childless mothers. For a creative writer, I wasn't that creative. When I was in high school, I fantasized that my mother would somehow come across my short stories and realize she should come home. In college, my intended audience changed. I gave up on my mother and started imagining that men might read my writing and come and save me. Every story I wrote was a love letter.

Getting into Wisconsin's MFA program was a dream come true. It was a two-year fully funded program with a teaching stipend.

Only six people were admitted for fiction every other year, and each year hundreds of people applied. I didn't meet Charlie until the fall of my second year. The first year of the program I went out on a few dates and hooked up with some guys, but mostly I wrote.

When I moved to Madison in August 2012, I met the other people in my cohort the night I arrived. We gathered at a dive bar called the Caribou, a five-minute walk from my apartment. One long wooden bar ran the length of the room and slot machines lined the opposite wall, with just a narrow aisle in between. I recognized a few of my classmates from their Facebook photos, circled together near the back.

Immediately I was intimidated by Vivian Spear, who was from New York City. She was loud and very tiny. Often I wondered how my life would be different if I were tiny. People seemed to respond differently to petite women. I was just under six feet. People asked me all the time if I played basketball, which I didn't. Sometimes they told me, "You're so tall!" as if I needed reminding.

Vivian Spear had long, reddish unruly hair and was wearing fuchsia lipstick that stood out, even inside the darkened bar. The straps of her black dress kept slipping down to reveal pale, freckled shoulders. She had a New York accent and a low, husky voice like a jazz singer. She snorted when she laughed, which only added to her appeal. It was hard for me to imagine her sitting quietly by herself and typing on a computer.

The rest of the cohort, besides me and Vivian, were guys in their twenties and thirties, and one in his forties. Wilson Barbosa, David Eisenstat, Rohan Bakshi, and Sam Fitzpatrick. Sam, the forty-two-year-old, was married. Everyone else, including Vivian, seemed to be single.

I expected writers to be weird and moody, but everyone seemed well adjusted and more comfortable socializing than I was. Rohan reminded me of the popular boys in high school—not the jerks, but the boys who became popular because they were cute and outgoing and just arrogant enough to not be irritating. He was wearing a Chicago Bulls snapback and a T-shirt with a bunch of people's signatures silkscreened across the front. There was a small diamond stud through one of his ears. Each time someone new from the cohort entered the bar, he gave them a giant hug. "You're here!" he'd say, like he was waiting especially for them.

Wilson was quieter than Rohan but he also generated a sort of gravitational pull. I found myself wanting to stand beside Wilson. He was short and slight, with kind, honey-brown eyes and thick black curls. His laugh was louder and more boisterous than his speaking voice, and each time he laughed at something someone said, I realized I was laughing, too. When he smiled, deep half-moon dimples formed in the cushions of his cheeks.

Sam was the only one of us who'd had a full-fledged career before the MFA. He'd left his accounting firm to come to Madison, and I think it surprised all of us to hear the word *accounting*. Out of everyone, he looked the most Wisconsin-y—blond and pale, big-boned. He was polite and gentlemanly in a way the other guys weren't. He was especially so with Vivian. He offered her his seat when he noticed she was standing, then glanced over at her with concern when Rohan made a crude joke. I found this insulting on several levels.

It was Wilson's idea to go around and say who our favorite

authors were. I hadn't read most of the writers people were talking about, but I nodded enthusiastically and told them that my favorite writer was Alice Munro even though I'd only read two of her stories.

"She's so good," Vivian said. "I loved *Lives of Girls and Women*."

Vivian already had a number of stories published in small literary journals and was halfway through writing a novel. "It's a hot mess, though," she said. A few others, it turned out, were in the middle of writing a novel or about to start one.

I wasn't sure which was worse. Watching the guys watch Vivian or watching her myself. She was everything I was not. I downed my drink and turned to David and asked him where he was from. David had shaggy brown hair and glasses and was wearing a long-sleeve button-down shirt even though it was late August. He had facial hair that he played with almost constantly, rubbing individual hairs between his fingers. His favorite writers were Philip Roth, Vladimir Nabokov, and David Foster Wallace.

"Connecticut," David said. "You?"

"Massachusetts. This is my first time to the Midwest."

David nodded politely and turned back to Vivian, who was telling a story about a workshop she'd taken with Zadie Smith. Understandably, a more interesting topic than the *where are you from* conversation. I tried to listen to Vivian with the same energy and generosity as everyone else, but I kept losing focus.

At that point I was still involved with Robbie, who wasn't exactly my boyfriend from back home, but I had been sleeping over at his place most weekends and some weeknights, on and off, since I was seventeen. Robbie had told me a few times he was in love with me, and I'd always said it back—mostly because I didn't want to stop going over to his house at night. I liked having sex with him and eating bowls of Lucky Charms with him and watching TV until we fell asleep. But I wanted more.

Robbie and I had been friends since kindergarten and he'd always had a crush on me, even when I'd gone through my especially awkward phase—glasses, braces, acne. I still wore glasses and had a decent amount of acne. But I had "grown into myself."

Robbie was cute, in a chubby, lumberjack kind of way. He was my height or a little shorter depending on both of our postures. And he was the only person in the world who loved me, outside of my family. But he didn't read books or think in the same way I did. Not that I needed to be with someone exactly like me, but sometimes I would tell Robbie something about my day or a thing that I noticed, and he would just nod or shrug without asking a question or adding to the conversation. We talked. We talked all the time. But I wanted him to say something that surprised me. Or look me deep in the eye and ask: *Why?* And really want to know.

After the dive bar on my first night in Madison I went back to my new, mostly empty apartment in Norris Court and called Robbie.

"How'd it go?" he asked. I heard him suck in air and I could picture him on his bed, smoking a joint. He was probably wearing sweatpants and no shirt, his hair a curly mess; his eyes soft, half-closed.

"I felt dumb," I said.

"You're not dumb," he insisted. But I wanted him to ask me why I felt dumb.

"They're all writing novels. And they were talking about authors I should have read already."

"Don't worry about it," Robbie said. "You're the smartest person I know."

I teared up then, because I knew that I was going to end things with Robbie, even though I loved him.

"Robbie," I said.

"Leah." I knew he was smiling.

"Why do you even like me?"

"You're crying?" he asked.

"A little."

"I like you because of all the little Leah things." He wasn't the type to list them. "Are you okay?"

"It's lonely here in Wisconsin."

"You're going to make friends before you know it."

"Are you lonely?" I asked.

"I'm all right," Robbie said. "I miss you, though. I miss you a lot."

Then he told me about the TV show he was watching while I stalked Vivian Spear on Facebook.

For our first workshop of the MFA, Vivian Spear and David Eisenstat submitted pieces. Vivian submitted the first thirty pages of her novel and David submitted a short story. I read Vivian's novel excerpt first. It was about a middle-age woman in Manhattan who was having an affair with her dentist. I finished the pages quickly and wanted to keep reading. Vivian was smart about people. She saw them exactly how they were. Reading her writing made me wonder how she saw me.

David's story was more self-conscious. Each sentence was beautiful; I liked the descriptions of the scenery. I had no idea what the story was about. It might have been about a man going on a road trip coming to terms with the fact that he was gay, but that was a guess. There was one sex scene between two people where no body parts were mentioned. I read the story three times and with each read I became more confused.

"This story broke my heart," Rohan said, when we got to talking about David's road trip story in class.

"I thought the end was really moving," Wilson jumped in. "When he goes to the diner and just sits in the parking lot in his car for hours."

"I also thought the juxtaposition between the stark, muted descriptions of his father's abuse and these longer, more drawn-out descriptions of the rural landscape was powerful," Sam said. "And when he has sex with that woman from the bar? The writing is amazing. We see her, but we don't. It's like she doesn't exist to him."

David was nodding and nodding, writing furiously, filling page after page with notes. The way workshop went was that David wouldn't speak for the entirety of our conversation. We would discuss his story almost as if he weren't there—what was working well, what wasn't—and then at the end, he could ask questions.

"It was hard for me to follow," Vivian said. "I didn't know where he was driving, or why. I think we need to know why he decides to get in the car in the first place. Same with having sex with the woman. I don't understand why he sleeps with her. Is it because he desires her or is it because he's trying to convince himself that he's attracted to her?"

Our professor nodded then, and the movement from her side

of the room made everyone look over. For the first time, she spoke. "This character describes the trees and the road with so much feeling, but then he withholds any kind of description when it comes to his own life or the people in it. Maybe he's in denial about who he is or what he wants. But he can still describe the way his father looks at him or the woman in the bar—and his desires or his repulsions can sneak through in those descriptions. Even if he's not aware of his own motivations, the writer has to be aware of them. We have to see around what he's not saying. That's the beauty of having a first-person narrator."

Everyone in the room was nodding. David was squinting at the page, bearing down so hard on his pen it looked like his hand might combust.

I was silently burning. Furious for not saying my thoughts about the story before Vivian had. But the truth was, I never could have articulated what I had been thinking the way she did. Vivian spoke with so much confidence. She'd said her piece without being scared that she was going to sound stupid, or that she'd gotten it wrong, or that she might wound David. And she'd said the right thing. The professor had validated her. I wanted to somehow indicate that this was what I had been thinking, too. But doing that would only make me look desperate and foolish. I turned the pages of David's story and tried to come up with something smart to say. Nothing came to mind.

After workshop the six of us went out to a bar on State Street called City Bar. City Bar was underground, down a long, steep staircase. It had low ceilings and no windows, big leather booths with Styrofoam padding bursting out of the seats. The drinks were half the price they were in Boston, and they had a full menu of burgers and fries and tater tots. There was a jukebox in one corner and dartboards in another. The biggest table was in the back—a high one with stools. That was the one we took.

We would continue going to City Bar every Tuesday night after workshop for the next two years. That night, we met the poets there, who were a slightly weirder and more emotionally demonstrative cohort of people than we were—more piercings and tattoos, more public tears.

I would come to realize over time that we fiction writers were just as emotional as the poets; we just did a better job of concealing it. Our group was a particularly buttoned-up group of fiction writers. The guys of the cohort were constantly vying for alpha male in the room, and for Vivian's attention and approval. Vivian was the most alpha of all of us. She was outspoken and brusque. She swore constantly. She kept up with and sometimes surpassed the boys' drinking without getting giggly. And when she spoke, everybody listened. I was the youngest and the quietest of the six. I saw myself as an outsider.

As the group debriefed at City Bar, I watched the poets. They'd already been here a year, and they drank their beer and ate their tater tots, listening patiently as Vivian and the boys talked endlessly about every small detail from the past two hours.

There was something all-knowing about the poets. They seemed more relaxed than the tense, hyper people with whom I was bound. I wondered if I would fit in more with the poets. I had no idea how to write a poem, though. I thought then about Vivian's thirty pages—the opening scene she'd written between the protagonist and the dentist. How much tension there'd been. How easy it was to turn the pages. She was talented. And it was obvious to me at that moment. Vivian was going places.

It didn't take me long to start opening up around Vivian and the boys; I could feel that who I really was would start to emerge. Things moved quickly in grad school. I'd always thought of quiet as synonymous with steady. Partly because that's what I'd always been. Leah: tall, quiet, predictable. I had emotions, though. Big, torrential emotions. But that was why I read. That was why I wrote. I wasn't one to call attention to myself in real life.

I settled into my life in Madison. I made friends. I became closest with Vivian and Wilson, and I spent most of my weekends and free time with them. And we had so much free time. I wrote during the day—and evenings Vivian and Wilson and I would hang out in one of our apartments, talking about books or what we were writing, the other people in the program, stories from our lives. There were also plenty of days I spent alone, taking long walks around the east side of Madison. Whole weekends working on stories in coffee shops—Johnson Public House, Mother Fool's, Colectivo. Coming home reeking of coffee and whatever scent lived in the fibers of that particular shop.

My apartment in Norris Court became cluttered with books and drafts and printouts of stories. I'd bought furniture from Craigslist and St. Vincent, the thrift store on Willy Street. I didn't buy a couch, but two massive armchairs that I put facing one another—one that was comfortable, and another one that sank so deep when you sat down you could feel the springs, but had only cost five dollars. The only thing I'd bought new was the rug—a plush blue-and-white floral-patterned one from Target. Nothing matched. But it was the first time I'd lived alone, and I loved everything about my apartment. It had a working fireplace and built-in bookshelves and French doors that led into a tiny study with windows that overlooked a courtyard. Each time I walked through my front door I felt peaceful—like this was where I was supposed to be.

I felt untethered and alive in Madison in a way that I never had in Boston. I don't know if things were actually so different in Wisconsin, or if it was because I was away from my family and everything I'd ever known, but I woke up each morning with a feeling that finally my life was happening.

I didn't have a car, so I walked everywhere. My apartment was two miles from campus, and though there was a bus, I preferred the walk, no matter how cold it got. Walking was when I would think about whatever story I was writing. Sometimes I'd write out entire scenes in my head, so that by the time I'd reach campus I was bursting with sentences and images, entire conversations between characters.

I felt lonely in Madison, but that was normal for me.

Our weeks revolved around Tuesday nights, which was when we had workshop. Our only real requirement, besides teaching an undergraduate creative writing class once a week, was to write things that we would submit for workshop, and to read each other's work.

My initial judgments about my cohort had been right in some ways, but mostly I'd been off. Everybody was far more complicated and vulnerable than they'd seemed that first night. We got to know each other, first through our writing, and then through talking about writing. From there, we became friends. We were "writing friends," though, which I learned was a particular sort of friendship.

Our lives were still separate. We could go days without speaking with or seeing each other—wrapped up in a draft or some particular mood. If someone didn't show up to an event or left early or flaked last minute, it wasn't considered weird. The social rules of this insular world agreed with me. It meant I could disappear, and no one would question me.

Writing came first. If you received a text saying "on a roll" or "in the middle"—you knew not to interrupt. Despite the fact that we had practically no obligations or commitments ever—ample time to write—as soon as we felt our writing time was being infringed upon, we became stringent and boundaried. We took ourselves so seriously that the poets stopped hanging out with us.

"You guys become kind of insufferable once you realize you could actually make money doing this," was how one of them put it. "Nobody gives a shit about poetry, though."

When we weren't writing, we were drinking. We'd go to the Tipsy Cow or Genna's or Mickey's or the Crystal Corner, or any number of bars. Madison was filled with them. Or we'd hang out at one of our apartments. We all lived within walking distance of one another. Rohan's house had a huge wraparound porch, and this became a common meeting place. Those were the nights I felt most like a teenager—playing beer pong and smoking cigarettes, gossiping about each other and the poets and what happened in workshop that week.

One night, while a bunch of people played flip cup, Vivian and

I sat on a mildewed couch on the corner of Rohan's porch and whispered about how much we couldn't stand David. The infuriating way he described women in his stories, how he always directed all his comments in class to Rohan, his incessant need to name-drop.

"I can't believe I thought David was cute when I met him," I said.

"I do think Rohan is pretty cute," said Vivian. I glanced over at her on the couch. Her cheeks were pink with cold and she was holding her beer close to her face, with both hands. Her face was partially hidden by her scarf, but I could tell she was smiling.

I followed her gaze to where Rohan was standing with the others, his arms lifted in a power pose. He was yelling something in triumph. For some reason he had on sunglasses even though it was dusk, barely any light left in the sky.

"Yeah," I agreed. "He is."

Most people's writing matched up with what I'd been expecting. It lined up, more or less, with how they spoke or the feeling I got when I was around them. All of us were able to express things on the page that we weren't able to out loud. Wilson's writing, out of everyone's, had surprised me.

Wilson was one of those people who was so universally liked— so quietly charismatic—that it was hard to know what was going on inside him. It was a slow unraveling—getting to know these people. But reading their fiction, a lot of it was right there.

When I started reading Wilson's stories, I was shocked at how sad they were. It wasn't that his laughter or his smiles were fake. The things that he saw humor in were the same things that made him sad. He couldn't separate the two. Or maybe it was the other way around. The things that made him sad, if you looked at them hard enough, in a certain way, were funny. His writing made you laugh while also giving you a sharp pain in your throat. It made you swallow hard.

The first time I read one of Wilson's stories I wanted to know him more. I felt attracted to him, in a way. Though it was less about wanting to be *with* him and more about wanting to be around him. I figured, based on the couples in his stories—he tended to write about romantic relationships between men—that Wilson was gay, but he never talked about his love life. Wilson's mysterious love life—or lack thereof—became a topic of conversation when he wasn't around. Sometimes people would bring up sex and dating around him as a way to dig or provoke a reaction, but he never took the bait. He was an incredible listener. Unlike the rest of us, though, he hardly ever spoke about himself.

For the first workshop of our second year, I wrote a story about a marriage falling apart. It was from the point of view of a father at his son's bar mitzvah, just days before his wife leaves the family. I titled it "Thirteen." I suppose I was channeling my father, although the man in my story was less passive than my father, and this wasn't how it went down in my family. My mom had still been at home for both of my brothers' bar mitzvahs.

My own bat mitzvah had been a somber affair. My mother had left just one month prior. She'd called a few times, but she wouldn't tell us where she was, and she wasn't coming home.

I had pretended not to notice, as I stood on the bimah, that my father was holding back tears in the front row, his face twisted in grief. My brothers, ages fifteen and eighteen, sat on either side of him, stoic and depressed. I sang "Oseh Shalom" alongside our elderly rabbi and prayed that my mother might show up in time for my Torah portion; for my speech; for her speech; for "Adon Olam." She'd been the one to plan this entire day, after all—book the caterer and the DJ, make the seating arrangements. She'd gone with me to buy my silk top and skirt for the service, the sequined spaghetti-strap dress I'd change into later for the party.

That night, when the neighborhood men hoisted me up on the chair and everyone danced in circles around me, grinning up at me like this was supposed to be the happiest moment of my life, I wondered where my mom was—at a hotel somewhere, or in her car. She had to remember what day it was.

My mother had been more religious than my father. I don't know if she believed in God, but she wanted to. You could tell by the way she recited the prayers, her lips moving even when no sound came from her mouth. And then how sometimes she'd close her eyes and disappear. My mother was always looking to believe in something bigger than herself. Whether it was through religion or art or some specific person or experience, she was on the lookout for the divine and the powerful. Ready, at a moment's notice, to be swept away.

The nice thing about writing was it took pain and warped it into something useful. I could shape it into a beginning and a middle and an end. It was manageable that way. And it was mine. Sharp and beautiful. By the time I was done with it, it was just a story.

———

Our workshop that semester was being taught by a writer named Bea Leonard, who was known mostly for her short story collection, which had won a prestigious award, and a slim novel that had gotten mixed reviews. Most people out in the world had no idea who she was, though she was a big deal to other writers. *She's a "writer's writer,"* Vivian had called her.

In her author photo, Bea looked thoughtful, wise, and amused. In real life, she looked frazzled—her red hair unkempt and going gray, her clothes wrinkled and odd-fitting. I'd imagined that she would start off the class with some sort of grand welcome speech: *You've arrived! You're so special!* But she passed out the syllabus and went through it matter-of-factly without making much eye contact with any of us. I'd read everything she had ever published. I loved her writing. She wrote about smart, angry women. Funny women, who always had a comeback. It was natural, I suppose, to assume she was one of these women. I realized, sitting across from her in the fluorescent-lit classroom, that I had no idea who Bea Leonard was.

I was nervous about my story. I wanted my workshop to like it. Especially Vivian and Wilson, who I thought were the best writers. And Bea Leonard.

That night we workshopped Rohan's piece first, which was a coming-of-age story that everyone seemed to like but agreed needed something. The writing was beautiful but it lacked tension. The beginning was slow and the ending was too tidy. Everything people said about Rohan's story I applied to my own, and by the time we finished workshopping his, I was convinced I already knew what they would say about mine. I wanted to call off my workshop before it began.

"Okay," Bea said, after our ten-minute break. "Let's talk about Leah's 'Thirteen.'"

For a minute nobody said anything. Then Rohan spoke. "I don't really know what to say to make this story better. I think it's phenomenal as it is. I loved the characters. It's fucking sad. I just don't know what to say. I mean, I have a lot to say. But I think it's done."

"I agree with Rohan," said Vivian. "I loved this voice. Reading it a second time, I do think there are some things that Leah could do to make it stronger, that I'll go into later. But this story blew me away."

The workshop went on like this. I tried to take notes, but my heart was beating too fast, and when I wrote words down, they came out scrambled. I didn't dare look up because I knew that my face was on fire. I was too in shock to feel happy just yet—but my happiness was there, brewing just beneath the surface.

After the workshop, when everyone handed their notes to me, I glanced quickly at Bea's. It was customary to wait until you got home, after City Bar, to read through the critique letters, but I couldn't help it. Bea's was brief. One long paragraph followed by a shorter paragraph. I only read the short paragraph.

> *I think you should start sending this story out to journals.*
> *Begin by submitting it only to the top places. The New*
> *Yorker, Tin House, Paris Review, etc. Even if it gets*

rejected by these places, keep sending. It will find a home
soon. Let me know if you want to talk about this.
Congratulations on writing a spectacular story.

BL

I stuffed the massive stack of papers into my backpack. As we all exited the classroom, Rohan threw an arm around my shoulder. "Not bad, Kempler."

"Thanks," I said. "You, too."

"I haven't seen Bea light up talking about a story that way."

His arm was still around me. We were walking down the hallway toward the elevators, the rest of the cohort around us.

"That's not true," I said.

"It is true," Wilson said. "She loved it."

All six of us stepped into the elevator, and someone pressed the button for the ground floor.

"Leah, you should show that story to the agent when she comes," Vivian said.

We all turned to look at Vivian.

"What agent?" Sam asked.

"They're bringing in a literary agent to meet with us," said Vivian.

"Who?" David asked. "Where did you hear this?"

"I don't know who," Vivian said, laughing. "She's going to be meeting with each of us individually. That's what Carla told me." Carla was the administrator of the program.

"Fuck," David said. "When is this happening? Why haven't they told us this yet?"

The elevator doors opened. We all stepped into the foyer of Helen C. White, taking a collective moment to zip up our coats before venturing into the Wisconsin night. It was a seven-minute walk to the bar.

"I don't think we need to stress about it," Vivian said.

"If I knew an agent was coming, I would have workshopped the first chapter of my novel," Sam said, "not that damn magic realism story."

"I thought that story was good," said Wilson.

"This is probably why they're not saying anything," Vivian said. "Also, I didn't know you had started writing your novel, Sam."

As for me, I couldn't have cared less about the agent. I didn't even care about the journals that Bea Leonard had typed out on my critique letter. It was thrilling, of course, to see the publications she thought my work was worthy of—*The Paris Review*, *The New Yorker*—but really, it was Bea Leonard's initials signed at the bottom that meant the most to me. The fact that she liked it. That, maybe, she liked me. And then how Rohan had put his arm around my shoulder. And now, walking to the bar with the five of them. I was quiet, still. But I was a part of it. Part of the group.

I didn't need to be the prettiest or the most successful or even the most talented. But I desperately wanted—*needed*—to be loved.

The agent came a week and a half later. It was the beginning of October—two weeks before I would run into Charlie in the grocery store. We were told to print out our most polished stories and novel chapters and be ready to talk about our work. We would each have twenty minutes alone with Maya Joshi.

We were scheduled to meet as a large group at nine a.m., before our individual meetings. Maya was dressed how I imagined an agent might dress—designer jeans and a leather jacket, boots with a four-inch heel, big tortoiseshell eyeglasses. Her hair, shoulder-length and blown out, could have been an advertisement for some kind of product. We gathered in the conference room across the hall from the MFA office, where chairs had been arranged in a circle for an "informal conversation" about finding an agent. The department had set out bagels and a pot of coffee. When we showed up, Maya was already there with a to-go coffee from Starbucks. She was chatting with Bea Leonard, who also had a to-go coffee from Starbucks.

I'd become accustomed to our faculty—the "grown-ups"—being a bookish, self-deprecating, and overall slightly awkward group of people. I could see right away that Maya Joshi was not awkward. She was friendly without being ingratiating, outgoing without being over-the-top. She smiled and said hello to each of us as we trickled in and poured coffee for ourselves, spread cream cheese on our bagels.

When she started her talk at nine, she exuded a vibe of professional warmth and success that filled the room. "Every year I look forward to my Midwest trip," she said. "You should be very proud to be at this program. Without fail, I always find incredible talent here."

She described to us what she was looking for—literary and up-market fiction, as well as narrative nonfiction and memoir. She was drawn to fresh, smart voices, multicultural and multigenerational stories, suspense with humor. "I want to see the world in a way I've never seen it before. I'm interested in writing that makes the familiar unfamiliar. I look for urgency. I want to be so wrapped up in the manuscript that I totally miss my subway stop." She smiled then, and her teeth were perfectly white.

There was nothing more exciting than discovering new talent, she told us. And she loved finding a writer at the beginning of their career; working with them not just on a particular book— but for their whole life. "I'm in it for the long game," she said.

I glanced around at my classmates. I'd never seen each and every one of them look so hopeful. Suddenly having an agent seemed crucial.

"I usually take on one or two new writers each year," she said. "So it really has to be just the right fit."

I could feel the deflation in the room. The odds were not good.

Rohan had the first meeting. When he went off with her, we all gathered in the MFA office to wait for our turn. I sat at my desk, looking over the two stories I had printed out. Right away I spotted two typos on the first page of "Thirteen." I still had an hour until my meeting, so I pulled out my laptop and fixed the errors. As I waited in the copy room down the hall for the story to reprint, I heard two voices around the corner.

"I think if she's interested in anyone it's going to be Vivian," Wilson was saying softly.

"Why?" came David's voice, a little louder. "Because she's working on a novel?"

"Well, yeah. She's the furthest along."

"Look," David said. "Vivian is good at what she does. And I have no doubt she's going to be successful. She has an incredible work ethic—better than all of us. And she's hot, so that doesn't hurt. But Vivian is writing about a divorcée in Manhattan who has an affair with her dentist. It's not really the type of book that makes you 'see the world in a way you've never seen it before.'"

Wilson made a *hmm* sound. "I see."

"Do I think it's going to sell?" David said. "Yes. Do I think a certain audience is going to eat it up? Absolutely. But I get the sense that Maya Joshi is looking for something more . . . literary. I could be wrong, though. Based on the authors she represents, I could see her being interested in Rohan." He paused. "Or you, man. Who knows? Especially with your latest story."

"Ha—because we're *multicultural*?"

"No," said David quickly. "Because you're good."

When Wilson spoke, his voice was stiff. "What do you think she'll think of your writing?"

"Oh, I'm sure she'll hate it. My stuff is all pretty raw at this point."

"Well, she just came from Iowa, so she's probably not taking any of us."

"That's probably true," said David. "Fucking Iowa."

I wondered if David had forgotten that Vivian had turned down Iowa—which was considered the best MFA program in the country—to come to Wisconsin.

"I'm going to head back to the office," said Wilson.

"Hey, Wilson, don't repeat what I said about Vivian's novel."

"Of course not."

"I do admire her. I actually feel like there might be some kind of . . ." David paused. "Attraction. Or something, between us."

There was silence.

"Do you think it would be weird if I made a move?" David asked.

"Weird for who?"

"Weird for . . . everyone," David said.

"Well, there's six of us," said Wilson. "And we're all going to be in class and socializing for another year. So I'd say weirdness is a possibility."

"Have you noticed anything?" David asked. "Like any tension between me and Vivian, when all of us are hanging out?"

"No," said Wilson. "But to be honest, I haven't really been paying attention."

"Fair enough."

Ten minutes later, Rohan came back into the office, his expression unreadable.

"What happened?" asked Sam.

"I don't know," Rohan said. He collapsed into his chair and ran a hand over his face. Then he laughed. "I don't think she liked my stuff, though."

We all exchanged looks. Rohan was good.

"What did she *say*?" asked David. All of us, minus Wilson, who was in with her now, gathered around Rohan's desk.

"Well, first, she sped-read my stories," Rohan told us. "And, I mean, I've never seen anyone read as fast as that woman. She started off by asking me why I made the breakup story first-person, and I said some bullshit about an unreliable narrator. Then she said that story was predictable, but the family vacation story could make a good novel—"

"Holy shit," Vivian cut in. "She said it could make a good *novel*? That's huge, Rohan."

Rohan reached to the collar of his shirt and undid the top button. He was dressed as nicely as I'd ever seen him, in a suit and jacket. His forehead was shiny with sweat. "Then she asked me which authors I'd compare myself to. I didn't know if I should just say my favorite authors, but if I say George Saunders and fucking . . . Baldwin . . . I sound like I'm full of myself. So I guess I paused for too long trying to think of an answer that didn't make me sound like a douche, and she told me it was important to know how to talk about my work in comparison to what else is out there." He smiled wearily at us. "So you should all probably start thinking of an answer to that question."

"The most important thing is that she loved your vacation story," Vivian said.

"Well, she definitely didn't use the word *love*."

"How did the meeting end?" David asked.

"She told me to write my email on the back of my story so that if she wanted to get in touch she'll know where to find me."

"That's good," Vivian said. "This is all good."

One of the poets walked into the office then, holding a breakfast sandwich and a pile of papers. "What's up, fiction writers?"

"Not much," Vivian said. "Trying to stay calm."

"Oh, that's right—today's the big day with the agent!" He grinned. "No wonder you all look like you work in a bank."

It was true that most of us were dressed up a little. Rohan and Sam had both shown up in suits. Wilson had dressed like he usually dressed—nicely—but he'd worn his glasses that day rather than his contacts. David had ironed his blue button-down for once, and he'd added a neon-orange winter hat to his look. Vivian, of course, looked the best, in jeans and a black turtleneck, black ankle boots—her hair pulled into a loose ponytail, her lips a deep red. As for me, I'd picked out my outfit the night before: a knee-length gray sweater dress from the Gap, black tights, flats. In the light of day, I wondered what had possessed me to pick such an outfit.

How much did that matter, I wondered—looking good? I thought about what David had said about Vivian: *And she's hot, so that doesn't hurt.* There was no denying that Vivian would look good on the back of a book. When the agent met with us, would she be assessing only our writing, or would it be our appearances, too? If this was the case, surely Vivian and I would be assessed differently than the guys. Our photos would hold a little more weight.

I went over to Vivian's desk. "Hey," I said softly. "Do you have any lipstick with you?"

She pulled a few black and silver tubes from her backpack and laid them on her desk. "Take your pick."

I glanced through the different shades.

"I think this one would look pretty on you." She took one of the tubes and drew a cranberry-colored line on the outer edge of my hand. "Unless it's too subtle."

"Subtle is good," I said. "Thanks."

I took the lipstick into the bathroom and applied it, then bared my teeth to make sure I hadn't gotten it all over myself. It looked nice, but it also seemed to call attention to the angry zit on my cheek and the small clusters of acne along my jawline. I smiled again and this time tried to exude confidence. My meeting was starting in forty minutes.

The others' meetings went similarly to Rohan's. Maya would speed-read the stories, ask a few questions, and then give some sort of feedback. So far she hadn't seemed especially in love with any-body's work, but no one could tell if that was because she wasn't, or if she was keeping her cards close to her chest. She ended each meeting by asking everyone to write their email address on the back of their stories.

When it was my turn, I marched down the hallway toward the office where Maya was waiting, my stories in hand, like I was heading off to war. I felt strong and brave and ready for anything.

"Hi," she said, smiling, when I walked in. "Please, sit down."

I sat.

She didn't ask me for my stories. "So," she said. "Tell me about yourself."

I didn't know how to answer the question. "Well. My name is Leah Kempler. I'm from Massachusetts. I write stories mostly about mothers and daughters. . . . But I actually just wrote a story from the point of view of a husband whose wife leaves him, and that was new for me, writing from the point of view of a man. I think it went okay, though. . . ." I trailed off then, as David's voice floated into my head, what he'd said earlier about divorcees; sto-ries that change the way you see the world, versus those that don't.

Across from me, Maya Joshi's face was blank. Not uninter-ested, but not interested, either. She was just waiting. She was on the clock. She was a businesswoman. And I was a girl wasting her time. I could feel my own breath start to quicken. I wished she would just take my stories and stop looking at me.

"What makes you interested in mother-and-daughter stories?" she asked.

"Well, I'm a daughter. Obviously . . ." I tried to laugh, and Maya offered me a quick smile. "And I have a mother. But I lost her. Well, I didn't *lose* her. As in, she didn't *die*. But she left. Which I realize is not a very unique story. But it informs my view of the world. Sort of."

"I'm sorry," Maya Joshi said, frowning.

Was she saying sorry because my mother had left or because it informed my narrow, uninteresting view of the world?

"It's okay," I said. "I'm over it."

The words sounded incredibly false considering everything I had just told her. For a moment, neither one of us spoke.

"I'm curious," Maya said. "Which authors would you compare yourself to?"

"Julie Orringer, Curtis Sittenfeld, Amy Hempel. And Bea Leonard," I added. "I'm really excited to be taking a workshop with her this semester."

For the first time, Maya's face lit up. "Bea's great, isn't she? Have you read her collection?"

"Yes. I've read it like a hundred times."

"One day more people are going to know Bea Leonard's name," Maya said. "Mark my words. She's a rare talent."

I nodded.

"Well, thank you, Leah." She pronounced it *Lay-ah*. "It was a pleasure to meet you and hear about your work. Keep at it. You're in the right place. You're going to learn so much from Bea." She stood up.

I felt a sinking in my chest. "Nice to meet you, too."

She glanced at her phone.

"Sorry, do you want my . . ." I held out my stories.

"Oh, absolutely. Thank you." She took them without asking

me to write my email on the back page, and placed them on top of the pile of Word documents sitting beside her purse.

"Bye!" I said, and then I ran out the door like a child in trouble. When I made it to the bathroom, I scrubbed furiously at my lips with soap and water until the color was gone. It seemed important, before I told the others about my meeting, that I wash away this evidence of my hope. It was my vanity, more than anything else, that humiliated me.

3.

AND THEN I MET CHARLIE.

He came by a lot those first few weeks. He usually had to leave, at some point, to meet up with his colleague. Or his boss. He used the words interchangeably.

"I thought you worked in construction," I said.

"I do."

"Wait, so who is this guy you keep going to see?"

"My buddy, Max. He's kind of an asshole when you first meet him, but he's actually a good guy. He's been there for me in tough times."

We were lying in bed on top of the sheets, the blankets kicked off. The sex had gotten better after the first time. Sex never seemed to be the first thing on Charlie's mind, though, like the other guys I'd been with—Robbie included. Robbie was never pushy, but once we got going, it was hard for him to have a conversation or focus on anything else until he had an orgasm. Charlie could be aroused and talk at the same time. And he touched me without expecting anything in return.

"Can I ask you something?" I said.

"Sure."

"Are you a drug dealer?"

I expected him to get defensive or start laughing, but he looked at me seriously and said, "No. I'm not."

"Okay. It's just weird how you keep referring to this Max guy as your boss and then you show up high . . ."

"I showed up high like once, right?"

"Yeah. It was just weird."

He nodded. "I can see why that would be weird for you." He sat up in bed. "Look, I want to tell you something. But I'm really nervous to tell you. Like, to be honest, I'm terrified. I didn't know the right time to say this. It's not the type of thing you say on a first date. And then on the second date I fell for you. I fell for you hard—more than I ever have so early on, and I was like: *Charlie, don't scare this girl off, this isn't the type of girl you find every day.*"

I sat up, my heart pounding, while also basking in his compliment.

He was leaning against one of my pillows. His body was relaxed, but his expression was pained. His long legs were stretched over mine. I reached for his hand, and he squeezed it. To my surprise, his eyes filled with tears and he blinked them away.

"Sorry," he said. "I just hate that I have to tell you this."

"Tell me what?"

"You can ask me to leave," he said. "I'll understand if you want me to leave."

"I won't," I said—but I could feel my heartbeat thudding in my ears; in my throat.

"You're, like, obviously super-talented and gorgeous—"

"I'm not, Charlie. Stop."

"You are, though. I didn't even realize it at first because you

hide yourself and you wear those sweaters like you're a librarian."
He smiled, his eyes brimming again. "And I'm not even talking
about your body, although I love your body. Your face is like . . .
unbelievably beautiful. You're like Lady Gaga. I can imagine you
all dressed up with tons of makeup, looking super-hot. Or how
you looked that morning when you woke up in my house with
no makeup at all. You were angelic."

I didn't know what to do with his words except commit them
to memory. Even if he was lying, it was the best lie someone had
told me. I wanted to tell him that he was by far the most beautiful
human being I had ever laid eyes on, but something stopped me.

"What is it?" I said. "You're freaking me out."

"Don't freak out. I'm not about to tell you I have AIDS or
something—"

"AIDS?"

"No, I don't—"

"Charlie, just tell me."

"Okay," he said. "Okay. I'm in recovery. I have been for a few
years. I'm not ashamed of it. It's made me who I am today. It's
made me a lot stronger. But it's hard to tell someone like you."

I nodded slowly. "Okay," I said. "Recovery for?"

He scratched his head. "It's the bad one." When I didn't say
anything, he said, "The Big H."

When I still didn't say anything, he said, "Heroin." He paused.
"I'm a recovering heroin addict."

I nodded, absorbing the information. A vague feeling of worry
washed over me. More than anything, though, I was relieved that
he hadn't just told me he had an STD, since we had continued to
not use condoms.

He looked down into his lap. "I understand if you want me to leave."

I got a flash then of what he'd looked like when he'd walked into the Weary Traveler—how his eyes had widened when he'd spotted me. And then two days later, that morning when he'd asked his mom for the credit card. *Gas, Charlie,* she'd said. *Nothing more.*

"No," I said, and I curled up beside him. "Please don't leave."

He closed his eyes and I could feel his relief, too. He buried his head into the space between my neck and my shoulder and wrapped his arms tightly around me. For a while he didn't say anything. "Thank you," he whispered finally. "Thank you so much, Leah."

When Charlie went home the next morning, I did some googling. The most I knew about heroin was what I knew from *Rent.*

Heroin addiction didn't look good. Reading about relapse rates and methadone clinics and fentanyl scared me. I texted Charlie.

> **Can I ask how long you've been sober for?**

> > **I've been in recovery for three years. There've been some issues with my meds along the way due to my health insurance that have caused me to substitute.**

> **What do you mean?**

> > **I'd rather explain in person. It's a long, personal story. But I'd like to tell you everything.**

Okay. Also, did you ever use needles?

Can we talk in person?

Of course.

I looked Charlie up on Facebook. I found his ex-girlfriend and looked at old pictures of them. She was so beautiful. Her features were precise and delicate—a doll-like nose, a small, pouty mouth, romantic-looking brown eyes. Her skin was dewy, flawless. Her hair, a pixie cut, short choppy bangs. They looked perfect together. Seeing pictures of him with her made me jealous. I saw that she and Charlie were no longer Facebook friends and wondered if it had been a bad breakup.

I downloaded Tinder onto my phone. I matched with a guy I recognized from around campus. His name was Peter and he was getting his PhD in political science. When he asked me if I'd like to get a drink with him that weekend, I said yes. I had been seeing Charlie for a few weeks by then. The more time I spent with him, the more I liked him, but the vague shiver of worry I'd felt when he'd told me about the heroin had started to grow. I tried to imagine introducing Charlie to my family and it seemed impossible. Going on a date with someone else seemed like a good thing to do.

Peter and I met at a wine bar near the capitol, and when I arrived, he was already there at a high-top table in the corner. He was wearing a navy-blue crewneck sweatshirt—the same sweatshirt he'd been wearing in his one photo on the dating app.

In real life, Peter had stunningly sad eyes, but when he smiled, it transformed his whole face. I sat down and we started talking easily about the cities we'd grown up in, how different the Midwest felt compared with the coasts. He was from Los Angeles and had done his undergrad at UC Berkeley. "I wasn't prepared for this kind of cold," he told me. "I showed up my first winter here with sneakers and a windbreaker."

Then we started talking about our graduate programs. He explained his dissertation and we talked about the social dynamics of both our cohorts. We didn't talk about superficial things, but we also didn't talk about anything especially personal. I realized that he was the type of guy who I wouldn't get to really know until a few dates in—maybe longer.

At one point I went to the bathroom and looked at myself in the mirror. Everything about my reflection looked wrong to me. I was freakishly tall. My lips were dry and chapped. It wasn't a pleasant face, I thought, as I stared at my oily skin, my unsymmetrical features. I ran my hands over my stomach and sucked in.

I thought about Charlie's words, *You're like Lady Gaga*, and turned away from the mirror before I could think too much about this.

"What do you write about?" Peter asked me when I returned to our table.

"I write short stories. A lot of them are about daughters losing their mothers," I said. "Sometimes I try to write something different, but it always comes back to that."

He looked interested. "I'd be curious at some point to read one of your stories. My mother died a few months ago."

I put down my glass of wine. I knew it wasn't his intention, but suddenly, I saw him differently. His sad eyes, his sweatshirt, his rare smile. I imagined the floods of emotion going through Peter—the few times I'd seen him around campus—and had no idea. "I'm so sorry," I said.

"It's okay," he said. "Thanks, though. It all happened quickly. Her getting sick, I mean."

I nodded and waited for him to say more.

"We all felt pretty helpless. Especially my dad."

"I can't imagine," I said. "How's your family doing? Your dad?"

"Everyone's coping in their own way. Some better than others."

"Right."

"My mom's white—Jewish—and my dad's black, and their families had some different ideas when it came to the funeral, so there was some friction around that."

"You're Jewish?"

"Yeah. You are, too?"

I nodded.

"I thought you might be."

"Oh?"

"Just your name, and, like, your—"

"Face?"

He smiled. "You look more Jewish than I do, anyway."

I shrugged. "I'm really sorry about your mom."

He didn't offer any more information after that, and I got the sense not to ask.

After we finished our drinks, we hugged goodbye outside the wine bar. I was half an inch taller than him in my boots, which meant that maybe we'd be the same height if I wore flats.

"That was nice," he said. "Want to do it again sometime?"

"Okay," I said. "I'd like that."

When I got home, I saw that I had three missed calls from Charlie, and a text.

Hey I have to come downtown tonight can I come see you for a little?

I put my phone down and started changing into pajamas. Three missed calls seemed excessive. I decided not to call him back. But as I was brushing my teeth, my phone began to buzz. It was Charlie. I felt a strange sensation. I couldn't tell if I was annoyed or a little bit aroused. I picked up. Hearing his voice, I was sure, would provide the answer.

"Hey," he said, his voice soft.

"What's up?"

"Are you home, by any chance?"

"Yeah. Why?"

"I just finished up with Max and I'm actually near your street. I don't want to bother you, though . . ."

"No," I said. "Come over."

Not even a minute later, my doorbell rang. When I opened it, Charlie was standing there, in a sweater and no coat, a blue winter hat with earflaps, hands in pockets. His eyes were wide and round. He looked like a little boy, except that he was over six feet tall, and he had the start of a beard growing in.

He smiled his slow, sweet smile and nodded hello. I realized I was expecting him to be angry; to ask me where I had been and why I hadn't been answering my phone. We hadn't seen each other since he'd told me he was in recovery, and when we had spoken, we'd both avoided the topic. But he just looked innocent and relieved, as though he'd been standing there for a while now, waiting for me to get home.

4.

ON MY SECOND DATE WITH PETER WE WENT OUT TO DINNER. I felt distracted and depressed. Thanksgiving was coming up and I didn't want to go home.

We went to a tavern in Atwood called the Alchemy, which served huge portions of colorful vegetarian food, things like coconut curry and grilled cheese stuffed with broccoli and roasted carrots and red onion. A live band was playing on the opposite side of the restaurant. Peter was wearing another crewneck sweatshirt—this one lime-green.

He also looked a little distracted and depressed.

"What are you doing for Thanksgiving?" I asked him.

"We get together with my dad's family in Oakland. It's usually a big event. Aunts, uncles, cousins, grandparents."

"That sounds nice." I didn't know how to make a sensitive comment about holidays and loss that was also not intrusive, so instead I said, "The older I get, the more I dread holidays."

He cocked his head to the side. "Why's that?"

"A yearly reminder of how fucked things are."

"Are things really bad?"

"No," I said, hearing how gloomy I sounded. "Things are okay."

There was a familiarity about Peter that made me feel both drawn to him and nervous. It was comforting being with someone Jewish, with someone who wasn't from around here. He was warm, but reserved. I recognized the ways he held back. It was harder talking to him, though, than it was talking to Charlie. Peter was quiet and he listened more closely, so there was more of a chance of saying something stupid, of messing it up. With Charlie and me, Charlie was the talker, and I was the one trying to make sense of it all.

We both loosened up after a drink. I told him about the literary agent. I made it all sound very dramatic and funny, and he laughed as I described, play-by-play, my conversation with her.

"It sounds kind of traumatizing," he said.

"It was," I told him. "I didn't realize what a poor first impression I make."

"I don't think you make a poor first impression." He smiled then—and it was the surprise of his smile, the way his whole demeanor changed, how his eyes brightened and the grooved lines around his mouth deepened—that made me realize that I did feel attracted to him.

After dinner, he drove me home. He pulled up outside my apartment and put the car in park.

"I know Thanksgiving is next week, but maybe we can see each other once more before we go home?" he asked.

"Yeah," I said. "Let's do that."

There was that extra beat of charged silence, and he looked down at the center console and then back up again. "I'm a little out of practice with this part," he said. "I just got out of a serious relationship . . ."

"That's okay," I said, and I leaned forward over the console, and we kissed.

It wasn't like my first kiss with Charlie—where everything around me disappeared and I felt delirious. The world was very much still going on around us. I liked Peter. But I was thinking about what he'd told me. That he'd just gotten out of something serious. And he was grieving. I don't know why these things scared me, but as I waved goodbye to him and walked up the path toward my apartment door, I felt uncertain.

"I wanted to tell you guys something," Wilson said. We were sitting at our table at City Bar after workshop, the tabletop covered with half-finished beers and baskets of cold fries. The poets weren't there—they'd stopped coming a long time ago—so it was just the six of us. It had been a good workshop. Vivian and Sam had been up, and they'd both handed in the kind of writing that made us all want to go home and write.

We turned to Wilson. He was frowning at his fries. "I wanted to let you know that Maya Joshi called me and she's . . ." He looked up, his eyes moving between the five of us. "She's interested."

It had been almost a month since Maya Joshi's visit, and we'd all finally begun to forget about it.

"Wilson!" Rohan said, swiftly breaking the silence. He clapped a hand on Wilson's back. "Holy crap, man. That's *fantastic*."

Everyone echoed Rohan, and Sam held up his beer. "Cheers to that!" We all clinked glasses and Vivian got up off her stool and went over and gave Wilson a hug. "Wilson," she said. "You're on your fucking *way*."

"Wait, so how did this go down?" David asked, leaning over the table. "Tell us the details."

"She just called me—"

David snorted. "So, writing our emails down was bullshit."

"I don't know," Wilson said. "I'm not sure how she got my number—"

"Probably from the department," said David.

"Right. So she told me that she liked my stories and that she'd also read my story in *Glimmer Train*."

"You have a story in *Glimmer Train*?" Sam said.

"Anyway," Wilson went on, blushing deeply. "She said to keep doing my thing here at school and whenever I wanted to send her something she'd be happy to read it. It all seems fairly informal."

"Well, I think we should celebrate with shots," said Vivian. "This is not just any normal Tuesday night. Is anyone with me?"

We all stood up. The mood was weird. We were smiling, but you could feel the collective anxiety. When we'd all had meetings in October, we'd been on even ground. Now there was a disruption. Wilson had been raised up; selected. I hung back for a moment with him, watching as he rummaged in his backpack for his wallet as the others migrated over to the bar. He was the only one not smiling. He didn't know how to act, so he wasn't acting at all.

"Wilson," I said. "Could you tell when you were in the meeting with her?"

He hesitated, then nodded. "Yeah. I could."

"How?"

"Just the way she was talking. She seemed serious. She asked about a novel."

"Wow, Wilson," I said. "That's so cool."

He smiled. "Thanks, Leah."

We were standing a few feet behind the others now. Sam and

Rohan were a little off to the left talking, and Vivian and David were in front of us, trying to get the bartender's attention.

The bartender turned to Vivian. "What can I get you?"

"We'll have six shots—" Vivian started to say, but David put a hand on her lower back, cutting her off.

"Let me get this round," he said. "We'll have six shots of tequila, please, and you can put that on my tab. David *Eisenstat*." His hand was still firmly on Vivian's back, so low that his pinkie was grazing her butt.

I was scheduled to leave for Thanksgiving on the very last day possible, Wednesday. On the Saturday before, Peter invited me over to his apartment for dinner. He lived about a mile from my apartment and as I walked down Willy Street toward his place, flakes of snow swirled in frantic circles in the sky.

Peter answered the door in a worn gray button-down, the first time I'd seen him without a sweatshirt. He was smiling when he let me in, eyes calm and warm in the soft lighting of his apartment. "Do you like salmon?" he asked, as I took my flats off in his front entryway.

"I do," I said. "You're cooking for me?"

"Attempting to."

He gave me the tour. The apartment was spare, but he had all the necessary furniture and a few framed posters on the walls. The kitchen had the most lived-in feel, with plenty of pots and pans, a gourmet knife set, and a huge rack of spices.

I prepared the asparagus while he prepared the fish, and we caught up on our weeks. Both of us were teaching that semester and we talked about our classes.

Teaching was something I hadn't expected to like. The first class I ever taught I let the students go an hour early because I ran out of things to say. After that it got easier. And I started preparing more. Some of the students took notes while I was talking, and this thrilled me and made me think more carefully about what I was actually saying. There were usually a few who came by my office hours to see if I would read a new draft of their story. I always said yes. I attracted the students who reminded me of how I was as an undergrad—shy but serious.

The part I liked most about teaching was that mysterious moment in the semester when the class no longer felt like a random group of strangers in a room. There was always a point when it occurred to me that everybody knew everybody else, and the classes, in a sense, began to run themselves.

I told Peter about my students and he told me about his. Then I told him about Wilson and the agent and there was a comfort in talking about this with someone who wasn't in my cohort, but who was in a cohort himself.

We moved into the living room and sat on the couch with our wine.

"I can't wait to be done with all this academia stuff," he said. "And Wisconsin."

"Oh?"

"I'm so tired of being here."

I tried not to show anything on my face, but when he said this, I felt sad. Though I barely knew him, I realized I didn't want him to leave.

"Where do you want to go?" I asked.

"I'd like to live abroad," he said. "Maybe Barcelona."

"Do you speak Spanish?"

"I do. But they speak Catalan over there. I think I could get by, though."

"Oh," I said, feeling dumb. "Right."

He stood up then and put on music. "Have you ever listened to Berry?"

The song he put on was French. The woman who was singing had a silky, sexy voice. The melody was beautiful and flirtatious.

"No," I said, "but this is nice." I paused. "I like being here. In Wisconsin."

"What do you like about it?" he asked, sitting back down beside me.

"I like the people in Madison. I like writing here. I like my life." I shrugged. "I guess I'm happy."

"That's good," he said. "Maybe it's just because I've been here for five years now, but I can't wait to get out. Besides, it's too cold here." He put his arms around me then, and it was the most physical contact we'd had, other than that one kiss in his car.

We readjusted on his couch so we were horizontal. There was a strength and solidity to him in comparison to Charlie, who was so thin he was almost frail. While we were kissing, he pulled back at one point and sang along to a line from the song, and I was so surprised to hear him sing that I laughed.

"That's my favorite part," he said, smiling.

I nodded. "I like it."

This meal together was different. We were less careful around each other. I ate without feeling like I was getting food on my face with every bite. I told him more about my family and he told me about his. He talked a little more about his mother's death. Mostly, though, he spoke about how his father had started dating someone immediately afterward, and how much he hated that. "It's not that I hate *her*," he said. "I'm sure she's a fine person. But I can't get behind the relationship. It's disrespectful to my mother."

"Will this woman be at Thanksgiving?" I asked.

He nodded. "And her daughter. I get if she and my dad have their own thing going on, but I don't understand why they need to involve the families."

I felt suddenly protective of him. If he had asked me if I would go with him to his family's Thanksgiving, I would have ditched my family in a second. I would have bought a ticket to Los Angeles right then and there.

We cleared our dishes and I started to wash the plates, but he stopped me. "I'll do that in the morning." Then he pointed toward the window. "Look outside."

It was snowing heavily now, big gentle flakes falling silently in the dark. There was already a thick, clean layer of white on the windowsill.

Whatever lingering formality that we felt around each other disappeared once we were naked. Suddenly Peter was all there. He touched me, not like a guy who'd been with a lot of women, but like someone who had been with one woman, for a long time. He knew how to listen and adjust. He figured me out so well that I began to laugh.

"What?" he asked, laughing, too.

"How are you so good at this?"

He kissed me, pulling me on top of him. He radiated warmth. "You give me lots of hints."

The only light in the bedroom was from the streetlights coming in from the window, and everything was soft and muted, different shades of blue. It was so quiet from the snow. We could have been the only two people in the world, right then, tangled together on his bed.

I sat up on top of him. "Do you want to have sex?"

"Do you?"

I nodded.

"Me, too," he said.

With me still sitting on him, he stretched his arm over to the bedside table and pulled a condom out from a drawer.

For several moments we were still, locked together, breathing slow. He closed his eyes, gripping my hips, and I was overcome with how good it all felt. I leaned down and kissed his ear and his neck, his other ear.

He held me tighter. Then, gently, he flipped me over so that he was on top. "Is this okay?"

I squeezed my legs around his waist and pushed myself closer against him.

"Tell me what feels good," he said, pushing back, almost like we were fighting, but it was soft, somehow.

"That does," I whispered. "What you're doing."

Sometimes, when I was having sex, I had an irrational fear that I would blurt out something embarrassing, or something I didn't mean—that I'd call the guy the wrong name or ask him to do something crazy, or I'd whisper my greatest fear or wish into his ear. With Peter, I kept having the slippery thought that I might accidentally say, *I love you*. I closed my eyes and bit my tongue.

Afterward I grabbed my purse and went to the bathroom. When I pulled out my phone, I froze. My lock screen was covered with Charlie's name. I had five missed calls, six text messages, and a voice mail.

I unlocked my phone and read his texts.

> **Hey I'm coming downtown tonight to meet up with Max can I stop by and maybe we can finish watching that tv show about polygamy and roses you like?**

> **I just tried calling you. Call me back when you get this? I'm only going to be downtown for a little longer.**

> **Is something wrong? Is there a reason you're not picking up or answering my texts? Did I do something unknowingly?**

> **I was kidding about the bachelor we def don't have to watch that I more just wanted to see you because I miss your cute smile and whatnot**

> **I'm getting a bad feeling and my intuition is usually right about these things but I'm really really really hoping I'm wrong so please call me back or text me or something. At least so I know you're not being held**

hostage by that creep David Einstein or whatever in your program I have a feeling that guy is going to end up on Dateline one day

Okay, Leah. I think I get what's going on. Have fun tonight. I'm going to try not to think about it and get some sleep.

Reading Charlie's texts had a physical effect on me. They took me out of Peter's apartment and transported me into the strangeness that was Charlieland. I started to text him back, but then something came over me. The right thing to do was not to answer. It was two in the morning. I powered off my phone. I flushed the toilet and stood up.

I crawled back into bed beside Peter.

"Your feet are freezing," he said, as we found one another in the dark.

"They're always freezing."

"Do you want socks?"

"I'm good. I'll just use your legs as a heater." I poked my feet into his calves.

"Jesus," he said, laughing softly. "Do you have some kind of circulation problem?" He reached under the covers and grabbed one of my feet. He squeezed it gently between his palms. "So," he said. "What should I read over Thanksgiving break? I don't read a lot of fiction."

"Do you want to read short stories or a novel?" I asked.

"Let's go with short stories."

"You should read Bea Leonard's collection. She's teaching our workshop this semester and she was the reason I applied to the program. She's very funny and dark."

Peter turned over in bed so he was looking at me. My foot was still in between his hands. "Okay. I'll take your word for it."

In the morning it was glaring white outside, with snow still coming down. We'd only slept a few hours but I woke up with all the energy in the world. Peter was leaving for the airport later that morning. When I rolled over in bed, he was sitting up, with a sweatshirt on.

"Morning, Leah," he said.

"Morning."

As I was getting dressed, he made the bed. "Do you want any coffee?" he asked, touching me briefly on my waist.

"No, thank you."

We trudged outside to his car and I sat in the passenger seat and watched him while he scraped snow off the windshield. He was wearing a black ski jacket and a maroon winter hat, no scarf or gloves. He looked serious while he did this, and I wondered what he was thinking. If it was about going home, or about his mother. Or if he was thinking about last night, or his ex. Or if maybe he was just cold and focusing on getting the snow off his car.

When he finally climbed into the driver's seat he said, "Shit, I didn't turn on the heat for you. I'm sorry about that."

"Don't worry about it."

When he pulled in front of my apartment I asked, "Want me to get that book for you?"

"Yes," he said. "I would love that."

I ran in and grabbed the book and then climbed back in the car.

"This one's special to me, so I'll want it back. Feel free to fold down the pages or whatever; I don't care about that."

He took it and read the description on the inside jacket. "I'm excited to read this. I'll take good care of it." Then he looked at me with his sad eyes. "See you in December?"

I nodded. "Definitely. Have a nice Thanksgiving."

We leaned in and kissed, lightly, on the lips.

I had three days ahead of me until my flight. Everyone from my program had already gone home for the holiday. I was nervous to turn my phone back on because I didn't know if I'd be hit with another influx of messages from Charlie, but when I did, later that morning, nothing came in except for one text from my dad.

> **Looking forward to seeing you for Turkey Day. What time does your flight get in on Wednesday?**

I lay on my bed and tried to read but I was too distracted. So I watched the rest of *The Bachelor* episode that I'd started with Charlie. And then I started to think about Charlie. Maybe I'd been a real asshole to him. I thought about how jealous I'd been when I'd seen the photos of him and his ex-girlfriend on Facebook. And those photos were from years ago. I'd be dizzy with jealousy—not to mention hurt and humiliation—if I knew he'd been with someone else while he'd been seeing me.

I opened my phone and looked at the photos of him and his ex, as if to prove to myself that jealousy was a real and powerful emotion. Looking at the photos of Charlie also elicited something else in me. Charlie didn't *look* like the crazy guy who sent all those texts last night. He looked like the guy who I'd met at the Weary Traveler; the guy in the glasses and the multicolored fleece who'd driven me home that sunny October morning. I could still feel that intense rush of affection I had for him.

Peter showed his affection in bursts—smiles here and there. Little windows in. Maybe one day he would love me. But maybe he was depressed and I was filling a void.

Charlie seemed wide open. He was vulnerable, like I was.

I texted Charlie, before I lost my nerve.

You're right, I wrote. **I've been seeing someone else too and I'm sorry for being dishonest about it.**

He responded several minutes later. **I get it. I'm at a place in my life and my sobriety where I need to respect myself more than that. Enjoy your fun and take care, hon.**

The last sentence of his text infuriated me, and I wrote back immediately. **It's also pretty messed up for you to text and call as many times as you did. And please don't call me hon.**

Wasn't trying to be passive aggressive calling you hon. Actually meant it in an affectionate way. If you got to know me more you'd come to learn that I use nicknames a lot: hon, honey, sweetheart, angel (just kidding I don't use that one, Paul calls my mom that and it makes me want to hurl) but I also understand those kind of names are kinda dated and sexist these days so I really am sorry if I offended you. But seriously, Leah, you're a cool girl and I'm sad this didn't work out. Like really sad.

I read his text, confused. Was he trying to fuck with me? Was he angry with me or not? Should I delete his number and put my phone away or should I respond? I closed my eyes and then opened them.

I'm sad, too, I wrote finally. **I know we've only known each other a short time, but it feels like longer. Goodbye Charlie.**

Then I started to cry. I rolled over on my bed and buried my face in my pillow. I was glad that everyone I knew had already gone home for the holiday because I would rather be alone and sad than try to explain this breakup with a guy who shouldn't matter but, for whatever reason, did. When my phone buzzed again twenty minutes later, I was no longer crying but staring blankly at my wall.

> **I understand if you don't want to, but would you be open to talking about this in person?**

I made myself wait five minutes before responding. **I'm free right now.**

5.

I WAS NERVOUS ANSWERING THE DOOR, BUT CHARLIE LOOKED
like he always did—sweet, innocent, gentle. He'd showed up wearing a sweater over a button-up shirt with the knot of a tie peeking out, like he was about to go to church. His hair was parted neatly on one side and had been brushed with a comb. He was holding a guitar.

"You're all dressed up," I said, once we were inside.

"My mom suggested I change. She thought I might have a better chance with you if I cleaned up a little."

I smiled. "You talked to your mom about it?"

"Not the details. It's too embarrassing."

We were in my living room, me in the nice Craigslist chair, him in the not-nice one. He had sunk deep into the cushions, his legs stretched out, his hands in his pockets.

"I'm sorry, Charlie. I didn't mean to make this embarrassing."

"So who is this guy?" he asked softly.

I shook my head. "It doesn't really matter."

"Can I at least know his name?"

"Peter."

He didn't say anything.

"You brought a guitar?" I gestured toward the big black case sitting in the entranceway.

"Oh," Charlie said. "I have band practice tomorrow and I didn't think it was safe to leave it sitting in my car."

"You're in a band?"

"Informally."

"Really?"

He smiled. "No, not really. But I had to find some way to compete with *Peter*."

When he played for me, his voice was soft and raspy, kind of like his speaking voice. I didn't know a lot about music but I knew that he was good. Really good. First he sang "Masterfade" by Andrew Bird and then "The Only Living Boy in New York" by Simon & Garfunkel. He wasn't making eye contact because he was reading the chords and lyrics off his phone, and I was grateful for that because I could watch him without having to think about what I looked like. He made lots of mistakes, but even his mistakes sounded good. They sounded like mistakes from someone who knew what he was doing. I felt like I was Maya Joshi in the room with Wilson. Like I'd *found* him—his talent, his potential, his charisma. I felt lit up listening to him. Completely alive.

Later in the evening, when he became bolder and he belted out the songs—"Space Oddity" by David Bowie, "Lola" by the Kinks, "Learning to Fly" by Tom Petty—his voice filling up the entire apartment, spilling out into the hallway of the building, I was speechless. I could have listened to him all night, all day. "Another," I told him, after every song. "One more."

Sometimes I'd sing along with him, but I was so quiet that my voice disappeared into his. Still, it felt good to sing with him—like we were doing something productive together. Hours later, he put his guitar down into its case and said, "I want to make you an omelet."

I laughed. "Okay."

It was past eight o'clock and had been dark for a while. I had almost no food in the house, so we drove to Hy-Vee, a grocery store on the outskirts of the city, cheaper than Madison Fresh and Whole Foods, which were more centrally located and where all the students shopped. Charlie parked in the giant lot and for a moment we sat in the car. When he turned to me his eyes were bright with tears.

"You have to know that I'm never going to use heroin again."

"How am I supposed to know that, Charlie?"

"You don't understand, Leah. For me, heroin equals death. The doctors told me it's a miracle I'm alive. I don't know if I believe in God or a higher power or any of that. A lot of people in recovery do. But someone or something has been looking out for me—I'm sure of it. I overdosed a few years ago, and for all intents and purposes I should be dead. But I'm *here*. With you, right now, in this parking lot of Hy-Vee." He wiped his face with the back of his hand. "The stuff that makes life worth living is everything I have. I own a guitar. I have a computer to write. I have all ten fingertips." He held out his hands and looked at them; they were trembling. "And if I get to spend more time with you, Leah, I'll be the luckiest guy in Wisconsin. And if I don't, I'll still be the luckiest guy because I had today, and that will keep me going. But I do want you to know that I am never going to use again. That part of my life is over forever. It has to be, if I want to live. And I do, more than anything."

I took his hand. His emotion seemed so big right then that I didn't know how to say anything that honored or matched it. I felt young and girlish. I felt as if he'd lived a life I didn't comprehend in the slightest. "I'm glad you're okay," I said. "I'm glad you're alive." And even though they were true, my words felt flat and small.

Once we entered the grocery store, Charlie's mood seemed to shift. Suddenly he was overjoyed; hyper. He practically ran down the aisles, pulling item after item off the shelves and throwing them into the cart, which I pushed behind him, hurrying to keep up. He picked out things that didn't make sense, like strawberry frosting and frozen bagel bites and sour-cream-and-onion potato chips. He narrated as we weaved through the mostly empty store, explaining to me why each purchase was necessary. The chips would be perfect if we got hungry late at night, and strawberry frosting was good on pancakes, which he wanted to make me. He wanted me to try this cheese and that kind of olive and he couldn't wait for us to have animal crackers dipped in hot chocolate like he used to when he was a kid.

"What about the omelet, Charlie?" I kept saying. "We have to focus on the omelet."

By the time we reached the register, our cart was teeming with an assortment of specialty items, junk food, cured meats, cheeses, and a few ingredients to make an omelet.

We loaded everything onto the conveyer belt and the woman behind the register scanned each item while Charlie and I loaded them into bags.

"That's going to be one hundred sixty-eight dollars and fifty-two cents," the woman said.

I looked at Charlie, who opened his wallet. "Shit," he muttered. "Leah, I forgot my EBT card at home."

The woman looked at me, and I looked at Charlie. "Charlie," I said. "I don't want all this stuff and I'm about to go home for Thanksgiving."

He nodded. "Kasey," he said then, glancing at the woman's name tag as she eyed us from behind the register. "Will you do us a huge favor? Can you hold on to these bags for me while I run home, grab my card that I left in my coat pocket, and then I'll be back so I can pay you?"

The woman frowned. "We don't hold groceries."

"You can put them anywhere. I mean, *I'll* put them anywhere. Right there on the floor, even. I'll be back in fifteen minutes, tops. I promise you, Kasey, I'm good for it. You can ask her." He touched my shoulder.

"Yeah, we don't do that," the woman said, glancing at me. "We would need to refrigerate the bags in case you don't come back for them and we don't have that kind of refrigerator space."

"That makes sense, but I swear to you—I'll even leave the rest of my wallet here as collateral. I'll make it back here before nine p.m."

"Charlie," I cut in, "let's just buy the stuff for the omelet. It's all in this bag, anyway. I can pay for it."

Charlie glanced at the bag. "Okay," he said. He turned back to Kasey. "I'll go put all this stuff back. I don't want you to have to do it."

The woman laughed a little. "How about you two just pay for what you can pay for and we'll deal with the rest?"

"Let's get the frosting, too," Charlie said to me. "I still want to make you pancakes." He took the frosting from one of the other bags and put it in the omelet bag.

I paid for our stuff and Charlie and I walked back out to his car.

"You're a little nuts, you know that?" I said, as we climbed into the car.

Charlie turned the key in the ignition. "I'm a lot better than I used to be."

We didn't leave the house again after that, except when Charlie went outside to smoke a cigarette. Our sleep schedules were off and I never knew what time of day it was. I was barely looking at my phone. There was nobody I wanted to hear from anyway. If Charlie had work those three days, he didn't go, and I didn't ask him about it. His mom called a number of times, but he never picked up the phone.

Charlie played more music, but mostly we had sex. I don't want to say it was the sex that hooked me, but it might have been. I came more than he did but he explained that it was the medication he was on, sub, and that it didn't matter to him. It happened easily. I'd never been so attracted to anybody in my life.

We showered each other with compliments—*your face is perfect, you smell so good, I feel like I've fantasized about you before I even met you*—and all of it was so much, so all at once, I could barely catch my breath.

It was different than whatever we'd been doing before. Now we couldn't get enough of each other.

His beauty only intensified for me. I could have stared at him all day, all night, done nothing else, and never gotten bored. I was in awe. And when desire overtook his face—he had a specific expression where his mouth turned downward a little, his eyes traveling across my body—I couldn't believe it was me he was looking at. I could practically be brought to orgasm that way, just being looked at by him. And when he did put his hand between my legs, his finger hovering so lightly in just the right spot that I thought I might die, my mind would go blissfully blank. Sometimes it only took a few seconds.

One evening I sat straddling Charlie. My bed was a mess of twisted sheets, the blankets a pile on the floor. He had one hand on my hip, the other behind his head. It could have been nine at night or two in the morning. I felt light-headed from pleasure and maybe hunger, but the idea of food didn't interest me.

"Charlie," I said.

"Yeah?"

"I feel bad for anyone in the world who isn't us."

A smile spread slow and wide across his face. Everything about him seemed to brighten. "I feel terrible for all of them," he said.

So, at the end of the three days, when Charlie started to cry, I had an idea of what was coming.

"What is it?"

"I'm happy," Charlie said.

"But why are you crying?"

"I didn't know I deserved to be this happy," said Charlie. "I didn't think it was ever going to happen for me."

I nodded.

"Leah," Charlie said. "I'm in love with you."

In that moment, an image of Peter flashed in my mind's eye—the steadiness in him as he brushed snow off the windshield. How calm I'd felt waking up beside him, the bright winter light pouring in through his window. I didn't really know Peter. And I'd never get to know him, or what he'd been thinking about that morning.

Saying it back to Charlie meant that I was really in it.

And when I did say it back, I felt an unease, but underneath it, an even deeper joy.

6.

MY PLANE LANDED AT LOGAN INTERNATIONAL AIRPORT ON Wednesday afternoon. I met my dad in the pickup lane. My dad had been driving the same green Subaru Forester since I was in elementary school, and over the years he'd been adding bumper stickers from mine and my brothers' various summer camps and colleges and graduate programs to the bumper. When I spotted his car, I saw the big red *W* from the University of Wisconsin, and I felt a pang of love for my father. He was a good dad, though we had nothing in common. He was a math professor at Simmons; he dealt with numbers and logic, and when he read, it was the news or the occasional presidential biography. The one time I'd given him one of my stories, he'd commented, "I thought it was interesting how all the characters take public transportation everywhere. Do none of them drive? Also, why are they all so angry?"

"There she is!" he said as I hoisted my suitcase into the backseat. "Here I am!"

We gave each other a brief one-armed hug after I'd climbed in. "Were there a lot of people on the flight?"

My dad liked asking questions like this: How was the traffic? Which route did you take? Was it crowded? I wasn't sure if it was his math brain or his dad brain, but I didn't mind his questions. There was something comforting about someone else caring about the logistics of my day. How I got from point A to B. I thought of Charlie then—showing up at his father's pharmacy. His dad looking at him—first blank-faced, then horrified.

"The plane was just about full," I said. "I got an aisle seat."

"Oh good," my dad said. "Easy bathroom access."

"Exactly."

When we got home, Monica greeted us right away at the door. I think she liked to remind me that she lived there now; that my dad was hers. She'd been with my father since I was seventeen, but they hadn't gotten married until I was twenty, after her divorce had been finalized.

Monica was nothing like my mother. She had blond hair that she got dyed and styled professionally every three weeks at a salon in the Back Bay. She had frameless glasses that magnified her small, watchful eyes. She possessed the qualities that good attorneys had—a steady, convincing voice, unwavering confidence, a poker face. She had a way of making you feel that as long as she was on your side, things would work out. I could see that it was good for my dad to be with someone like her. I'd watched the way Monica was with other people, like her daughter and my dad and her clients. But she was never that way with me.

Today she had on a gray turtleneck and a red apron. There was a useless barrette holding back one tuft of her bangs. "Leah, you look well," she said, air-kissing me on the cheek. "How was the flight?"

"The flight was good," I said. "How are you, Monica?"

"Cooking up a storm. Everyone's bringing their significant other this year, so I had to double all the food. But it's okay!" She threw up her hands dramatically. "There *will* be enough." Monica turned to my dad. "Dave, did I tell you Christina is bringing Stephen?"

"I don't think you mentioned that."

Monica rolled her eyes at me. "In one ear and out the other. Leah, my daughter is bringing this very interesting man she's seeing who's a journalist at WGBH. Or a reporter. Anyway, I thought you and Stephen would have a lot to talk about since you have *the writing connection*."

"Sure," I said. I realized then that I was still holding my suitcase. "I'm going to go bring this upstairs."

"Of course," said Monica. "You'll notice I moved a few boxes into your room to make more space for your brothers' girlfriends. But I'll be sure to clear out everything as soon as everyone leaves."

My bedroom, it turned out, had been converted into storage space. The room was overtaken by boxes, plastic crates, a few unplugged, dated computers, and an old exercise bike. I dropped my duffel bag onto some bare floor space and then collapsed on my bed. I closed my eyes and let the last three days with Charlie wash over me like a sedative.

My middle brother, Ben, arrived first. He'd brought Soo Min, a gastroenterology resident at Tufts, whom he'd been dating for three weeks. All Ben had told us about her ahead of time was that she was from out of state and it was impractical for her to go home for the holiday. Soo Min seemed confident and accomplished—as Ben's girlfriends tended to be. She had a blasé demeanor, as though going to a random family's Thanksgiving dinner were par for the course. When she presented a bottle of Merlot to Monica and Monica gushed over it as though she'd never been given wine before, Soo Min smiled thinly. "My pleasure," she said, unfazed. Her outfit—jeans and a long wool sweater that went down to her knees—was somehow both understated and trendy. I wondered what had attracted her to my brother.

Next to Soo Min, Ben looked even sloppier than usual. He still dressed the way he had back in high school. That night he had on a flannel over a yellow T-shirt. His hair was too long, curling up on the sides, and he had a disheveled, un-showered look about him. "I'm starving," he said by way of greeting, as they entered the kitchen. He reached his hand into a glass bowl of maple-roasted Brussels sprouts with bacon that was heating up on a warming plate and popped a sprout into his mouth.

Monica looked over at my father in alarm, but my father chose to tune this moment out. "Ben, I've set appetizers out in the living room," Monica said.

"Great," he responded, reaching in again for a bacon bit.

I glanced at Soo Min to see if she was bothered by this, but she was looking at her phone.

It was obvious to me, when Ben spoke about his students—he was an eighth-grade social studies teacher and he also coached the boys' JV soccer team—that he'd be a good dad and that he wanted a family. But the way he treated the women he dated suggested otherwise. His relationships never lasted more than a few months, and the excuses he gave us for ending them—she says *like* too much, she has weird feet, she wants to talk every day—gave me reason to believe that my brother was not a great person to become romantically involved with.

My oldest brother, Aaron, was softer and kinder than Ben. He wasn't scared of vulnerability. But unlike Ben, who always answered my phone calls, Aaron could vanish for long periods of time. It was impossible to get him on the phone and he canceled plans last minute. He blamed this on the busyness of his work— Aaron was a psychotherapist—but I suspected that Aaron was depressed, and that hibernation was his way of coping.

Aaron arrived next, with his longtime girlfriend Haley. Haley was also Jewish—"culturally, not religiously," was how she put it whenever it came up. She'd grown up in Westchester, New York, and then moved to Massachusetts for college, which was where she met Aaron. Now she taught ballet to children. She'd been in our lives long enough that I did feel some sort of tenderness for her. I appreciated her loyalty, especially to my brother. But I could only stand her cheeriness for a few hours at a time. Her go-to way of connecting to people was to give unsolicited advice.

Someone like Haley—the ultimate caretaker, oozing with maternal energy—made sense for Aaron, but I could see he got irritated by her. There were times she'd speak for him or she'd state her opinion as if it were their shared opinion—"We're avoiding artificial sweeteners these days," or "We get all of our news from Twitter"— and a look of masked agitation would come over my brother's face. A clenching of his jaw muscles, a caginess in his eyes. They'd been together since they were nineteen, though. They'd met at Harvard, their sophomore year of college. Haley was a part of Aaron, and he was a part of her.

She showed up to this dinner, as she did to most of our family dinners, in a floor-length dress and bearing a homemade dessert. "It's lemon yogurt pound cake," she said, handing a plate over to Monica. "Made with Greek yogurt."

"Yum," Ben muttered to Soo Min. "*Yogurt* cake."

Soo Min smirked. "Don't be a dick."

My brothers never showed up to family events without girlfriends. For Aaron, it was Haley, and for Ben, it was always somebody different. I was the one who never had a *partner, significant other, better half, whatever*—and I think my family assumed this meant that I was perpetually alone. They'd be shocked to know what actually went on in my life.

Still, I hated family events for this reason. Because, when it came down to it, I was alone. Everyone else had a partner with them as their own personal emotional shield.

We sat around in the living room, drinking wine and eating appetizers, pretending to enjoy one another's company. Haley told us about changes at her dance school—a new director, a scholarship program and everyone nodded enthusiastically. The nice thing about the significant others was that they often distracted from the underlying tension of the immediate family.

"Soo Min," Monica broke in, bored by Haley. "Tell us about *medical school*."

"Well, I'm technically not in med school anymore," Soo Min said. "Now I'm in residency. It's a lot of work, but it will be worth it."

"And what kind of doctor do you want to be?"

"Technically I already am a doctor. But I'm completing my training in GI."

It was clear from the way Soo Min was speaking that she was asked these questions all the time.

"Good, Ben." Aaron grinned. "Now someone can finally help you with your IBS."

Ben put his arm around Soo Min. "She's not a big fan of the poop jokes."

"You must deal with a lot of colon cancer, Soo Min," said Monica sympathetically.

"Some of that, yeah. GI is a whole range of things." Soo Min turned to me. "Leah, your brother tells me you're a writer."

"I write, yeah."

"Are you working on a book?"

"I am."

"*Really?*" said Monica. "I had no idea."

I turned to Monica. "Everybody is. At the end of the program we all hand in a book-length manuscript."

"What are you going to do with it?" asked Soo Min.

"Depending on what shape it's in, I'll send it out to agents," I said. "Try to get it published."

"Good for you, Lee," Aaron said. "That's great."

"You know, Leah," Monica said, "you should talk to Christina's boyfriend, Stephen. He could be a useful resource to you in terms of reaching out to publishing houses with your book. He interviews authors all the time on WGBH."

"Maybe," I said. "But that's not really how it works. First I have to find an agent, and it's the agent who reaches out to the publishing houses—not me. Our MFA program has already started introducing us to them."

Monica stood. "Well. It sounds like you know exactly what you're doing. I'm going to check on the turkey."

I pulled out my phone and pretended to type something.

"We just read *The Red Tent* for my book club," Haley said then. "I think it should be mandatory reading for every woman. Leah, have you read that?"

"Not yet," I said.

I glanced at my father, who had been silent throughout the entire conversation. He was staring off into space. There was a look of unrest on his face, as though he were trying to multiply numbers in his head—which was very likely what he might have been doing.

Things were better before my mother left. Ben says differently, but that's because it makes him too sad to remember.

There are certain memories I'd never write down or tell anyone. I know what happens when you write things down. They change shape. Some of the feeling goes away. Things on the page are never as rich as they are in your head, as they were in real life. There are parts of my mother I could never bear to lose.

And some things I write over and over again because it's the only real story that I have. Like her particular scent, how she always smelled good, no matter what. The way her closet and her bed and her clothes held her scent—powdery and springlike. On mornings when I'd climb into bed with her, how safe I'd feel, protected in her bubble.

Losing her has never stopped. While her disappearance happened fast, overnight—it's been a slow, endless transformation of our lives.

We used to do a lot together. We celebrated holidays and we'd pile into the car to go on family trips. We were always getting into arguments over trivial things. Childhood was a constant loop of playing and fighting and singing, the same fights and songs and games over and over again, but I never remember getting bored.

When Aaron broke his ankle on Thanksgiving one year, we all spent the day in the emergency room. We crowded into the hospital room and ate turkey and pie from the cafeteria. The food was terrible and Aaron was drugged up on painkillers. I was nine at the time, and Ben was eleven, and Aaron fourteen. We played charades and tried to make Aaron laugh, and Ben and I fought over who got to press the button on the elevator. My family functioned best that way—in a crisis. The five of us against the world.

That Thanksgiving in the hospital was one of those days with my family that had morphed, over the years, into a distinct memory, a story I liked to return to in my mind. Proof that there was a time when we were whole and happy. I do know what that feels like.

After she left, it was hard not to be angry. We'd be out and we'd see a certain type of family—two parents and a couple of kids—and I hated that family. I hated them because we used to be them. I knew that if my father or my brothers saw the family, they would feel the same thing. None of us would say it, but we'd all be feeling it, and that feeling would be enough to ruin the day.

I'm not angry anymore. Now, when I'm back home, I stay

quiet and wait until it's over. It's fine while it's happening, but afterward, when I'm by myself again, I feel blank and flat—like a half person, and I badly want to feel alive again.

My mother's presence was bigger than my father's. She talked more, hugged tighter, cried harder, laughed louder, yelled scarier. We inherited our father's height, but other than that, we all look more like her.

My mother's nose was the most distinct thing about her face. When I was younger, I thought it distracted from her prettiness. And I hated my own nose. It was too big and it had a bump; it wasn't girlie or cute. I would have done anything for one of those button noses. But after she left, I'd look at photos of my mother and I began to like her nose, its distinct topography. How her face looked different depending on the angle. I'd look at my own reflection and instantly see my mother.

My mother's eyes and mouth were almost sensual in their ability to express emotion. Sometimes it was hard to look at her, because everything was all there, all her feeling—in the shape of her mouth, trapped in her gaze.

There are moments when I catch my brothers like this—all their vulnerability mixed up in their expressions. I never know if I should acknowledge it when this happens. I don't know how to reach my brothers, or if they want to be reached. I know that my face is readable in the same way. Sometimes I'll make eye contact with a stranger, usually a man, and I can tell they are seeing something on my face—something totally naked.

I don't think of my mother all the time. There are days or

weeks or even months when I don't wonder about her—where is she, what she's doing—at all. But her absence is part of me, a void I carry around.

My mother was an artist, but she rarely made any money from her art. She didn't need to, because my dad's job—and my dad—was steady. She was always starting new projects. She beaded jewelry and sewed her own clothing and sculpted pots out of terra-cotta clay. Each time she started something new, she acted as though she'd finally found the thing that would make her happy. When she quit something, she never looked back. I was aware, even as a young child, that I, too, was one of her passions, the same way her other obsessions were. Sometimes she seemed enthralled with me—even more than with my brothers. I was the girl, and the youngest, and I was the most like her. That's what she told me.

But there were also times when our life and our house and our family seemed to depress her. She would disappear on weekends. My father would be comatose those days, glued to the phone, waiting. He did nothing else those weekends but wait. Any small movement from the window, any hint of noise from outside, his gaze would jolt to the door, hopeful. Eventually, it really would be her, coming home. Then the two of them would disappear to their room for a while. Sometimes there would be voices or crying—mostly hers—but there'd never be any explanation as to where she'd gone. It became something we lived with, our mother's disappearances. But also, the relief of her coming back.

"Where do you go those times when you leave, Mom?" I asked her once, when it was just the two of us. Sometimes we did things together, my mother and I, like go hiking or to museums or take long drives to random destinations just to have something to do.

"When I leave where?" she asked, looking confused. I understood she was pretending not to know what I was talking about, and I played along. I knew I had to be gentle and patient with my mother, if I wanted to get a truthful answer from her.

We were sitting in a little town square, hours away from home. We'd parked the car on a side street and eaten sandwiches at an old-fashioned diner. My mother seemed to know the town, though I'd never been there before. She'd brought me into a used bookstore and a jewelry shop and told me to pick out whatever I wanted. She always spoiled me on those excursions.

"When you leave on the weekends. Like two weeks ago." I said it like it wasn't a big deal.

"*Oh*," she said, as if remembering. "Don't worry about that, okay, Lee? That has nothing to do with you." She smiled at me then, which made me feel both relieved and confused. "That has to do with me living my own life. It's important that I still live my own life, right?"

"Right," I said. And that explanation suddenly made so much sense to me. I never questioned it. A year later—when she left for good—it was those words I kept coming back to. My mother had to live her own life. My mother's life, even when she was at home, was a mystery. Sometimes I was allowed in, and sometimes I knew to wait. I instinctually understood what my mother wanted, and at times what she wanted was to not be a mother.

The only thing I wanted was for my mother to be happy, and I did everything I could to make her happy. When she was happy, I felt loved.

My brothers talk about my mother as someone unpredictable, with terrible mood swings. She cried easily and would leave rooms abruptly, announcing that she was having a panic attack. My father would hurry after her, but she never seemed to want to be comforted by him. Aaron says she was mentally ill, and Ben uses words like *psycho* and *loony tunes*. I remember my mother as someone who was always searching for something. She seemed lost. Like she'd ended up in our house, in our family, by accident.

I could tell that I had an effect on her, though. Even if she didn't like being a mother, she at least liked being *my* mother. I wasn't a normal daughter; I knew that from an early age. I was a perfect daughter. I was well behaved and always nice. I was affectionate but I knew when to pull back. When she left us, the part that hurt most was that she didn't take me with her.

After she left, Ben and Aaron and I bickered less—bonded together not so much by the loss of our mother, but by the shared task we then had of trying to keep our father happy.

It wasn't that my father had been an especially happy person when my mother was around. But up until that point, my father had seemed content. And he took pleasure in being a dad. He liked helping us with homework and making meals for us. To him, a nice night was grading his students' tests at the kitchen table while we read or watched TV in the next room—my mother somewhere close by, working on whatever project she was into at the time. After she was gone, my father, who'd always been steady and reserved— a numbers guy—suddenly turned into a romantic. I'd never seen my father cry before. Now the smallest things set him off. A Joni Mitchell song, a birthday card, a commercial for Cheerios.

More upsetting than my father's tears were the ways my broth-

ers changed. They grew up quickly. The first few weeks, when it
was clear that she wasn't coming back, it was unbearable, like a
sudden death. We hid from one another, not knowing what to do
with all our embarrassing grief, the way we'd suddenly start crying out of nowhere. Then we adapted. My brothers understood
that with our mother gone, it was up to them to fill in and step up.
We all took different roles. Aaron was better with emotions and
Ben was better at being funny. *We're having a great time! Things are
normal!*

It was Aaron, though, who really took care of us—making
sure Ben and I woke up on time for school, asking if we needed
help with our homework. My father still made dinner every night,
but dinners were a performance, trying to pretend that we were a
happy family. Ben seemed desperate to make sure that nobody
cried at the table, so he would act outrageously—doing bits and
impressions, constantly making fun of Aaron and me—though he
didn't make fun of our father.

I felt that my feminine presence was crucial. Without me, it
would just be a group of lost men. I was there for them—sweet,
sturdy, agreeable. And I never brought a boyfriend home.

The first few years, she sent me cards on my birthday. The return address on the envelopes was in St. Paul, Minnesota, where
my mother was from. The messages inside devastated me—*Happy
birthday. Love, Mom.* No real note. Still, when I turned seventeen
and for the first time no card arrived, I cried. First because I was
hurt, but then I panicked.

"Do you think she's dead?" I asked Aaron. He was the only one
who could handle a question like that.

"She's not dead," Aaron said.

"How do you know?"

"I look her up online. She's living in St. Paul and she works at the public library. She teaches some sort of ceramics class."

This stunned me. "She forgot my birthday."

"Listen, Lee. You have to adjust your expectations. That's what my therapist told me. You have to expect literally nothing from her. Otherwise you're always going to be disappointed."

Several weeks after my seventeenth birthday, I had sex for the first time. Robbie and I did it on an unzipped sleeping bag in his parents' basement. Robbie was the nicest guy I knew. It hurt a little, but I didn't care. I cried afterward, not because I was upset, but because I was relieved. He held me the entire night, and that part was better than the sex.

Our lopsided family was starting to grow. Aaron met Haley. My father met Monica. Home looked the same but I didn't recognize it anymore. It was just a group of people.

When Christina and Stephen arrived, Monica forgot all about Soo Min and her residency. Now it was on to Christina's recent promotion as digital marketing manager, and Stephen as broadcast journalist at WGBH. Monica peppered them with questions, less for her benefit, since it was obvious she already knew all the answers, than for ours—so we understood just how impressive her daughter and her daughter's boyfriend were.

And they were impressive. They were good-looking, fit, polished. They were the kind of couple you'd find on the glossy black-and-white photo that comes inside the frame before you replace it with the real, more unfortunate-looking photo of whoever you were—zits and all. Christina and Stephen sat beside one another on the couch, saying all the right things, laughing at all the right moments, smiling like all of this was so much fun. I found myself wondering what their sex life was like. What did these two people do behind closed doors?

I was grateful, in that moment, for everyone back in Wisconsin. Vivian and Wilson and Rohan and Sam—even David. I was grateful for the stories they wrote; all those messy first drafts, the trust we put in each other week after week to read our attempts at *something* that hit a nerve. I was grateful for Bea Leonard and her unevenness; her strange clothes, her kindness, her awkwardness. Also for Peter and his sadness, his startling smiles.

But especially Charlie. How passionate he was, how every moment with him was unexpected. How he sang for me for hours. All those mistakes. Everyone in Wisconsin was imperfect, but nobody there was trying to pretend otherwise. It made being around them so much easier.

We ate. We went around and said what we were thankful for. We talked about politics. We'd all voted for Obama to be reelected, but sometimes Ben liked to say inflammatory devil's-advocate-type things to rile people up—mostly Aaron—and this went on between my brothers, while the newcomers watched and the people who were used to it tried to change the subject. My dad and I mostly didn't say anything.

"Leah," Christina said from across the table, once my brothers' bickering had died down. "I've been meaning to ask you. I actually know someone at UW; we went to Princeton together. He's getting his MBA. I don't know if you'd be interested in meeting him, but he's a very nice guy and *very* smart."

"Sure," I said. "It's always nice to make another friend."

"Great." She clapped her hands together. "His name is Glen Douglas. I'll make sure to get you his information before I leave."

"Cool." I returned to my cranberry sauce.

"Very cool," Ben intoned from across the table. "A date with a businessman."

I raised my eyebrows at my brother. "I didn't just agree to a date." I looked over at Christina. "Did I?"

She shook her head. "Not if you don't want it to be. I mean, he is single and so are you. I thought you two might hit it off. But it could absolutely be a friend thing. I just thought—you know—you're both from Boston, way out there in Wisconsin. Why not meet up?"

I could feel my face heat up. "I'm not single."

"Oh!" She glanced at Monica. "I'm sorry. My mom told me . . ."

"Who are you seeing, Lee?" Ben asked.

I paused. "This guy named Charlie."

"And what does Charlie do?" asked Monica, smiling.

"He's a musician," I said. "A really talented musician."

"Wow," Monica trilled. "So that's what he does for a living? Play music? Or is he studying music at the university?"

"No, what he does for money is construction."

The table was silent.

"So, tell us about him," Aaron said. "What's he like?"

"Why?" I said. "It doesn't matter."

"Of course it matters," Aaron pressed, in his therapist voice. "We want to know about your life. Is he from Wisconsin?"

"Yes, he's from Wisconsin. I don't know what you want me to say." The entire table was staring at me, waiting for what I was going to tell them about Charlie. "He's an interesting person," I said finally. "He's smart and funny. Really nice. Also, he's a recovering heroin addict."

This time the silence was longer. I took a sip of my wine. I didn't look at my father or my brothers. The person I did look at was Soo Min. She'd been calmly leaning back in her seat this whole time, watching the conversation unfold, her face betraying nothing. When our eyes met, she gave me the smallest hint of a smile that I wasn't sure how to interpret.

Finally, Ben broke the silence. "Are you fucking with us?"

"Why would I joke about that?"

Ben pushed his chair back, his face red with fury. "Leah, are you an idiot? You can't fuck around with a heroin addict."

"Okay," Aaron cut in. "Relax, Ben. I think we should talk about this somewhere else, not with the whole group. Leah, let's go up to your room?"

"My room is stuffed with other peoples' crap, so it's unusable," I said. "Also, did you not hear the word *recovering*, Ben? He's been sober for three years. You don't know anything about him or the situation."

"Actually, I know more about it than you do, apparently," Ben said. "Heroin changes your brain chemistry, Leah. It doesn't matter how long this person has been clean—he is now physically dependent on this drug for the rest of his life."

"You don't know him, Ben," I said, and I felt then that if I stayed any longer at the table, I was going to bawl.

I looked at Monica hard, even though she hadn't said anything.

"I'm not hungry anymore." I left the table and went up to my room full of boxes.

Upstairs, I thought about calling Charlie, but the memory of our three days together—the singing, the sex, the closeness—all of it seemed too perfect to risk disrupting. What if he didn't answer? Or, worse, what if he answered and he sounded different than I remembered? Perhaps his enthusiasm for me had faded. Maybe I was clinging to the memory of those days with Charlie too tightly; blowing them out of proportion. It was possible I liked him more than he liked me.

Instead I texted Robbie. **Happy Thanksgiving!**

Hey, you too! he wrote back, within seconds. **With the fam?**

Unfortunately. You?

Back home now. Not going well?

Usual BS. Can I come over?

It was as if no time had passed. When Robbie and I hugged, he smelled like weed and the drugstore shampoo he used. I considered lingering in the hug a little—it would be easy to fall back into our old routine—but that wasn't why I was there.

We settled into our normal spots in his room—me on his rumpled, unmade bed, him at his desk chair. Robbie packed a bowl, while Radiohead crooned softly from his laptop speakers. There were a few dirty dishes piled on his desk and bureau. He still had his same setup for a night table—an upside-down milk crate with a desk lamp, a power cord with a mess of wires, and various chargers. I set my phone and keys down beside the lamp, ignoring the texts I was getting from my brothers to "come back and talk." I already felt better being at Robbie's. My family and Monica and Soo Min and Haley seemed far away and inconsequential.

Robbie rolled the desk chair over to the bed. "Ladies first," he said, handing me the small blue pipe.

I held the mouthpiece to my lips and inhaled as Robbie lit the bowl of weed until it glowed orangey-black. I held the smoke in for a few moments, and when I exhaled I began to cough uncontrollably. Robbie grabbed his water bottle from his desk and handed it to me.

"Thanks," I managed, gulping down the tepid water.

"How was it with your family?" Robbie asked, after he'd taken a hit.

I thought about trying to describe it to him, but it seemed too complicated—having to explain Charlie. I didn't want to risk making Robbie jealous. "Monica was being a bitch," I said. "And Ben brought a rando."

"Oh yeah? Who this time?"

"A doctor named Soo Min. She seemed fine but I'm sure I'll never see her again."

Robbie smiled softly at me. "Want to watch something to take your mind off it?"

"Sure."

We watched the first episode of *Game of Thrones*. I made him stop it every few minutes to explain what the hell was going on.

"Robbie, this is too confusing," I said, laughing.

Robbie started laughing, too. "Trust me," he said, "it's worth it when it starts to make sense. I'll put on subtitles. It's easier that way."

We were lying on his bed with his computer between us. I started to drift off during the second episode and Robbie lowered the volume on his computer and pulled the blanket over me. This woke me up a little because of how nice it was, but I pretended not to notice.

I startled a while later to the sound of an incoming text. I glanced at my phone. It was Charlie.

> **I miss you beautiful Leah. I hope it's okay but I told my extended family about you at Thanksgiving and they're all super happy for me. I know your family stresses you out so just know that if I was there with you right now I'd be holding your hand under the table.**

I shivered in delight. I wasn't making it up; he liked me as much as I liked him.

"Everything okay?" Robbie asked from the other side of the bed.

I put my phone down. "Yup."

"Are you going to stay here tonight?"

"Is that okay?"

"Of course."

When we went to bed, I could sense Robbie awake beside me, trying to decide whether to initiate something. He was waiting for me to turn over and open my eyes; or to say something—some kind of sign it was okay to touch me.

I kept my eyes closed and my back to him. After a while I could feel his body relax into sleep. Soft snores.

Finally I texted Charlie back. **I miss you Charlie. Your text made me really happy you have no idea. xoxo.**

A few days later, my brothers dropped me off at Logan. On the drive to the airport, Ben said, "So, Leah, what are you thinking in terms of your relationship?"

"What are you thinking in terms of *your* relationship?"

Aaron, who was in the passenger seat, turned around to look at me. "We're worried about you, is all, Lee."

"Well, don't be."

"What you've told us about Charlie doesn't sound great, to be honest," Aaron went on. "He's still living with his parents, he's working in construction, he smokes weed. It just doesn't seem like he's in a solid place in his recovery."

I pressed my nose to the window. We were passing the Charles River and Harvard Square on one side, Harvard Business School on the other. The day was cold and gray. According to my weather app, it was snowing in Madison. I couldn't wait to get back there. The last few days at home had been miserable. My brothers had brought Charlie up several times, though it had mostly been during stolen moments when Soo Min and Haley were out of the room. Aaron had asked questions about Charlie's job and family and past, but Ben seemed to want as little information about Charlie as possible.

My father had broached the subject only once. He'd recited a few unsettling statistics about the opioid epidemic. Then he'd said:

"You want to consider if Charlie can make a suitable living in construction, and whether he'd be a consistent husband and father."

"Thanks, Dad," I said. "We only just started dating. I'm not thinking about marriage."

"Be safe, is all I'm saying."

It was the most we'd ever spoken about relationships.

The only semi-good conversation had been with Soo Min, earlier that morning. We'd mostly avoided one another since Thanksgiving dinner—or, really, it was me who was avoiding her. I didn't want to make small talk with someone who I was sure must think I was a loser.

"About your boyfriend," she'd begun abruptly, during our chance encounter in the hallway. "Do you know if he's on any kind of medication for his opioid use disorder?"

"He is," I said. "I think it's called sub?"

"Suboxone," she said, nodding. "I don't know a ton about this, but three years sober is no joke. If he's getting the treatment he needs and going to meetings regularly, plenty of recovering addicts go on to live full, productive lives and have healthy relationships. The stigma . . . well. You saw. That's hard to overcome."

"I don't actually know how often he goes to meetings."

"I tried to explain to Ben that he was jumping to conclusions." Then her eyes and voice softened. "I think your brother is protective of you. He's doesn't want you to get hurt." She smiled. "I'd never actually seen that side of him before."

I understood then that Soo Min might actually be falling for my brother. I recognized the look on her face; she was starting to imagine a future with him. It pained me, because I knew that my brother was going to disappoint her. He would hurt Soo Min, just like he'd hurt the others.

"I shouldn't have told you about Charlie at all," I said now, to my brothers in the car.

"I'm glad you did," Aaron said. "Obviously there's a lot of nice things about him, but—"

"Just break up with him," Ben interrupted. "Find another guy. You're at a university with thousands of about-to-be doctors and lawyers. Or the guys in your program! Go out with a fucking poet! I don't know. Just don't date the heroin addict."

I didn't say anything.

Ben glanced at me in the rearview. "I'm yelling at you because I love you."

"Shut the fuck up, Ben," I said.

When we pulled into the drop-off lane, I grabbed my duffel and climbed out of the car. "I'll see you guys at Christmas," I said through the window as I stood on the sidewalk outside the terminal.

"You're going to end it, right?" Ben said, leaning over Aaron.

"Yup."

Ben flashed me a thumbs-up.

"Have a safe flight, Lee," Aaron said, giving me a wave. And then my brothers were off.

7.

FOR OUR FIRST WORKSHOP BACK, WILSON AND I HANDED IN stories. At the bar afterward we talked about workshop and about our Thanksgiving breaks. My new story had been well received and I felt pleased. When I finished my drink I got up to get another and found David leaning heavily on the bar, a full beer in front of him.

"Nice workshop tonight," he said, when I approached.

"Thanks. I appreciated what you said about the ending."

"Sure. It was powerful. What'd you think of Wilson's story?"

"I loved it," I said. "I think it's his best yet."

"You think he'll send it to Maya Joshi?"

"I don't know. Maybe."

"Do you think she's sending his stories out to journals for him?"

"I have no idea. You should ask him."

David grunted. Those were the most questions he'd ever asked me in a row.

I ordered my drink. "How was your Thanksgiving, by the way?"

"It was nice," David said. "My sister and her husband came. They just had a baby, so my parents were excited about the baby."

"I had no idea your sister had a baby."

"Yup. A girl. Emily."

"How is it being an uncle?"

"It's good. The baby is pretty cute."

I smiled. "Well, I'm going to get back."

David almost never went out of his way to talk to me, and when he did, he often seemed distracted, always looking over my shoulder and around the room, glancing at his phone, giving one-word answers. When I first met him, this offended me. I felt invisible—or, worse, a nuisance to him. I wanted him to like me, as if getting David Eisenstat's validation would mean I was worthy. Now I couldn't care less.

Later that night I got a text from Peter asking if I was back in town.

I waited several days to write back because I didn't know how to break things off with him. A small part of me felt hesitant to.

I ended up getting back together with my ex over break, was how I eventually put it, although this didn't really feel like the truth.

I'm happy for you, he responded. And then he wrote: **I probably wasn't very emotionally available anyway.**

For reasons that I did not completely understand, his text message felt like a slap. I tried to take this as a sign that I'd made the right choice.

He told me that he'd finished Bea's collection and enjoyed it, that he would make sure to get it back to me.

Thanks, I wrote. **I'm glad you liked it.**

I didn't hear anything else from him after that.

The next evening, Vivian and I met for dinner at our favorite place to eat, a no-frills, American-fare restaurant on East Wash.

When I arrived, Vivian was already there, tucked into a booth near the back, her head bent over her phone.

"Sorry I'm late," I said, sliding into the bench across from her.

"Martin is texting me," she answered, without looking up. "His sister is *pregnant*. Not on purpose. Fuck."

Martin was Vivian's most significant ex. They had been together for eight years in their twenties, after having dated all throughout college. The relationship hadn't ended in infidelity or any huge betrayal. They were still good friends, and the way Vivian spoke about Martin—often, and with a kind of private, knowing smile—I got the feeling she still loved him.

"Of course I still love him," she'd said, when I'd asked her. "He's essentially family."

"So, why . . ."

"We were like brother and sister by the end."

Now Vivian was thirty-three. None of her other exes sounded as nice as Martin.

"Shit. What is his sister going to do?" I asked, piling my coat and scarf at the end of the booth.

"Probably get an abortion. I'm going to call him later tonight."

The waiter came by then and took our orders, and we settled into our regular conversation—the latest workshop, the classes we were teaching, the books we were reading.

I was eager for the conversation to turn to men, though. I wanted to tell her about Charlie. I trusted Vivian's take on people more than my own. The steadfast way she listened to her own intuition made me trust in her gut instincts, too.

"I'm kind of in love with this guy," I blurted out.

She looked at me wide-eyed. "Wait, *who*?"

"His name is Charlie."

I told her the whole story. How he'd asked me out, our first date, our second. I told her about his slightly druggy vibes, how I hadn't been totally off, what he'd told me about his addiction. I explained all the stuff with Peter. And then how Charlie and I had worked it out those days before Thanksgiving. "He told me he's in love with me," I said.

The more I talked, the more worried she looked.

"Wow," she finally said, sitting back in her seat.

"I know," I said. "It's a lot."

"I don't know," she said, shaking her head. "It's not the heroin part, exactly. It just sounds intense, very quick."

"Yeah," I agreed. "It has been."

"He sounds kind of jealous."

"I think he just doesn't want to get hurt."

Vivian nodded.

"I've never felt this way about anyone."

"How long have you been seeing him?" she asked.

"About a month."

She nodded again. "Well, I look forward to meeting him, Leah."

Her lack of enthusiasm disappointed me. Actually, it annoyed me. I wanted her to be happy for me. I wanted her to lean across the table and ask for every small, intimate detail. To say, *Show me a picture.*

She glanced down at her phone then, which was glowing with several new text messages. "Martin," she muttered, shaking her head. "God, he's *meddling*. He's not really giving her space to figure out what she wants."

It struck me then that maybe Vivian was jealous. Maybe her lack of enthusiasm didn't have to do with Charlie at all. Perhaps she was just lonely and regretful. For a moment I felt cruel and condescending toward Vivian. It was time she moved on from Martin. It had been almost six years, after all.

But then she put her phone down and took a bite of her burger. She chewed slowly—her eyes glazed over in thought—and the meanness I'd felt a moment ago went away. I just felt sad that we weren't connecting like we usually did.

8.

EVERY YEAR AROUND THE HOLIDAYS, CHARLIE'S FAMILY WENT out for lunch and drinks in downtown Madison with their friends to celebrate the season. This year, Charlie asked if I would like to go with him as his date.

He picked me up wearing his church outfit. "You look nice," he said, as we got in his car. It was only the second time we'd gone out in public together, the first being our date at the Weary Traveler. Even though we were only going to spend an afternoon at a restaurant with Charlie's parents, I was excited.

When we arrived, Charlie smoked two cigarettes in the parking lot. "I haven't been to one of these things in years," he said.

"You're nervous?"

He nodded and tossed his cigarette on the pavement.

"Let's go in," I said. "It'll be fine."

It was more of a beer hall than a restaurant, all wood and forest-green accents inside. The room was loud with voices and laughter, the sounds of afternoon eating and drinking, glasses and silverware clinking. We found Faye and Paul at a large group table in the middle of the room. I could tell their party was drunk before we sat down. When Faye spotted us coming toward them, her eyes widened. "They're here!" She patted a burly man's shoulder beside her. "Honey, Charlie and Leah just arrived." When she stood and hugged us, I was struck again by how pretty Charlie's mother was. She was wearing a shimmering gold sweater and a thick gold choker necklace. Her hair was pulled back with a clip, loose tendrils framing her face. She was made-up that day—her big eyes lined and her lashes curled and dark, so that the blue of her irises looked almost electric. With her heels, she was as tall as I was.

She addressed the whole table, her voice clear and lively: "Can everyone scooch? My son and his girlfriend just got here and we need to make room!"

People nudged their chairs and waved at Charlie and me. I waved back, feeling happy and special being called Charlie's girlfriend.

Someone grabbed two chairs and brought them over for us.

"I want to sit next to Leah," Faye announced, and she smiled at me, gesturing to the empty seat beside her.

The man next to Faye held out a pink, beefy hand. "I'm Paul Nelson," he said. "Faye's husband."

"Hello," I said, shaking it. "Leah."

"And these are Charlie's stepbrothers," Faye said loudly, above the din. "Ty-ty and Chad."

Across the table were two hulking, almost identical-looking men. They both had thinning hair, shining pink scalps, slightly bugged eyes, and big, perfectly square jaws. They resembled their father.

"Great to meet you," said one of them. "Chad Nelson." Then he turned his attention to Charlie. "Long time, buddy. How's work been?"

Charlie was stiff and wide-eyed in his chair, like a kid who'd just sat down at the dentist's. Underneath the table, his hand found mine. "It's good, man," he said, and though I knew his voice intimately, I was taken aback by the softness of it. "How's it going at Epic?"

"Tyler is at Epic." Chad slapped his look-alike brother on the shoulder. "I'm over at Nordic."

"Oh fuck," Charlie said. "Tyler, then. How's Epic?"

"Living the dream, Charlie," Tyler boomed. "They put in a rock wall. It's like summer camp over there."

Charlie nodded several times fast, smiling. "Not bad."

"So, Leah, what do you do?" Tyler asked me, shifting his tone to a softer register.

"I'm a student at the university," I said. "I'm getting my MFA in fiction writing."

"What was that?" He cupped his hand to his ear.

I leaned in and repeated what I'd said.

"Good for you for going back to school and getting that degree. So you want to go into publishing?"

"I guess the plan is I'd like to write a book." I could feel Faye watching me.

"Look at that!" Tyler said. "Charlie, you got yourself a smart one."

"You know," Faye said to me, "Charlie is a very good writer, too. He studied writing in college."

"I know——" I started to say, but Charlie cut me off.

"That was a long time ago. Leah's in one of the best writing programs in the country. When she says she's going to write a book, she's actually going to write one."

Faye put her hand on my shoulder. "That's incredible, sweetheart," she said. "That you're following your dreams."

"Thank you," I said. I leaned in close to Charlie. Our hands were still entwined under the table, and every time he squeezed, I felt I knew exactly what he was telling me.

We got up to play darts. I went first and hit the board once out of my six tries. When I was done with my turn, Faye whooped and gave me a double high five.

Chad and Tyler went next, whipping the darts at the board like maniacs while making loud grunting noises each time they made contact.

"All right, champ, let's see what you've got," Tyler said, when it was Charlie's turn, thumping him hard on the back.

I realized I was nervous, watching Charlie take his first throw. When it landed dead in the bull's-eye, Faye and I jumped and cheered.

"Not bad, Charles," Chad said. "Not bad at all."

When Charlie threw again, he missed the board completely.

"Well, that's what happens when you throw like a pussy," Chad said, and then he mimicked Charlie's throw—an exaggerated flicking motion in his wrist while kicking up his foot in a girlish hop.

Charlie laughed loudly at Chad's imitation of him in a way that was painful to watch.

Faye put her beer down. "Honey, will you watch my drink?" she asked me. Then she marched over. "All right, boys. Let your old mom have a try."

As I watched the Nelson family continue to play darts, I found myself hating Charlie's stepfamily.

Paul and Chad and Tyler were big and insensitive; solid and obtuse as brick buildings. *Man, champ, dude, buddy.* It hurt me to think of Faye and Charlie being swept up by this family. Charlie, as a kid, growing up in all that chaos. He looked different from them, too. Even though he was just as tall, he was slighter, his jeans slipping off his slender frame, so he kept having to pull them up. His posture was bowed, from his hands so often stuffed in his pockets. His features were darker and softer. His brown hair, while plentiful, was as fine and silky as baby's hair.

A little while later, I ran into Faye on my way out of the bathroom. "Leah," she said. "I'm so glad that you and Charlie found each other."

"Me, too."

She gazed at me with her big round eyes and she looked so much like Charlie in that moment that I felt as if I knew her more than I did.

"He's had his struggles, but he has the sweetest heart," she said. "He really is so sweet."

"I can tell," I said. "I like him a lot."

"He's smitten with you, too. At home it's *Leah this, Leah that.*" She laughed. "I haven't seen him like this for a long time. It makes a mama happy."

"Really?" I said.

"Oh yeah." She winked at me. "You're big in his heart, honey."

Charlie and I left and drove over to Lake Monona. It was four in the afternoon but the sun was already setting, the sky bleeding stripes of magenta and lavender. We stood in a field of dried wheat.

The lake was a rippled wintry blue. Charlie stood beside me without a coat, smoking.

"I love you," he said, breaking the quiet.

"I love you, too."

"It's easier to do those kinds of things with you there."

"I hope it's okay to say that I don't like your stepbrothers."

He smiled. He was trembling in the cold, but his eyes were warm and bright. "It's okay to say that," he said. "They're assholes."

"Charlie?"

"Yeah?"

"Can I take your picture?"

"I'm not very photogenic. But, sure."

So I took a photo of him in the dried wheat in front of the lake. It turned out to be the best photo of him I ever took. I would go on to take quite a few others. And he was right. For someone so handsome, he wasn't photogenic. He blinked a lot and made a lot of awkward smiles. But the photo of him I took that afternoon was perfect.

I wanted to introduce him to my friends. He agreed to come meet them on Saturday night but then he complained of a sore throat and fell asleep in my bed for most of the afternoon.

"Can't we just stop by for a little?" I asked once he woke up, an hour before we were supposed to leave. "Just so we can say hi?"

"I want to be at my best when I meet them," he said. "You go without me. I'm going to sleep."

So I left him, in my darkened bedroom with a glass of water and a bottle of ibuprofen on the nightstand. But when I came home around midnight, my apartment was ablaze with activity. It smelled like weed. In the kitchen, I saw that Charlie had started and then abandoned making a mug of hot chocolate. I found him on my living room floor, leaning against the good Craigslist chair, his guitar in his lap. There were clementine peels and loose sheets of paper scattered all around him. He was squinting at my laptop, which was open in front of him. On the coffee table were rolling papers and an Altoid tin full of marijuana. The pillows on both armchairs had been thrown off and tossed onto the floor.

"I thought you were feeling sick."

He looked up. "Hey, babe. I'm feeling much better. I realized it must have been allergies."

For the first time, I felt irritated by him. "Charlie, you can't use my computer." I went over and snapped the laptop shut.

He looked up at me. "I'm sorry. I didn't realize."

"All my writing is on there. It's very important. You can't be, like . . . touching it with your clementine hands."

"I would never treat your things with disrespect, especially your computer that you use to write. I should have asked," said Charlie. He paused and bit his lip. "It's just that mine is so slow from all the porn." He was trying to make me laugh.

I sat down beside him. "Charlie," I groaned.

"I learned how to play a song for you. Joni Mitchell. You said you liked her."

"Okay," I said, softening. "Play it for me."

"So what did this Peter guy have that I didn't?"

We were sitting on the bench outside my apartment, Charlie smoking, me inhaling the secondhand fumes. He finally had a jacket—a long black overcoat he'd found in the back of his closet, which I thought made him look like a British rock star.

"Nothing. I don't want to get into all that."

"He had a really big dick, didn't he?"

I looked at Charlie. "Stop. I'm not having this conversation."

Charlie sucked hard on his cigarette and didn't say anything. The two bus slowed to a stop on Gorham and several students wearing backpacks climbed out.

When I looked at Charlie he was frowning, his eyes glazed with worry. "What's wrong?" I said.

"It's just hard to think about."

"Well, don't."

"Sorry," he said listlessly. "I just didn't realize you'd actually slept with him."

"Oh," I said. "I'm sorry."

I glanced at him from the corner of my eye. He was squinting into the gray, the cigarette quivering between his fingertips. His lips and cheeks were pink with cold.

"There is something you could do to make it up to me," he said.

"What?"

"For this outpatient program I'm in, my doctor needs to drug test me every month. Obviously I'm not using hard drugs. But I do smoke weed. As you're aware." He glanced quickly at me. When I didn't say anything, he kept talking: "They're super-strict, though, so even marijuana is a problem if it shows up on the test. I've cleared it with my psychiatrist and she knows I smoke for my anxiety and she's fine with it. Actually, she supports it. But for this test I need to be clean. So what I'm asking—and I know this sounds weird but it happens more than you'd expect—is . . . can I borrow your urine?"

"No."

"No?"

"Whatever you work out with your psychiatrist is your business, but I don't want to get involved."

Charlie leaned back against the bench. "Okay," he said. "I understand."

I realized, after some time had gone by, that I was waiting for our relationship to begin. When were we going to start doing relationship things? Go on day trips, wander through museums, browse bookstores together? When were we going to go to the movies? But we never even went out to dinner. First of all, Charlie didn't have any money. The money he made at his construction job went to Faye for safekeeping.

"It's better if I don't have cash on me," he explained.

Also, Charlie never felt well enough to do anything. He was always tired or coming down with something. His work schedule was erratic, and though I heard from him multiple times a day, and saw him almost every day, we never made plans in advance. He would text me to tell me that he was free and could he come by now.

I was starting to get tired of the dynamic, but I always said yes. Despite my frustration, he was my favorite person to spend time with.

One night we lay in bed listening to music in the dark. There was a dramatic pause in the song that somehow lined up just as we pulled back to look at one another. It was so funny to me, and a little embarrassing, too, as though we were in a movie with a corny soundtrack, and I started to laugh and couldn't stop. Charlie began laughing, too, equally hard. We completely lost it, laughing together.

"Did you notice that?" I asked him.

"What?"

"The thing with the music?"

He shook his head, still laughing, eyes shining.

"Then what are you laughing about?" I asked.

"I'm laughing because you're laughing," he said. "I've never heard you laugh so much."

Looking back, I think this was when I actually started to fall in love with Charlie.

Charlie finally did meet my friends, one night after workshop at City Bar. He arrived an hour later than he said he would, when we were all finishing up our second round of drinks. When he got there, Rohan, Sam, Wilson, and David all looked Charlie up and down, assessing him. When they shook Charlie's hand, they did so seriously, as though they were finalizing some kind of somber deal.

"You're the one from New York," Charlie said, when Vivian introduced herself.

Vivian smiled dazzlingly. "Born and raised."

"You look like you're from New York."

It was true—Vivian did look like she was from New York—but I could feel my friends' silent reactions. It was just a weird thing to say. And it was practically the first thing he'd said to Vivian—the first real thing he'd said in front of all of them.

Vivian just laughed. "What does someone from New York look like?"

I held my breath.

"Bold."

Charlie sat down beside me. "So this is where you guys come every week?" he asked me.

"After every workshop." I said this loudly, so as to invite everyone else into the conversation, but no one else said anything.

"I used to get hammered here when I was in college," Charlie said, looking around the bar. "I think they threw me out a few times. Do they still have darts?"

"In the back."

"We should play."

"Maybe." I glanced over at my friends, who were taking the final sips of their drinks. Sam and Wilson had started talking softly with each other.

I was mortified. Charlie wasn't making eye contact with anyone else at the table besides me. He wasn't even acting like we were sitting with other people.

"Charlie," Rohan said then. "How long have you been in Madison?"

"I grew up here," Charlie said. "I moved back home about a year ago."

"Nice," said Rohan. "How's it being back?"

"Not bad. Just getting my feet on the ground."

Rohan nodded warmly. There was a long pause when I prayed Charlie might ask Rohan a question in return, but Charlie didn't say anything.

"Must've been a nice place to grow up," Rohan said finally.

Charlie smiled. "It's a good place to raise a family, yeah."

My friends didn't stay long. They left like dominoes—first

Wilson—and then ten minutes later they'd all closed out their tabs and Charlie and I had the table to ourselves.

"I guess they didn't like me very much," Charlie said, smiling, but his eyes were sad.

"That's not it, Charlie. You just showed up really late. We'd already been here for hours."

But he was right—they hadn't liked him. That had been clear. When Sam's wife, Katie, had come to visit from Kansas City, we'd spent all night with her—asking her questions, getting to know her, understanding how Sam and Katie *were* together, as a couple. And she'd asked questions, too. Katie had known how to be in a group. In fact, Katie was better at being in a group than Sam was. Even if she wasn't interested in the MFA world—Katie was a biochemist—she'd joined in when the conversation turned to writing. She'd made comments about how our world compared to her world in the lab. She'd joked around. She'd fit in.

Sitting with Charlie at the table at City Bar, surrounded by all the empty beer glasses, I put my arms around him. Now that we were alone, he seemed more relaxed, more himself. His posture was self-possessed; his face looked older, more thoughtful. I wished that he could have looked that way around my friends.

"I like being out with you," I said.

"Really?" he said. "What do you like about it?"

"It makes you real. You're a real person. Not just a figment of my imagination." I ran my hand down his face and he smiled into my palm.

"How do you feel about PDA?" he said, sliding a hand up my leg.

"I don't mind it."

"No?"

I shook my head.

As he kissed me, his hand wandered higher, his thumb grazing the seam on the inside of my jeans.

I asked Charlie to show me one of his short stories. He found the only one he'd saved, from over a decade ago. He'd written it for a creative writing class he took in college. I could tell by the first paragraph that I liked his writing. His story was about a fourteen-year-old boy who starts calling a sex phone line after school. The boy ends up on the line with another teenage boy, essentially doing the same thing, although both boys are pretending to be adult women and don't realize they're on the line with another kid.

They end up getting caught by their parents and it's mortifying. A lot of Charlie's nineteen-year-old humor was offensive to women and to sex workers, and if he were to submit it to workshop he would get eaten alive. Underneath the offensive stuff, though, it was about the boy—his loneliness and his family life, the ways he keeps trying to connect and messing up. I loved it.

"Charlie, this is so good," I said, once I reached the end.

"Really?"

"It's amazing. Why don't you write anymore?"

"I don't know. I can never think of things to write about."

"Are you serious? You have so many things to write about."

That night I emailed Charlie one of Rohan's stories. Rohan's story was far more mature than Charlie's—which made sense, given that Charlie hadn't written since he was a teenager. But they both wrote about sex and masculinity, and they did so fearlessly.

Rohan's writing reminds me of yours, I wrote. *Let me know what you think.*

In the morning I checked my email but Charlie hadn't responded.

I had my students read a Mary Gaitskill story called "The Other Place." It was told from the point of view of a man who has fantasies about hurting and killing women.

"I don't understand why we read this," my student Jenna said, starting off the class discussion. She was someone I could always count on to do the reading and participate. "It was sexist." She looked at me, eyebrows raised, daring me to object.

I turned to the class. "What do others think?"

"It made me uncomfortable," a student named Taylor spoke up. "If the author really felt the need to write about a sociopath, maybe she could have done it in the third person so we don't need to hear every one of his thoughts."

"Or maybe the story could have ended with the man and his son having a conversation about their issues," someone else suggested.

The rest of the class remained silent.

I looked around, sweaty. Suddenly I felt ashamed. What was I subjecting my students to? I felt vaguely predatory.

A girl named Nina raised her hand.

"I liked it," she said. "I thought the whole point was that Mary Gaitskill wasn't afraid to go there. She wasn't saying it was okay or giving him an excuse—she was just saying, here's this fucked-up person, and he could be your next-door neighbor or your realtor or the guy in class who doesn't talk a lot—and there's a lot more men like him out there than we realize."

"There's not supposed to be a lesson or a moral here," said a student named Evan. "I don't think she's trying to teach us something. That's not what stories are supposed to do. Not all stories have happy endings or are about *good* people." He put *good* in air quotes.

"Well, I wouldn't mind reading a happy story every once in a while," someone muttered, though I didn't catch who.

For the last twenty minutes of class I told everyone to take out a blank sheet of paper and a pen. There was a pause and rustling as everyone unzipped their backpacks and pulled out their notebooks.

"This writing exercise is not what I would call fun," I told them. "But I think it's useful. I'd like you all to look back on your lives, and think about your most shameful moment. You're going to write about that moment. We won't be sharing these. At the end of class you can rip the paper up or burn it—do whatever you want with it. If you really want, you can spend the next twenty minutes writing your name a hundred times over and I'll never know. No one except you will read it, so there's no need to give it a happy ending or make it pretty or even worry about making it well written. Just focus on making it real. I'd like you to bring the reader—the imaginary reader, that is—into the moment with you and then lead the reader out of the moment, too. And write in the first person, using *I*. Any questions?"

Jenna raised her hand. "What if we can't think of our most shameful moment?"

"Any shameful moment will do. It doesn't have to be the *most*. As long as you can make that moment come alive."

I watched the students turn to their notebooks. Some started writing immediately and others sat with their pencils poised on the page, their faces furrowed with concern. I turned to my own notebook and started to write. Pretty soon the room was filled with the sound of pencils scratching, the occasional flipping of pages.

Twenty minutes later, everyone was still writing.

"How was that?" I asked, breaking the quiet. Half the class continued writing, and the rest of the students looked up at me. Their faces seemed gentler and younger than before.

"Brutal," said one kid, Andrew, and then he smiled.

That night in Charlie's car on the way to the suburbs for family dinner, I asked if he'd read Rohan's story that I'd emailed him.

"Oh. Yeah, I think I started it."

"Did you like it?"

"It was pretty good. I don't really see how our writing is similar. It's not like I write about being an Indian."

I looked at Charlie. He was tapping on the wheel, bopping his head to the song that was playing. In the cup holder was a gigantic iced coffee from McDonald's.

"I know that," I said. "Rohan's story is about much more than being Indian."

Charlie shrugged. "I only read the first few pages, I think." Then he turned up the radio.

9.

FAYE USED TO WORK IN CUSTOMER SERVICE. NOW SHE WORKED
a few mornings a week in the financial aid office at the university.
Even when she wasn't working, she was always busy. Whenever I
saw her she was halfway through a list of errands—a trip to Target, a car wash, Paul's dry cleaning had to be dropped off or picked
up. And she had countless friends. She belonged to a book club and
a walking club and a Bible study group and she took tennis lessons.
But she was home every evening by five to make dinner. Each
meal had a theme. Make Your Own Tacos Night! Italian Night!
Breakfast for Dinner!

Charlie and I would serve ourselves from the stove and then
bring our food to the den and eat in front of the TV. Faye and Paul
would eat in the living room together in front of that TV.

"Why don't we eat with them?" I asked Charlie.

"We could," Charlie said. "But Paul likes to watch shitty TV
while they eat."

"How come your mom is always in such a good mood?"

"I think she's just relieved that things are calm right now,"
Charlie said. "They haven't always been that way."

When Faye had talked about family dinners, I hadn't expected for us to be eating in different rooms, in front of different television sets. The Nelsons had a formal-looking dining table but I'd never seen it used.

My brothers and I had never been allowed to watch TV while we ate. Now I watched shows on my computer all the time while I had dinner alone in my apartment. Sometimes I'd watch cheesy TV like *Full House*, or reality TV like *The Bachelor* and *Keeping Up with the Kardashians*. I liked the hometown dates on *The Bachelor*— the way the moms would cry when their daughters walked through the door, how the dads would act overprotective—how the most important thing in the world to those families was their children's *hearts*. It was all bullshit. But sometimes I'd be watching one of those shows and I'd realize that I was crying or I'd see my face reflected in the computer screen—smiling like an idiot. I hated myself in those moments—that that's who I was.

My family wasn't like those families. It wasn't that we didn't know how to show each other love. I had no doubt that my family loved me. We didn't know how to show each other pain. We didn't know how to comfort one another. We were shadows; a shadow of a family. When I thought about it from an outsider's perspective, I didn't blame my mother for taking off. I hoped, in some weird way, that she'd found a new family. I wanted that for her in the same way that I hoped that someday I, too, might find myself a new family.

When I imagined my mother and me reuniting, it was in the context of a wedding or a baby being born or a funeral. Those were usually the reasons people showed up for one another. In my imagination, our reunions were never like they were on *The Bachelor* or how they happen in airport terminals: running full speed toward one another, arms out, tears streaming. That would be nice, but it wasn't our style.

There was the fantasy of my wedding. My husband—some faceless yet handsome man. My bridal shower populated by fun, spirited women—who these women were, I wasn't sure. In my mind, Monica was far nicer than she was in real life—and we were close. Ben and Aaron would be there. My father, happy and steady. When my mother showed up, she was late, and everyone was already having a great time. I imagined her in a simple dress, her long dark hair straight down her back. She never wore makeup, though she wore lots of jewelry, necklaces layered upon necklaces, rings on every finger, a dainty diamond in her nose.

In my fantasy, she'd be overwhelmed by all the people in my life. She'd be filled with regret. We would catch eyes across the room. She would look at me, and it would all be there in that look. *I'm sorry. I'm here.* This was where the fantasy stalled and came to a close. It felt good to see my life through her eyes. My full, beautiful life.

When I imagined reuniting with her at a funeral, it was often the same group of people who had been at my wedding. A doting, faceless husband. Numerous friends. A family who resembled mine, but wasn't, not really. It was my own funeral I was imagining. Everyone was there, except for me. In my fantasy, they'd all get up to make gushing eulogies. I liked to imagine what each person would say about me—my father, Ben, Aaron, Robbie, my husband. My mother would know then that it was too late. Afterward, when everyone was weeping into each others' arms, my husband would approach her.

"You're Naomi," he'd say.

She'd nod. "Leah's mom."

Then my dad would come over. My brothers. Sometimes Robbie, too. In my mind, everyone was a little warped, a dream version, or an extreme of who they really were. Everyone except for Robbie. The Robbie in real life and the Robbie in my imagination were always the same. I think that's what made him feel so safe for me.

10.

FAYE AND PAUL WERE GOING AWAY FOR CHRISTMAS TO VISIT their friends in Arizona, as they did every year. They would be gone for a week—from December nineteenth through the twenty-sixth—and Charlie would be staying at the house with the cat. My flight back to Boston was on the twenty-fourth. Charlie asked if I would stay with him and Butterscotch in the suburbs. I didn't know how to tell him that staying at his house was somehow less appealing, knowing that Faye wasn't going to be there.

A few days before the Nelsons' trip, I was over at Charlie's house, and Faye said, "When you two are here taking care of Butterscotch, I'm going to leave some money so you can treat yourselves to takeout a few nights. And, Leah, I want to show you where I keep my hair dryer and all my girlie stuff." I realized then it had already been decided. I was staying.

Faye brought me into her massive bathroom—granite counter-top with two sinks, a Jacuzzi tub, and every type of beauty product imaginable. "Use anything," she said. "What's mine is yours."

"Thank you," I said, glancing through the dozens of bottles and lotions and tubes of makeup.

"Also, could you remind Charlie while I'm gone to take his

meds every night at nine? And it would be good if he could make it to a meeting or two."

"Okay."

"And let me get your number, sweetheart," she said. "In case anything comes up while we're away."

The first day at the Nelsons' I woke up around nine and took a long shower in his parents' bathroom, using Faye's expensive shampoo and conditioner. Then I looked around the house. The biggest room was the living room, with vaulted ceilings and big glass windows overlooking the backyard—and beyond that, a man-made pond with a circle of identical-looking houses surrounding it.

I'd spent plenty of time in there before, but never alone, and as I peered around, I wondered how much of the home had been decorated by Faye—what the house had looked like before she and Charlie had moved in. The Nelsons' furniture was formal. Each piece looked new, despite the fact that it was used daily by Faye and Paul. The floor was carpeted and meticulously vacuumed. There was a Christmas tree in the corner of the room, decorated with lights and ornaments, but Faye had unplugged the lights before they'd left town.

Framed portraits of Charlie and Chad and Tyler when the boys were little hung above the mantel. Three in a row, as if they were all blood brothers, as if they'd known each other at that age. Chad and Tyler had small beady eyes, reddish skin around the nose and eyes and mouth, smiles that looked like grimaces. Charlie was achingly cute as a boy. His blue eyes were gigantic, and he was missing a front tooth. His smile was the same as it was now. There was also a wedding photo of Faye and Paul. Faye was mid-laughter, making direct eye contact with the camera, beautiful in a white satin dress, her hair, longer and much darker than it was now, twisted over one shoulder. Paul had both arms around Faye's waist. His hair and mustache were now gray, but when he was younger, he was blond, like Chad and Tyler. He was beaming at Faye.

Every surface in the room was bare. Where was all their stuff? There was a feeling of pride in there. This house belonged to a family who saw itself a certain way. On some visceral level, it repulsed me. But also, I loved being there—it was clean and comfortable and wholesome, and it made me feel safe.

When I was growing up, our living room had been in a constant state of madness, piles everywhere, cluttered with things. We had a surplus of stuff. Books and junk mail, magazines, loose papers from school. Random items that should have been thrown out, or that had no obvious home: those little goody bags dentists give out at cleanings, bottles of expired Advil, stray cords and wires, CD cases with no CDs inside.

We didn't have professional portraits of ourselves. We had Kandinsky and Edward Hopper prints, my mother's art. If there were images of faces on the walls, they weren't of people we knew.

I wandered into Faye and Paul's bedroom. I left the door wide open so I'd be sure to hear if Charlie woke up, but the house was silent. Their bed was a California king and had a million throw pillows on it. The room was spotless—every drawer closed, everything in its place.

On either side of the bed were matching night tables. On one table there was a bottle of Tums and a watch. On the other, a stack of books: *Parent of an Adult Addict*, *Addict in the House*, *Don't Let Your Kids Kill You.*

There weren't any photos of Chad and Tyler in the bedroom, but there were more photos of Charlie. One framed, on the bureau—a photo of Charlie at graduation from college, holding up his diploma. He was heavier than he was now. A photo of him with the beautiful ex-girlfriend, which made me burn with jealousy. A photo of Faye holding Charlie as a baby—their smiling faces pressed up against one another. That one made my breath catch. I ran out of the bedroom and shut the door.

In the living room I pulled out my computer and worked, half-heartedly, on one of my stories, but it wasn't working. The pages I'd previously written irritated me and every new sentence I wrote came out dull and tired, like a sentence I'd already written before, in some other story. Eventually I grew hungry and went in search of food. The Nelsons' pantry was stocked. I was angry, though, that I was stuck there, instead of at my own apartment. I stood in the silence of the Nelsons' kitchen and turned around slowly in a circle. I glanced at my phone. It was almost two in the afternoon.

In the den, the room was bright with winter sunlight. Charlie was in the same position, curled under the blankets, his hair poking out, dark against the white pillowcase. I climbed onto the sofa bed beside him. Despite the fact that he'd been sleeping for close to fourteen hours, I still loved how he smelled.

"Charlie," I whispered.

He didn't respond.

"*Charlie.*"

After a few moments his eyes blinked open.

"It's one fifty-five," I said. "Do you want to do something?"

"I'm gonna sleep more," he said foggily. "I'm really tired."

I got out of bed and went back into the living room and waited for Charlie to wake up.

It was dark outside by the time I heard Charlie's footsteps. I was still on the couch, my computer in my lap, refreshing Facebook and the other nine pages I had open. When he appeared, he was wearing the clothes he had slept in and his hair was sticking straight up. There were pillow lines across his face and jaw.

"Why are you sitting in the dark?" he asked, his voice raspy.

"Can you drive me home now?" I responded.

He rubbed his eyes. "Why?"

I closed my computer, but that cut off our only light source, so I opened it again. "Because I've been sitting here all day waiting for you to wake up."

"Babe, I was really stressed out by my parents leaving yesterday. They made it into this massive deal and we got into an argument and I think my body just needed a day to recuperate. I didn't mean to sleep the whole day. You should have woken me up."

"I tried."

"Well, next time jump on me or something."

"Can we go stay at my apartment instead?" I said. "I don't want to be stuck here in the house. There's nothing for us to do."

"I told my parents we'd take care of Butterscotch."

"You can drive back to feed the cat. It's not like she needs twenty-four-seven attention."

"Leah, I'm sorry, but my mom wants me to be at the house."

"Why?"

"She's more comfortable if I'm here."

"Well, I want to go home. So can you drive me home?"

He came over and slumped on the couch. "I had this whole surprise planned for you. It got all messed up because I was an asshole and slept the whole day." He put his head in his hands.

"What was the surprise?" I asked.

He lay down then and curled into a ball. "It doesn't matter anymore."

"No, what was it? Were we going to go somewhere?"

"Leah," he said softly, "I feel really sick. I think I might be coming down with something."

"Really?" I touched his forehead.

He nodded. Then he glanced up at me. "What was that show you were telling me about? The one with the girls living in New York and all the bad sex?"

"*Girls*?"

"Yeah. Can we watch that? And then I can do the surprise for you tomorrow? I really want to do it."

"Okay."

Charlie scooched beside me. He figured out how to access HBO on the big-screen TV and pulled a throw blanket over us. We watched, huddled up together, holding hands under the blanket. Each time Charlie laughed at a joke, I found myself burrowing closer to him. Halfway through the second episode, Charlie paused the show and made us nachos for dinner. The soft light of the kitchen at night and the sounds of Charlie getting our food ready made me feel calm and happy.

The next day he had to go to his doctor's office, which meant he woke up at a more reasonable time—ten a.m. for an eleven o'clock appointment. He had thirty minutes to prepare his friend's urine for the drug screening, which he'd be sneaking in with him in a heat-protected thermos.

"It has to be hot enough to make it seem like it just came from my body, but not boiling," he said, as he microwaved Danny's pee in his parents' microwave. He was still wearing the same clothes he'd worn and slept in the last two days. The good Charlie smell had started to wear off and something stale and odorous was setting in. His hair was doing this thing where it was spiking straight up with its own natural oils.

"Do you want to take a shower before we go?" I asked.

"No," he said, peering into the microwave. "My skin gets really dry in the winter and the water pressure kind of hurts."

"Okay," I said.

We got in the car and Charlie turned on the radio, rolled down the windows, and lit a cigarette. As we started the drive into Madison, the cool winter air washed over us. I was so relieved to be out of the house, out of the suburbs, and that Charlie was awake again. The trip to the doctor and the task of preparing Danny's urine seemed to have invigorated him.

"If your psychiatrist is okay with you smoking weed," I asked, "why do they care if it shows up on your screening?"

"It has to do with my insurance and getting prescribed my suboxone. Also, Wisconsin is fucked. If I lived in a place like Massachusetts where weed is decriminalized, this would be a totally different conversation." He tossed the cigarette butt out the window. "I actually want to move to Massachusetts. I don't fit in, in Wisconsin. I never have. It's probably one of the reasons you and I get along so well."

"Who is Danny anyway?" I asked. "And why did he agree to give you his pee?"

"Danny's, like, my best friend. I think he feels he owes me. He introduced me to all this shit. I don't blame him or anything. I would have started using heroin some other way if it wasn't with him. I was destined to become addicted to heroin. If it wasn't with Danny, it would have happened with someone else, but it just happened to be with him."

I looked over at Charlie, stunned. His eyes looked a little crazed—bright with purpose and conviction—as he pulled into the lot where his doctor's office was.

"Jesus, Charlie. How do you even know that his urine is clean?"

"Oh, I trust him. We're both sober now. He's the best. I actually really miss chilling with Danny. I used to hang with him all the time. Every day, for years. He's practically a brother."

"So why don't you get together with him now?"

"That's the thing. All I've ever done with him is drugs." He parked and turned to look at me. The thermos of pee sat between us in the cup holder. "All I've ever done with anyone is drugs. That's why I love you, Leah. You're the one person I know whose life doesn't revolve around getting high. We do so many things together and it's never about that."

I wanted to tell him that we never did anything together. But he was already ten minutes late.

I could tell by his posture that things hadn't gone well. He was holding the thermos in plain sight instead of hiding it inside his jacket like he'd done walking in. "What's wrong?" I asked when he got back in the car.

"The appointment was yesterday."

"Really?"

"*Fuck*." He banged his head on the steering wheel.

"They wouldn't just let you do it today?"

"The fucking nurse said they tried to call me yesterday, but I never got any calls." He lifted his head up and turned on the car, then backed out of the spot without bothering to look behind him or check his mirrors.

"Charlie," I said. "It's going to be okay."

"I don't know."

He was driving fast and smoking at the same time. When he barreled straight through a stop sign, I tensed up. "Drive safe, okay?"

"I always do."

I thought about asking him to drop me off right then. We were only ten minutes from my apartment. He was upset, though, and I didn't know how he'd react to this. Also, all my stuff was at his house, including my computer.

"Well, what does this mean moving forward?" I asked him.

"I might get kicked out of the program. Maybe my psychiatrist will fight for me. She likes me. But they're assholes there. They don't really understand recovery."

"They're going to kick you out for missing one test?"

"This is the third time I've missed, or so they say. *Three strikes and you're out*. They say they call me to remind me, but I never get their calls. To be honest, I think they call the wrong number on purpose."

"Do you think you should get in contact with someone? Your psychiatrist?"

"I really need to get home and rest," Charlie said. "I didn't sleep well last night because I was nervous about this stupid test."

"What if you called your mom?"

"Leah, I really just need to take a nap."

Charlie disappeared back into bed for the rest of the afternoon while I sat on the living room couch. I tried to read but I kept reading the same paragraph over and over again. I wanted to go home. I thought about calling a cab, but leaving abruptly seemed more frightening than just staying still. I wished Faye were home.

Around dinnertime I went to check on Charlie but he wasn't in bed. I looked in the bathroom but the door was ajar, the lights off. "Charlie?" I called. I did a lap around the house, although I couldn't imagine he was inside, because I would have heard him walking around. I checked all the bedrooms and the bathrooms, the sunroom, the back porch. "Charlie!" I yelled. I looked at my phone but I hadn't missed any texts or calls. When I tried calling him, it rang and rang. I put on my shoes and stepped outside.

That's when I saw him, sitting in his darkened car in the driveway. I ran over, calling his name. I was furious.

But when I approached the window, I saw that even though he was upright in the driver's seat, he was asleep, his head back on the headrest, his mouth slightly open, his hands placidly in his lap. He wasn't wearing his black overcoat, but an oversized orange puffer coat that I didn't recognize.

I felt scared.

I tried the door, but it was locked. I knocked, hard, on the window.

He came to and looked at me, through the glass. Then he opened the door. "Sorry," he said. "I fell asleep."

"What the fuck, Charlie?" I was practically crying. "What are you doing out here?"

"I came out to smoke a cigarette. But it was too cold, so I smoked in my car. And then I fell asleep."

"Why are you sleeping this much? It's not normal."

"I think I'm sick. I think I need to go to the doctor."

"You were at the doctor today. Why didn't you say something?"

"I need to go to my PCP. Not a drug counselor. I think I have some kind of virus."

"Charlie," I said. "Are you using? Is something going on?"

He shook his head. "This isn't what happens when you use. If I was using I wouldn't be able to have a conversation with you right now. Also, the medicine I'm on makes it so that I couldn't get high even if I wanted . . ." His eyes fluttered closed when he said this.

"Charlie, I need you to take me home."

He opened his eyes. "I really want to do the surprise for you." His voice and eyes were so deadpan when he said this that I burst out laughing, but he just stared at me.

I stopped laughing. "I don't think it's a good idea."

"Please," he said. "I think you're going to like it." He got out of the car then and closed the door. When he hugged me, he held me close to him, and underneath his unwashed smell, I could smell Charlie—whatever it was about him that I loved.

I shrugged against his chest.

We walked inside the house together and Charlie led me into

his parents' bathroom. He put on one of the overhead dimmer lights to the lowest register—a soft, dusky amber. He was still wearing his shoes and the huge puffer coat. It was at least two sizes too big. Then he leaned over the tub and turned on the hot water, swiped his finger underneath the faucet several times. "Okay," he said, touching my shoulder. "Wait here for a second."

He left then and I stood in the bathroom. I watched the Jacuzzi fill with water, steam billowing off the top. After some time, I turned off the water and took off my clothes. In the mirror, I looked slimmer than how I pictured myself. My hair had gotten long and it fell far past my shoulders, over my breasts. I looked sad and unfamiliar. I climbed in. I sat in the steaming tub, waiting. Finally, Charlie came in with a tray. On the tray were two cans of root beer with pink plastic crazy straws coming out of them. There was also a lit candle. He still had on that jacket. He smelled of a fresh cigarette.

"Hey," he said.

"Hi."

He eased the tray down on the side of the tub. "This candle floats in water. I thought you'd like it." Gently, he placed the floating candle down on the surface of the water and we watched it bob and sway.

"Thanks," I said. "I do."

He took off his coat and then his clothing, leaving them in a pile on the floor. When he climbed in, I was amazed by his thinness. His stomach was concave and his limbs were long and gaunt. It occurred to me how little Charlie ate. He slept most of the day, it seemed, and ate only once, usually at night. We sat on opposite ends of the tub, looking at each other. The bathroom was dark, the only lights the dim ceiling bulbs and the flicker of the floating candle.

"I know this isn't much," Charlie said. "But I hope you like it, honey."

I began to say something back, but Charlie had already started to fall asleep, right there in the water.

11.

THE NEXT DAY I MADE CHARLIE BRING ME HOME. WHEN WE GOT
to my street in Madison I felt as though I were returning after
months of being away. My days in the suburbs had been like living
on another planet. Hours of silence in the Nelsons' living room.
Eating bowls of cereal alone, waiting for Charlie to wake up.

For a few minutes we sat without speaking in Charlie's car in
front of my apartment.

"I can't handle it if you're about to break up with me," he said
finally. "I don't think I could take that right now. Obviously, it's
your choice and you can decide whatever you want, but if you're
going to break up with me, can you just wait a few days, maybe
until after Christmas?" He looked at me. "We don't have to talk or
see each other or anything, but at least I can pretend that things
are normal and you're just busy writing and I'm going to see you
again in a week."

"Charlie. Just answer me one question honestly. And I won't
break up with you if the answer is yes, but I need to know. Are
you using?"

He unbuckled his seat belt and turned so he could face me

head-on. "No. I'm not." He took my hand. "Look, I'm a work in progress. I'm not perfect. I know you said I have a perfect face or something crazy like that, but I think you're the only one in the world who actually thinks I'm that handsome." He smiled, but his eyes were scared. "And I've messed up a lot. But I know that there's this *thing* between us." He squeezed my hand. "Like this buzzing electric hum that when we're in the same room it's *there* and we both feel it, and probably other people can feel it, too. But I'm serious, Leah. It's not something I want to give up on."

"I don't know," I said. "I feel that hum, too. But you don't seem . . ." I paused. "Healthy."

"Every day I'm trying to get healthier. I'm trying to be the best possible Charlie Jacob Nelson that I can be. That's all I can give you."

"I need to be on my own for a while," I said, letting go of his hand.

Charlie didn't say anything as I got out of the car.

The first few hours I reveled in my freedom. I showered and then walked around the apartment naked. I tidied up my small, beautiful rooms. I sprawled out on the blue-and-white rug in the living room in my underwear. It felt good not to have to answer to anybody; not to ask Faye for the credit card; not to feed Butterscotch; not to think about suboxone or the temperature of urine.

I got dressed and went to the mini-mart a few blocks away. I bought frozen burritos and dark chocolate and clementines. Next I headed to Johnson Public House to get a coffee. As soon as I stepped inside, I spotted a guy in a blue crewneck sweatshirt sitting at the counter. I began to sweat inside my winter jacket.

I pretended not to notice him while I waited in line and ordered. But after I paid, I looked over. "Hey, Peter."

He smiled. "Hi, Leah."

"How's it going?"

"It's good. Just working on these applications."

"Oh?" I said. "What for?"

"I'm trying to go to Barcelona over the summer. There are a few internships through the department."

"That's great. I remember you said you wanted to spend time over there." It was strange, accustoming myself to the normalcy of the conversation. Applications, internships, departments.

"What about you? How's writing going?"

"It's okay," I said. "Kind of slow these days."

The barista came over then with my to-go cup of coffee and set it down on the counter. I nodded thanks.

"Well," Peter said, when I turned back to him. "I'll be anxiously awaiting your first book."

"You might be waiting a long time."

He laughed. "I'll be patient. It'll come—I have no doubt."

I was about to say something else, but then Peter gestured toward his computer. "I should get back to work. Good running into you."

"Oh, you, too," I said.

I was almost at the door when I heard Peter call my name. I turned back.

He reached into his backpack and pulled out Bea Leonard's collection. "I've had this in my bag for weeks," he said. "Now I can finally give it back."

"Thank you," I said. I took the book from him, crushed. I

wanted to ask him what he'd thought of it, but I could tell by his face that he really was busy. Peter had a life and he needed to return to it.

As soon as I stepped out of the shop onto the sidewalk, I realized I had forgotten my coffee on the counter. It was too late, though. I couldn't bring myself to go back inside. My eyes blurred with tears. I hated myself.

I wrote for the rest of the day, without taking any breaks. Charlie hadn't texted me since he'd dropped me off. I decided the only thing that was going to make me feel better was to write something good—something to hand in to workshop that I could be proud of.

When I got tired of writing in the good Craigslist chair I moved to the bad one, and wrote more there. Then I went over to the kitchen table, which was where I kept giant stacks of papers. I found the note from Bea. *I think you should start submitting this story to journals.*

My heart began to beat quickly and I sat up straighter. I typed "New Yorker fiction submissions" into the search bar. Suddenly my world felt so much bigger. I composed an email. *Dear Editors, Attached please find my short story, Thirteen. Thank you for reading. Best, Leah Kempler.* I pressed send.

That night as I was falling asleep I kept thinking I heard vibrations, but each time I checked my phone, nothing. Finally, I put my phone on silent and turned over in bed and fell into a restless sleep.

In the morning I walked in the snow for two hours through

the quiet east-side neighborhoods. The houses on Willy Street and Jenifer Street and Spaight were old and colorful—blush-pink and periwinkle, pale yellow, hunter-green. Most had big porches out front, signs of life out on the porches—snow shovels and twinkle lights, furniture like couches or small patio tables, ashtrays. There were remnants of gardens in the snowy yards—wire fencing, stone borders, bare trellises. There were snowmen with carrot noses and winter scarves, imprints of snow angels, candles in people's windows. I walked up and down the streets, the wind sharp and frigid.

By the time I returned home, my face and hands were frozen numb and I felt excited to work. I took a scalding-hot shower and started writing and didn't stop until dark. That's when the loneliness hit.

My loneliness. Sometimes I was sure I had a sickness. It had been there for as long as I could remember, a heaviness that pressed down on my chest at night, and sometimes during the day, too. It was a feeling that separated me from other people, even though the core of the feeling was wanting, in a terrible way, to feel close to someone. When I was young I'd always known that the antidote to my loneliness would be to fall in love someday. I looked forward to love more than anything else about growing up. More than leaving home or learning to drive or doing drugs—things that other kids were excited about. I didn't care about those things. The only thing I wanted was to be known completely by someone, to know someone completely. When I did fall in love for the first time—not with Robbie, but with a boy from college—and it was as good as I imagined, it only confirmed what I believed to be true. Being in love made the heaviness go away. And being alone again after having been in love was even worse than the original loneliness.

Now my loneliness was so vast and endless it was sure to scare off anybody normal.

I closed my computer and lay down on my living room rug again. How was it that just yesterday I felt free and happy to be lying here, by myself? Today it felt unbearable. I'd been alone with my thoughts for over twenty-four hours. I hadn't spoken a word in that long. I opened my mouth and said, "Hello."

Then came the beautiful sound of an incoming text. And it wasn't a phantom vibration this time. It was loud and real. I knew, before I looked at it, that it was Charlie.

Hey, he wrote. **I had this horrible feeling in my stomach and I got in my car and I ended up outside your place. I feel like a creep. I can go home though.**

This was both better and more alarming than what I was expecting.

Do you want to come in? I wrote.

When I opened the door, he was wearing his black overcoat, not the weird orange puffer one. He'd recently showered and he had on his glasses, and for some reason, all of this made everything better. He'd brought his guitar. When we hugged, we held on long and tight, as though we hadn't seen each other in years. I turned my face up and we kissed, and his lips were soft and pillowy. I could have cried, I was so happy.

That night he sang "Shelter from the Storm" by Bob Dylan. Then he sang "Have Yourself a Merry Little Christmas" and "Silent

Night" and "Auld Lang Syne." The next day was Christmas Eve and I was flying back to Boston in the morning. I took videos of him singing on my phone. By the time we stopped, it was almost midnight.

"You could be famous, Charlie." I lay down on the rug and he lay beside me.

"I'm not that good," he said.

"That's not true. You're so talented. You could do anything you want."

He rolled over on his side, and so did I. We got close, so our foreheads and our knees were touching.

"Do you actually think so?" he asked.

"I do."

"Maybe I'll try to do one of those open mic nights or something."

"You should."

"There's one every Thursday at Michaelangelo's."

I nodded. "Would you ever want to read one of my stories?"

"Of course, Leah. Send me one while you're gone, okay? So when I read it I can feel like you're here with me."

Then we had sex, right there on the living room rug.

12.

MY DAD AND MONICA HAD PLANNED A WEEK-LONG FAMILY VACA-
tion at a beach resort in Florida. By my dad and Monica, I mean
Monica. And by family, I mean everyone who had been at Thanksgiving minus Soo Min. Ben was told he was not allowed to bring
her along since she was not a "serious partner."

"Bullshit," Ben muttered to me in the terminal at Logan, while
we waited to board our flight. "Soo Min is more serious than
fucking Vegan Ballerina." He nodded toward Haley, who was another row down, already dressed in her summer wear and floppy
straw hat. She was stretched over three seats, her head in Aaron's
lap, her sandaled feet dangerously close to a stranger's hip.

"Soo Min is a *physician*," said Ben. "She's fucking serious."

"But are *you* serious, Benjamin? Are you two in *love*?"

Ben made a loud *ha* noise. "Hell no."

I turned to look at him. "Well, then it's good she's not coming
on this trip." My voice emerged hostile and I noticed that a few
beads of my saliva had landed on his face.

"Jesus." He wiped his nose. "It's seven in the morning. Relax."

"Only people who are in love are allowed on vacation," I said,
altering my tone. "You know. Like Christina and Stephen."

Ben laughed. He was quick to switch back and forth between anger and humor. I was grateful for that. Really, I was relieved that Soo Min hadn't been allowed to come.

Several hours later we emerged into the Florida heat, pale and blinking, our winter coats slung over our elbows, our jeans heavy and oppressive. Everyone except for Haley, of course, in her linen frock and Birkenstock sandals. "Palm trees!" she announced gleefully.

Ben rolled his eyes at me.

We were staying in a giant condo that overlooked the beach. Every couple had their own room, and Ben and I would be sharing.

"If you snore," Ben said as we unpacked, "I'm booting you to the couch."

I didn't answer. I had just gotten a long text message from Charlie. Faye and Paul were back in Madison and apparently they were angry with Charlie over the state of the house.

"Who are you texting?" Ben asked.

"Vivian," I said, and it shocked me, how easy it was to lie to my brother.

To be safe, I'd changed Charlie's name in my phone to Cynthia. Everyone in my family was under the impression that I had ended the relationship.

We spent our days doing nothing on the beach. Each morning I spread my towel close to my brothers, and as far away from the others, as I could. The sun was strong and I had to use a book to create shade in order to read Charlie's texts. His messages were getting longer and longer. Often the texts would break off into tangents. Sometimes every sentence was its own tangent, its own separate mood. Things were escalating in his house. When his parents returned home they had cornered him in the kitchen, he told me, and raged at him because he'd left "crumbs of food" out on the counter.

Then he got into childhood stuff. He told me that when he was younger, Paul used to chase him around the house and hit him, but when Charlie had reported this to Faye, she hadn't believed him. Charlie said he was scared of Paul. He said Paul cheated on his mother. That, as teenagers, Chad and Tyler had spent his mother's hard-earned money on cocaine and strip clubs and prostitutes. That he was certain he could find evidence of all of this. His mother was in denial. That Faye had a pattern of being in denial about the abusive men in her life.

Then the texts would veer off into the romantic.

> **Even with everything happening with my parents I
> just feel so grateful to have you in my life. I think
> about you and everything bad just disappears. I try to
> articulate exactly what you mean to me but words
> don't do it justice. Kind of like how the words
> beautiful and hot and sexy and cute all mean slightly
> different things and you're all of them, encapsulated
> into this one specific LEAH hotness. And when I see
> you I get this feeling, like the whole is bigger than the
> sum of its parts, all these things about you add up to
> YOU, and I don't know what the feeling IS, there's not
> a name for it, but I think you probably know what I'm
> talking about. I write you letters in my head telling
> you how special you are, that's kind of how I fall**

asleep at night, talking to you in my head. And I've been working on a song since that is really the only way I think I could actually express how I feel about you or come somewhat close. Warning you it's going to be cheesy as fuck

When I wrote back with follow-up questions about the fight with his parents, the stuff about Paul—and what was going on with Charlie's treatment—he never answered the questions directly.

I was in the middle of reading his latest text when I got an incoming call from Faye.

"I'll be right back," I said to my brothers, and I jumped up and ran across the beach to where the sand turned to pavement.

"Leah, I'm calling about Charlie," Faye said, when I picked up. "We're really worried. We think he's relapsed."

I felt her words in my entire body. I'd never heard her sound so serious before. "He hasn't," I said. "I was with him almost the whole time. I do think he's going through some sort of emotional breakdown, though. He's really upset."

"Honey, this is what he's like when he's using. The boy I came home to a few days ago—that's not Charlie. He turns into somebody else."

"It's Paul, I think," I said, lowering my voice, as though Paul might somehow overhear me. "Charlie doesn't feel safe around Paul."

"Leah, we can't find Charlie," she said, as though she hadn't heard what I'd said about her husband. "He left the house yesterday and he didn't come back home and he's not answering our calls. Do you know where he is? Has he been talking to you?"

"We've been talking," I said. "But he didn't tell me he left."

"Can you tell him that I love him and I want to help him?" Faye said. "I'm on his side."

"Okay," I said. "But Faye, I don't think he relapsed."

"I hope not." Faye sighed. "I don't know what to do anymore, Leah. He's a thirty-one-year-old man. What am I supposed to do?"

It seemed like she was actually asking me, and I didn't know what to say.

"Well, I'm going to call the police," she said then, her tone firm and resolved. "I need to find him."

When I got back to our spot on the beach, Ben and Aaron were drinking beers even though it was eleven a.m. "What was that all about?" Ben asked.

"Nothing," I said. "My friend is having boy drama."

Ben and Aaron put their beers down and ran into the ocean.

I texted Charlie. **Can we talk on the phone? I just spoke to your mom. She loves you a lot. You should call her.** When he didn't answer, I tried calling him. His phone went straight to voice mail.

My brother met a girl on the beach. She was an undergrad from the University of Florida, had pink hair and a rhinestone belly button ring.

"I'm going to need you to sleep on the couch tonight," Ben told me at dinner.

"Why the fuck can't you go to her place?"

"She has three roommates, unfortunately."

"You have issues," I said. "Serious issues. What about Soo Min?"

"The couch is comfortable," Ben said. "I fell asleep there this afternoon."

That night, as I tried to get comfortable on the fake leather sectional in the living room, I got an incoming call from "Cynthia."

"Charlie," I said quietly into my phone.

"Babe."

"It's good to hear your voice."

"Yours, too," he said. "So good."

"Where are you?" I asked.

"I'm really embarrassed to tell you."

I sat up. Out the big glass picture windows were the silhouettes of palm trees moving gently against a purple-black sky. It was strange to think of Charlie back in the biting cold of Wisconsin. "Tell me."

"Leah, I've been realizing something. My parents are abusive. I have to cut ties. There's no other choice. If I stay in their house there's a good chance I'll use again." He paused, and I heard commotion around him, voices; the sounds of people walking in an indoor space. "I'm at a homeless shelter right now."

"Oh my God, Charlie."

"I know this is a huge ask. But could I stay at your place until you're back? It's awful here. It's really crowded and it smells, and I already had some of my shit stolen. I just want somewhere safe and warm to catch my breath while I figure out a plan. It just can't be with my parents."

I put my head in my hands. I thought about all the stuff in my apartment—my books, my jewelry box, my little portable speaker. Nothing was that valuable. I had my computer with me. "Okay,"

I said. "I'll call my landlord tomorrow and figure out if she can get you a key. But Charlie, your mom is convinced that you relapsed. Are you okay?" I paused. "Did you?"

"This is just her way of controlling me. When she doesn't like what I'm saying—especially if it's about Paul or his kids—or if I start putting up boundaries of any kind, she'll blame it on drugs. This has always been the pattern between me and her. But I've actually never been clearer than I am now. Leah, I have to go, but thank you. I don't take this for granted. You're saving me right now. You are."

We hung up, and I lay back down. I closed my eyes and tried to push away my gnawing disappointment. That he hadn't asked me how I was doing. That he hadn't said anything about my story, which I'd emailed him days ago, like he'd asked me to. But he was at a homeless shelter. To expect him to be thinking about me or my vacation was nothing less than selfish.

The next day on the beach, the undergrad from the University of Florida came along and talked in a loud voice about people she went to college with. Ben pretended to be interested and fake-laughed at her jokes. I fumed on my towel. When I started getting calls back from my landlord, I welcomed them.

It took a while—both convincing my landlord to give Charlie a key, and figuring out logistics, especially because Charlie was not making himself easy to reach—but by the end of the day Charlie texted me from inside my bedroom in Norris Court.

You have no idea how good it feels to be here. Your pillows smell like you. And don't worry I took a triple

**shower to get all the homeless shelter off me. Also, I
won't touch anything that's yours unless I absolutely
have to. Just the shower and the toilet and the bed.
And I'm going to hug the shit out of your pillows all
night. Love you.**

The next morning, while we were eating breakfast, I got a call
from an unfamiliar Wisconsin number.

"Excuse me," I said. "I have to take this." I ran outside and
answered just in time.

"I'm trying to reach Leah Kempler. This is Officer Ron Dowl-
ing with the Madison Police Department."

A sharp pain cut across my lower abdomen. I leaned against the
side of the house for balance. "Yes?" I said. "This is Leah."

"Leah, I'm calling about your boyfriend, Charlie Nelson."

"Boyfriend?"

"Is he not your boyfriend?"

"Well, kind of. Is he okay?"

"We're trying to figure that out. Is he staying with you?"

My mouth went dry and I tried to swallow. "He's staying at
my apartment for a bit, but I'm out of town. My landlord said it
was fine."

"And is it correct that you live in the Norris Court Apartments
on the east side of Madison?"

"Yes."

"We'd like your permission to do a wellness check on Charlie.
We're concerned he's relapsed and might be in extreme danger
right now. A wellness check means that we would go inside your
apartment, simply to see if Charlie is there."

"Look," I said, "I talked to him last night. He hasn't relapsed. No one is listening—"

"Heroin addiction is very serious, Ms. Kempler. I've walked into too many bathrooms with kids dead inside the tub. This wellness check isn't to get your boyfriend in trouble. It's to make sure we help him before it's too late. I just need permission from you to go inside your apartment."

I nodded into the phone. "Do whatever you have to do."

After we hung up, I ran to the bathroom. I got there just in time. I threw up the eggs and coffee I'd had for breakfast. Then I sat on the cool tile floor for several minutes, staring into the toilet bowl. I thought of calling Charlie to warn him, but I didn't.

A few hours later I got a voice mail from the officer saying that when they went into my apartment Charlie wasn't there. "Charlie left your door unlocked, though," the officer said. "I wanted to make sure you were aware of that."

At the end of that week, we all flew back to Boston. I had a few days at home with my dad before my flight to Wisconsin. I spent that time trying to write, but mostly I hung around, waiting for texts from Charlie. I went on a couple long walks around Brookline, imagining that Charlie was with me—pointing out to him my old high school and elementary school; where I used to take dance lessons; the hill where I had fallen off my bike and sprained my ankle. One night I got a text from Robbie. **When are you home for break? Want to chill?**

I didn't respond to Robbie until my plane was about to take off from Logan.

**I was in Florida with my family. Sorry I missed you!
How are you?**

Robbie wrote back right away: **I miss you too! Doing alright.
How was vacation with the fam? Make it through?**

But then a voice came over the sound system in the plane telling us to power off all electronics. I turned off my phone and forgot all about Robbie's text.

13.

CHARLIE WAS AN HOUR AND A HALF LATE PICKING ME UP FROM the airport. When he finally got there, we hugged but he didn't kiss me. He had a full beard grown in and he was wearing the orange puffer coat. He looked confused, his huge eyes darting all over the place.

"Charlie," I said, kissing his cheek. I was so happy to see him; it had been almost two weeks. "I missed you."

"I missed you, too."

His text messages had been so filled with passion and affection— **I can't wait to squeeze you and kiss your face a million times**—but now he seemed to be having trouble even meeting my eye.

There were a few times on the drive home that his eyes started to drift shut, when I needed to shake him to keep him alert. "What's up?" I said. "Why are you falling asleep?"

"I had a ton of cereal before I picked you up," he said. "Carbs make me so tired."

I laughed. "That's bullshit."

He smiled blearily. "It's true. I'm gluten-intolerant."

We stopped at the grocery store on the way home—the same Hy-Vee from before Thanksgiving—and halfway through the fruits and vegetables section Charlie said he had to go to the bath-room. I continued shopping. After I had everything I needed, I did a quick loop around the store, looking for Charlie, but I couldn't find him. I texted him: **Where did you go?**

Twenty minutes later he found me, standing near the checkout lines with all the bags of groceries.

"Where were you?" I asked.

"Sorry. I'm really constipated." He was holding a bag of Cool Ranch Doritos. "Can we get these?"

"I already paid for everything. I've been waiting for you for a long time."

He nodded and put the Doritos down on a nearby shelf.

In my apartment, dirty dishes and take-out containers covered every surface. Charlie must have gone back to his house and picked up his belongings, because his stuff was all over the place— laundry baskets full of clothing, his guitar, stacks of books, a be-hemoth of a speaker system from another era. There was a giant, filthy looking bong sitting on the side table next to the good Craigslist chair.

"I'm going to clean it all up," Charlie said. "I didn't have time before you got here."

I nodded and didn't saying anything. Then I went into the kitchen to make pasta. I thought he would follow me in there. Say something to make it better. Hug and kiss me and work his charm. But he didn't follow me. I made the pasta, banging the pots around, and then ate it alone, sitting on the kitchen floor. Every minute that he didn't come in, I got angrier. By the time I was done eat-ing, I had decided I would break up with him. I walked into the living room and found him passed out on the bad Craigslist chair, still in his coat. "Charlie," I said, shaking him. "*Charlie.*" He didn't budge.

I went into my room and lay down. After a while I heard Charlie stir. When he came in, he'd taken off his coat and he sat down on the edge of the bed. "I love you so much," he said, his voice barely audible.

"I love you, too." I had started to cry, but he didn't notice.

He pulled gently at my jeans, but I mostly had to do it for him, and then he took off my underwear and he started to kiss me. Soft kisses on my stomach, moving lower, but after a minute or so, he stopped.

He had passed out again, his head resting between my legs, a hand on each of my thighs. I crawled out from underneath him and pulled him into bed.

The next day I told Charlie that he needed to move out. He tried to convince me that it would be good for our relationship and beneficial for my writing for us to live together, but I wasn't interested. I'd take the loneliness, I decided. I'd dealt with it before; I could do it again.

"So you're breaking up with me?" he asked, and there was something knife-like in his tone that made me nervous.

"I'm not saying that," I said. "But I want my apartment back."

He didn't leave. He didn't leave the next day, or the day after that. For an entire week, each morning we both left my apartment at the same time, like a married couple on our way to work. Except, instead of going to work, I'd head for campus, and he'd go to meet up with Max. Every night around ten he would text to say he was on his way back. He acted like everything was normal between us, like this was our new life.

He told me that he and Max were working on an entrepreneurial project together—a documentary film about race relations in Madison. "I've started recording all this stuff on my phone," he told me. "You have no idea the kind of fucked-up shit black people have to deal with in this racist city. When Max is driving, we get pulled over all the time for no reason, and when I'm driving, no one bothers us. The documentary is going to reveal everything."

"What about a job?" I asked him. "Are you looking for a job?"

"That's what we're doing, babe. Dropping off applications."

"Do you think you could stay with Max?" I asked.

"Max lives in a motel," he said. There was a cigarette tucked behind his ear. "I'm going to go smoke."

We slept beside one another but we weren't having sex. In bed, I alternated between wanting to scream at him to get out, and to beg him to touch me and look at me the way he used to.

"Are you still attracted to me?" I whispered one night, as he lay beside me, passed out.

He muttered something I couldn't understand and put one hand on my thigh.

On the seventh day of this routine, I told him that he and all of his stuff had to be out of my place by seven p.m. that night. We were standing in the front hallway of the apartment with our coats on.

He looked at me, shocked. "*Tonight?*"

I nodded.

"Leah. I don't have anywhere to go."

I bent down to tie my winter boots. "Sorry."

He showed up at the apartment that night at quarter till seven. He stormed back and forth between the building and his car, hauling his stuff in armloads. "If things were reversed," he ranted, "I would never kick you out. You would always be welcome with me."

I didn't respond. I stood in a corner of the living room while it went on for half an hour. I didn't help with the moving and Charlie didn't ask for help. I was scared that he might take something of mine if I left him alone in the apartment.

At the end I asked him for the key.

He looked at me, eyebrows raised. "Why do you want it?"

"Because it's my key."

"No, it's mine," he said. "The landlord made it for *me*."

My stomach dropped. "Charlie, I let you stay here as a favor. I want my key back." My voice was beginning to shake.

"Well, I don't have it anymore."

"Are you serious?" I said. "My key is just floating around somewhere?"

He shrugged. "You can get the locks changed if you really need to."

"Do you have it?" I said. "Please just tell me if you have it."

He furrowed his brow and squinted like he was trying to discern something. "Do you not trust me, Leah?"

"No, I don't," I said. "You're scaring me right now, Charlie." Tears were starting to pool in my eyes.

"Leah," he said. And suddenly his voice was soft and gentle. "It's me. It's *me*. You seem really anxious. Are you okay?"

I squatted down and took a few deep breaths and Charlie knelt down beside me.

"You're freaking me out, Charlie," I whispered. "Please just give me my key."

"I honestly would, but I don't have it." He looked at me, and his face was back to normal—those big, innocent eyes.

"Okay," I said. "I need to get back to work. I'll talk to you later, okay? Do you have somewhere safe to stay?" I felt it was important, suddenly, to end this interaction on good terms.

"Yeah. I'm going to crash at my friend Danny's. I'll call you later?"

"Okay," I said. "Good. Let's talk later."

As soon as he left, I locked the door. Then I dragged one of the kitchen chairs over and propped it against it in a precarious way, so if anybody were to open it, I would be sure to hear the crash.

Several hours later, I sent him a text:

> **Charlie, I love you but this relationship isn't healthy. I'm going to be on my own for a while and focus on school. I think you're an amazing person. I'm really sad but I think this is the right thing. Please take care of yourself. I can see that you're hurting.**

That's when his texts really started. Long messages about why we should be together, his plans for the future, and his thoughts about the past. The texts were dramatic, seductive, manipulative, romantic, long-winded, and in many places made no sense.

I got hundreds of them a day. I read all of them.

14.

I GOT A DRINK WITH WILSON AT THE CRYSTAL CORNER, A DIVE
bar with neon lights in the frosted glass windows and arcade games
in the back. I checked my phone so many times that Wilson asked
me if something was wrong.

"It's Charlie," I said. "He won't stop texting me."

My friends hadn't said much to me about him after they'd met
Charlie at City Bar, but I knew they didn't approve. None of them
had conveyed this in words, except for Rohan. "You're the shit,
Kempler. You deserve the best. You know what I mean?" Everyone else just avoided mentioning him and never invited him out
again.

Only Vivian had said something nice. "He's charming, Leah.
There's something intriguing about him."

Wilson took a sip of beer. "How's that going?"

"We broke up. He's not taking it well."

"Christ," Wilson said, glancing at my iPhone, which was
blowing up with texts. "Why don't you block him?"

I shook my head and slipped my phone into my purse. "I can't."

"Why not?"

"I just . . . need to know what he's saying."

Wilson looked interested. "Why do you need to know?"

"He's going kind of nuts right now. It makes me feel better to know where his head is at."

Wilson frowned. "This doesn't sound good."

"Don't worry. It's not like that. He's harmless; trust me."

"You've been glued to your phone all night, Leah. That kind of texting isn't normal."

"I know," I said. "I know it's a lot."

"I'm not saying it's the same thing, but these things can escalate. My dad stalked my mom for years. When I was a kid he would show up to our house all the time. She used to be scared to answer the door. We weren't allowed to even answer the phone."

"Wilson, I didn't know that."

"It's changed her life. Wherever she is, she feels like he could turn up. It's not paranoid when it turns out you're actually being watched, you know?" Wilson's expression was hard, and I realized I'd never seen him look angry before. "He told her that if she told anyone, they could get sent back to Brazil. For a long time she didn't say a word, because she was scared that my brother and I might get taken away."

"I'm so sorry, Wilson. That's awful." And I did feel sorry. But Charlie wasn't like that.

"I ended it with Charlie really abruptly," I said. "I think he's confused. I did it over a text message."

"If you broke up with Charlie," Wilson said, "he should leave you alone."

I glanced at my phone, which was glowing in my purse. Another huge block of text flashed up at me.

**Leah when you tell someone you are insanely in love
with them, that you've never had such good sex before
and that they are your IDEAL partner emotionally
spiritually and physically, you can understand why
suddenly being broken up with feels like having the
rug yanked out. Were you just lying to me about all
that stuff? Maybe I am too gullible for my own good
but I really believed everything you said. You were it
for me, Leah. I was starting to envision a future. Not
just next month future, but real life. Taking out a
mortgage and babies and fighting over who does the
dishes. I honestly just want to talk so I can start the
process of understanding. Just a conversation. If you
saw me in person you'd see that I'm not angry, I'm just
heartbroken**

I looked back up at Wilson. "What happened with your dad?"
I asked.

"We don't know. He probably met someone else. But my mom
still goes back to court every year to renew the restraining order.
Getting that order was a huge deal for her."

I felt guilty then, as if by not blocking Charlie I was somehow
condoning Wilson's father's behavior. "I just want you to know,
Charlie has never hurt me. He's just in a bad place right now."

What I didn't tell Wilson, because it was too pathetic, was that
woven into Charlie's insane op-ed articles in the form of text messages were long passages about his love for me. They were even
more histrionic than the usual stuff. Those were the parts I was

reading for, more than anything else. Those were the parts that I read, over and over again, like a fiend.

After we finished our second drink I asked Wilson if he wouldn't mind walking me home. I'd been feeling nervous at night since my argument with Charlie. The Crystal Corner was on Willy Street and to get back to Norris Court, we had to cross from one side of the isthmus to the other, about a twenty-minute walk. Wilson and I made our way past the bike path and empty fields, crossing the train tracks and the quiet bus terminal, the city buses lined up in rows for the night. As we waited for the lights to change to cross East Wash, I looked to my left at the capitol building up the hill—white and gleaming against a creamy black sky.

Next to me, Wilson was standing seriously with his thumbs hooked into the straps of his backpack. I was grateful for him. I knew, deep in my bones, that Wilson was a man who would never make me feel unsafe.

When we arrived at my apartment complex, we walked up to the entrance of the building. I unlocked the door that led into the front foyer. "Thanks for walking me home," I said. "I appreciate it."

"Sure, Leah. Anytime."

I smiled at him and pushed open the door. I saw that a container of strawberry frosting was sitting on the welcome mat outside my apartment.

"Everything okay?" Wilson asked.

"Yeah." I was unsure if I should tell him about it. "I think Charlie left frosting at my door."

"Jesus. Is this safe, Leah? Are you safe?"

"It's fine."

"Listen. If you want to apply for a restraining order, I'll come with you. You know that."

"Thank you. But it's really not like that. I promise."

He nodded.

"Good night, Wilson."

15.

STAYING WITH DANNY HAD NOT PANNED OUT. CHARLIE WAS now sleeping in his car. His texts to me were getting more and more strange. I wasn't responding to any of them but he kept writing, and I continued to read them.

Then on a Wednesday at ten p.m. my doorbell rang twice in a row. My heart began to pound. I went to the bathroom and checked my reflection before going to answer it. As I was making my way to the entrance of the building, the bell rang again.

When I opened the door, he looked terrible. He was wearing the orange coat and his hair was sticking straight up in oily tentacles. He had on his glasses but they were crooked on his face, making him look deranged. There was acne across his cheeks and forehead that had never been there before. The coat was unzipped and underneath was the church outfit, but it was clear he'd been wearing it for days—maybe longer. I could smell him from several feet away.

"Hi," he said pitifully.

"Are you okay?"

He nodded.

I wondered then what I had been so scared of. He looked as though he might break in two.

He was holding a broken-down cardboard box. "I know you want me to leave you alone," he said. "I'm really sorry to bother you. I was wondering if I could sleep in the basement of your building, just for tonight? It's getting really cold in my car."

"Jesus," I said, looking at the box. I glanced behind him, through the windowpane that looked out onto the courtyard. Snow was falling in the dark. The temperatures that week had been dropping down to the single digits. "You can sleep in the living room," I said.

He swallowed. "Are you sure that's okay?"

"Just for tonight," I said. "But then you have to find somewhere else. Talk to your mom, okay?"

He nodded. "I will. Thank you, Leah."

While he was taking a shower I brought out a pillow and a few blankets and made a makeshift bed for him on the living room rug. I found sweats that would fit him for pajamas, and brought out a glass of water and heated up some of my dinner from earlier. He came out wrapped in a towel, looking clean and more like himself.

"I can't thank you enough for this," he said, as he changed into the sweats and sat down on the bed I'd made him.

"Have you eaten?" I asked.

"I had McDonald's earlier. But thank you. Really."

"There's food here if you want it."

Then I went into my bedroom and shut the door. For a while I lay in the dark. I wasn't anywhere close to sleep. I could tell by the sharp quiet in the apartment that he was up, too. I opened my bedroom door and stepped into the living room. "Are you still awake?" I whispered.

"Yeah. Are you?"

"Yeah."

"Are you okay?" he asked.

"Kind of. It's hard for me to sleep with you out here."

"Do you want me to go?" he asked.

"No," I said. "Do you want to sleep in my bed with me? But no sex. Just sleep next to me."

Charlie paused. "Are you sure you want that?"

"If you do."

I watched him stand in the dark, pick up the pile of blankets and pillows from the floor, and then make his way over to my bedroom. We crawled into bed together and for a few minutes just lay beside one another, breathing, not talking.

"I know you said no sex, but can I hold you?" Charlie asked.

I turned to him and he gathered me in his arms. He didn't try to kiss me or anything, though I wouldn't have minded. But he held me close the entire night. We fell asleep that way, our arms wrapped around each other, my head resting on his chest.

In the morning I checked my email on my phone from bed. Charlie was still sleeping beside me, one arm draped over my middle. When I saw that I had a response from *The New Yorker*, I sat up.

> *Dear Leah, I just read your story "Thirteen" and the bottom line is I think there is something great here. I couldn't put the story down. I don't think it's quite working yet—the ending didn't land for me in the way I think it was supposed to and I*

wonder about the backstory and about how much it's adding.

Are you willing to do a revision? Either way, no promises.

Happy to discuss more if this is something you're interested in.

"Holy shit," I whispered. Then I jumped out of bed. "Holy *fuck!*"

Charlie's eyes fluttered open. "What's wrong?"

"Nothing's wrong. I just got the best email of my life. From *The New Yorker.*" I tossed him my phone and began to laugh. "I think I need to call somebody. My dad's going to freak! Oh my God, Charlie, I'm going to remember this day for the rest of my life. Did you read it?"

Charlie smiled faintly and dropped his head back on the pillow. "That's great."

"I need to go," I said.

"Do you mind if I sleep longer?"

"Ten minutes while I shower. And then I'm going to the library."

Charlie rolled over.

As I shampooed my hair, I was filled with a new take on my future. I didn't care about love. I couldn't care less about it. I was going to have a story in *The New Yorker.* I was going to be a *writer.* I would pour everything into this.

When I got out of the shower, Charlie was in the same position in my bed.

"I need to leave in five minutes," I said. "Please be ready to go."

Twenty-five minutes later, Charlie and I walked out of the apartment together. "Are you going to talk to your mom?" I asked, when we hugged goodbye.

Charlie shrugged.

"You should," I said. "She loves you."

"Hey, Leah," Charlie said, before I walked away.

"Yeah?"

"I'm happy for you, about the story and everything. But just be careful."

"What do you mean?"

"One thing I've learned from recovery is that your sense of self-worth has to come internally. Not from external validation. And if this whole *New Yorker* thing doesn't work out for you—which I'm sure it will—I want you to be okay."

I didn't have time for his recovery psychobabble. "Got it, Charlie. Right now I just have to focus on my writing, which is why I'm in Wisconsin to begin with. It doesn't have to do with validation."

He nodded. "Well, good luck."

I wrote the editor back. We exchanged several emails and then I got to work. I worked all day, every day, for the next two and a half weeks. I went to the same cell in the stacks of Memorial Library. And that's what it was—a cell enclosed with a metal cage-like door. Five feet by five feet, with a built-in desk, a chair, and a fluorescent overhead light, one small window that looked out onto the frozen lake. Those weeks were the best of my life. Not the happiest, exactly. But I was alive. I woke up every day, my brain already at work. When I ate meals or drank coffee, it was simply to fuel up to get back to the story. I'd never wanted anything more.

I texted Charlie. **We both have to move on. I want space. I need to focus on writing now. Please respect this.**

He wrote back epically long text messages. He berated me for blaming him for my unproductivity in writing, and that if I let him, he could be a good influence on my work. That together we could write and make music and have a healthy, loving, creatively inspired relationship.

I didn't respond. I continued to go to my cell in the library. Charlie continued to text, but I kept my phone on silent and didn't read his messages until I was back home, after dinner.

I sent the editor at *The New Yorker* my revision of "Thirteen." Without the draft to work on, I was lost and purposeless. After clicking send, I sent out a batch of my other, less accomplished stories to other, less prestigious journals. I felt crazed, writing cover letter after cover letter, uploading attachment after attachment. *Take me, take me, take me.* I thought about what Charlie had said about external validation. I understood I was fucked. I kept sending.

One night my phone started ringing. It was Charlie. I was in bed, watching a movie on my laptop. I stopped the movie and waited for his call to go to voice mail. A few seconds later he called again. Then I heard knocking on my door. Not the door to my apartment complex—it was the front door to my apartment unit. I tried to take deep breaths, but something kept catching in my throat. A text came in:

Leah please can we just talk

The knocking continued. Another call. Then another knock. It went on like this for twenty minutes. Knock, call, knock, call, knock.

Then a voice mail. I listened to it, under the covers.

Leah—Charlie's voice emerged from my phone, soft but urgent—*when I was driving over here I almost did something really bad. Something I could never take back. But then I thought about you. I realized you're the only person in my life who really matters. I'm outside your door and I know you're there and I just want to talk to you about what's been going on in my life because I think you're probably really confused or someone's been telling you something untrue about me. I love you.*

I started to cry. **You're scaring me,** I texted, finally.

Two minutes later he texted again:

This is freaking me out. Something has gone really wrong because it seems like you are actually scared of me. I think it's really important that we talk. I need to tell you some things from the past month that will explain a lot.

I stayed under the covers until the knocking stopped and my phone went quiet. Finally, he went away.

In the middle of the night I glanced up and Charlie was standing at the foot of my bed, staring at me. I screamed. My scream woke me up suddenly. I sat up in bed, panting. I was alone in the room. He wasn't there. It was a dream.

16.

THE NEXT DAY I WALKED OUT OF MY APARTMENT TO CATCH THE bus to campus and I saw Charlie leaning against my building smoking a cigarette. He was talking with someone—the woman who lived across the hall from me. Charlie said something and the woman laughed and waved before walking away from him. This gave me an awful, nauseating feeling.

I ran up to him. "What are you doing here?"

He eyed me coolly. "I live here now."

"What?"

"I moved in across the hall with Ariana and Nick."

My body turned prickly with heat. "You can't do that, Charlie."

"Actually, yeah," he said. "I can."

"This is my *home*. We broke up." I thought about what Wilson had said to me at the Crystal Corner. "Charlie, when you break up with someone, you leave them alone."

"I've made a lot of friends around here, Leah," Charlie said. He was sneering, and it shocked me—how mean he could be. "Besides, Ariana and Nick need me. I'm Toby's new babysitter."

"Who's Toby?"

"Toby is their cat. It's my new job." He tossed his cigarette butt on the ground and it landed an inch away from my boot. The end gleamed bright and red in the dirty snow. "This is my life now, Leah. So you should get used to seeing me around."

I didn't go to campus that day as planned. I went back inside my apartment and sat in my living room and listened for Charlie's voice out in the hallway—for the sound of his footsteps, for the creak of doors opening and closing. I watched out my window, waiting for him to go back out for another smoke. Then I closed my blinds and wept into a blanket.

I was scared. And I hated him. I *hated* him.

My beautiful apartment with the built-in bookshelves and the fireplace. These two years, which I'd worked so hard for. And now he really wasn't going to go away. Would I have to move? Could I convince Ariana and Nick to kick him out? How did he even know Ariana and Nick? *I* barely knew my across-the-hall neighbors. I couldn't imagine how he'd charmed his way into their home.

But actually, of course I could imagine how.

I called Vivian and told her what was going on.

"Holy shit, Leah. He's harassing you. Why don't you call the police?"

"I don't know," I said.

"Could you get a restraining order?"

When she said this, I knew that she and Wilson must have been talking, and I felt ashamed for getting myself into this mess.

"It's not like that," I told her.

I couldn't call the police. I had been complicit in all of this.

And what would I even tell the police? Why wouldn't he have a right to live here? It was my fault for letting him in to begin with.

I didn't leave my apartment the next day, either. When I heard Charlie's voice out in the hallway, I called Robbie. Even though I hadn't seen or spoken to him since Thanksgiving, I knew he'd pick up.

"Leah!" he answered, and the warmth in his voice brought me to tears immediately. "Jesus," he said. "Are you okay? What's going on?"

I told him everything—about the first couple dates, about the time I'd spent at Charlie's house in the suburbs, Charlie moving in, kicking Charlie out. About all the texts and the calls and the showing up at my apartment at night. I told him about the key and that now he was living across the hall; that I could hear his voice in the hallway. "I'm scared to leave my apartment." I wept into the phone.

"Leah," Robbie said, when I was done. "I don't care that this guy is an addict. Lots of people are. Fuck, I probably am. But he's not treating you well. This stuff is scary."

"I think what people don't understand about this situation is that it's more mutual than it sounds."

"You're not treating him well, either?"

"No. I'm in love with him."

"I see," said Robbie stiffly.

"Anyway," I said, wiping my eyes and nose on the sleeve of my sweatshirt, "thanks for listening."

When he didn't say anything, I asked, "Are you seeing anyone?"

"No, Leah. I'm not." His voice was distant, which was not how Robbie ever sounded.

"Is something wrong?"

"I'm just not sure why you called to tell me this story about you and your boyfriend."

"He's not my boyfriend anymore. But I'm sorry that I called you. I just . . . you're someone I trust," I said.

"It's hard to hear, that's all."

I didn't say anything.

"You use people, Leah. It's something that you do. You're really scared of being used yourself, but you do it to other people."

I felt hot and sick. "I'm sorry, Robbie. I didn't mean to . . . I can see how . . ."

"I still have feelings for you, so it's hard to hear that you're in love with someone else. Especially someone like this guy."

"I shouldn't have called you about it," I said. "I won't call you about it again. I promise."

"It's okay," Robbie said, his voice softening. "You know that I'll always pick up. No matter what."

Charlie didn't stay across the hall for long. I don't know if he left of his own volition or if Ariana and Nick asked him to leave, but a week later, he was out, and I got back to my life.

I was spending time with Vivian and Wilson again. I'd been telling them more about the relationship—especially Vivian, since she'd said the thing about Charlie being intriguing.

It was hard for me to talk about Charlie with people who already had made their mind up about him. I tried to explain the nuance of my relationship to Vivian and Wilson. I thought, if anyone was going to understand it, it would be them—fiction writers. We wrote about messy situations, unlikable yet sympathetic characters. We dealt, not in the black-and-white, but in the gray. Often, when I spoke about Charlie, I felt like I was trying to paint him in just the right way. I knew that certain details would make people dislike him—or, worse, dislike me. Think that I was weak. I was pathetic. Desperate. So I left out parts of the story—things he said and did, things I said and did. And it's not like Charlie had ever hit me. It was difficult for me to imagine Charlie even raising his voice. Where my fear came from—if it was even fear at all— was still unclear to me.

17.

VIVIAN AND I WERE TAKING A WALK. IT WAS FEBRUARY AND there was snow on the ground from a storm the week before, mounds of it, packed and dirtied, lining the sides of the road. We were talking about Vivian's novel, what we'd thought of Rohan's latest story, David's most recent attempts to woo Vivian, when my phone started vibrating in my pocket. It was Faye. I hadn't heard from her since that phone call I'd gotten in Florida.

"This is Charlie's mom," I said to Vivian. "Do you mind if I take it?"

"Not at all," said Vivian.

"Leah, I'm sorry to bother you," Faye said.

"That's okay," I said. "Is everything all right?"

"No, honey. Is Charlie with you?"

"He's not," I said. "We broke up. He didn't tell you?"

"He told me." She didn't sound mad, though. "If you see him, will you call me or make sure he goes to a hospital?" Faye's voice was low and breathy. "We can't find him and Paul just found needles in the garage."

I stopped walking. "Needles?"

"Yes. Charlie's in trouble and needs to go to a hospital as soon as possible. So if he shows up, just try to get him there or you can call me—any time of day or night. I have to get going, but thank you."

I put my phone in my pocket. "He relapsed," I said to Vivian.

"He did?"

"They found needles . . ." I trailed off. "I know it sounds crazy, but I really believed him when he kept telling me he wasn't . . ." My stomach was starting to hurt, and it took all my strength not to sit down on the snowy curb. "He told me he was never going to use again."

Vivian leaned in and hugged me. The top of her head came up to my chin.

"You must think I'm so stupid," I said, after we pulled away.

"No," said Vivian. "I don't. I hope it's okay to say this, Leah, but I think you were in denial."

The word sounded clinical and faraway—like it had nothing to do with me. *Needles.* That sounded real.

We walked back to Norris Court silently. I couldn't stop imagining Charlie with a needle in his arm. I'd never allowed myself to picture it before. Now it was the only thing I could think about. All those times he'd disappeared for hours. Every time he hadn't been able to keep his eyes open. The night I'd found him passed out in his car. I wondered if he'd ever used in my apartment—in my bathroom or my bedroom. I wondered what he'd done with the needles afterward. Then I was scared in a new way. I thought of all the times we'd had sex without a condom. I almost said this fear aloud to Vivian but I couldn't bear to tell her how irresponsible I'd been.

When we got to Norris Court, I stopped short. "That's Charlie's car."

I hadn't seen his car for several weeks, but there it was, parked in front of my apartment complex—a blue Honda Civic, splattered with dirty sleet, the familiar orange and red and green Wisconsin license plate, ending in RH3.

Beside me, Vivian looked scared, which frightened me even more. Vivian almost never looked scared.

"Will you stay with me?" I asked.

"Of course."

Vivian followed me over. I saw from the sidewalk that Charlie was in the driver's seat with his head down on the steering wheel, his arms hanging limp by his sides. My heart was beating so hard I was breathless. I climbed over the small mountain of snow between the curb and the car and knocked hard on the window.

After a few knocks, Charlie raised his head and I exhaled. I backed up so that he could open the door.

"Hi," I said.

He gave me a small, weak smile.

"Remember Vivian?" I said, nodding toward Vivian, who was watching us from a few feet away. "From my program?"

"Of course," Charlie said. "It's nice to see you again." His voice was so soft I could barely hear him. I could tell he was trying to hold it together—for me, for Vivian.

"You, too," said Vivian. She smiled at him.

"Charlie, I think we should go to the hospital," I said. "We can go together."

"I don't know." His eyes were dim—there was no light in them at all—and his face was pale and waxy. I saw him then from Vivian's point of view, and understood, in a single flash, just how sick he was.

"I'll go with you," I said, and I held out my hand. "I love you, Charlie." I said it so he'd agree to come along. But it was also true. I loved him.

He took my hand.

We took Charlie's car. Vivian drove and Charlie and I got in the backseat. Charlie smoked cigarettes the whole way there and didn't let go of my hand once. None of us spoke except for Charlie, who gave Vivian directions every once in a while to the closest hospital.

After we parked in the visitors' garage, Vivian and I were about to climb out when Charlie said, "Sorry. Do you guys mind if I smoke once more? Before we go in?"

Before we answered he pulled a small vaporizer out from his pocket. He closed his eyes and sucked in hard, the way an asthmatic would pull breath from an inhaler. I felt embarrassed in front of Vivian, but she didn't seem to mind. He did this a few times. Small tears sat in the corners of his eyes.

"I'm really sorry," he said then, mostly to Vivian. "You're not seeing me at my best."

"Don't worry," she said, meeting his eye. "Truly."

It was empty inside the emergency waiting room. We checked in and then sat in a corner to wait for them to call Charlie's name. Vivian picked up a magazine and began flipping through until she came to a crossword puzzle. "What's a seven-letter word for a dessert in a glass?" she said.

Neither Charlie nor I could think of the answer, but it was nice, the way she was trying to distract us.

"I'm so bad at those," I said.

"Me, too," said Charlie. He offered a smile. He wasn't wearing his coat. I wondered where Charlie would be going, and if he would need one when he got there.

"Charlie Nelson?" a nurse called. She was standing across the room, holding a chart. My own stomach filled with nerves, as though she'd just called my name.

Charlie and I both stood, and Charlie looked at Vivian. "Maybe I'll see you again one day under better circumstances?"

Vivian nodded. "I hope you feel better, Charlie."

"Thanks. Me, too," he said. He gave her a little wave.

Then Charlie and I walked into the exam room together, hand in hand.

Charlie went straight to the exam table. Wordlessly, he held out his arm for the nurse to take his blood pressure, and he breathed in deeply, then out slowly as she checked his heartbeat. He did each of these things automatically, without being prompted. He looked feeble and resigned sitting on that table, his shoulders hunched, like a meek adolescent, or an old man.

"So, Charlie," the nurse said, after she'd made note of his vitals, "what brings you in today?"

"I need to detox," he told her—though he didn't sound ashamed, like he'd sounded with Vivian. "I'd been doing well, but then things spiraled. My doctor is Kristin Mitchell at the Opioid Addiction Treatment Center downtown. I'm in their outpatient clinic. They can probably send over my files. Or the hospital might already have them."

I expected the nurse to have some sort of reaction—even just a flicker of repulsion across her face—but she only nodded kindly. "We'll see what's open, Charlie. There's a chance you might have to stay here for a night or two until there's an available bed, but we'll get you in somewhere."

"In August you guys got me into that place in Milwaukee. Safe Haven, I think? I liked it there."

I felt it in my stomach, like a punch. I looked over at Charlie but he didn't notice. August had been just two months before we'd met. I tried to integrate this new information into the picture of Charlie I had in my head—of the guy who asked me out at the grocery store, who'd met me for drinks at the Weary Traveler. Would it have made a difference, if I'd known? I wondered then how many times Charlie had relapsed in the three years he'd been in recovery—if it had even been three years at all. I wondered how much of our relationship Charlie had been high. I would probably never know the answers.

"Charlie," I said.

He looked at me, his eyes heavy.

"I should go now."

He nodded. He held out his arms, and I could feel the nurse watching us. Maybe she thought this was pathetic. Maybe she assumed I was an addict, too.

I hugged him and he hugged me back, tighter than I was expecting.

"I love you," he whispered to me.

"I love you," I whispered, and my throat closed up.

In the waiting room, I found Vivian crying. "Are you okay?" I asked.

"I see it," she said, wiping her eyes. "I see why you love him."

No one had ever said anything like that to me before, and I sat down beside her and began to cry, too.

I called Faye and told her we were in the UnityPoint emergency room with Charlie.

"I'm on my way," she said, her voice thick. "I'll be there soon."

We waited until Faye arrived. I wasn't expecting Paul, too, but they came together, Faye first—rushing through the doors in a long wool coat with fur lining—and Paul several strides behind, lips pursed, hands in jacket pockets. When Faye saw me, she held up her hand and hurried over. She hugged me urgently and then she hugged Vivian, too.

"How's he doing?"

"He's in with the nurse already," I said. "He seems okay."

"Thank you for getting him here." Her hair was pulled up into a knot on the top of her head and makeup was smeared underneath her eyes—from crying or not sleeping, I didn't know.

Paul had joined the circle and put a hand on Faye's back. "Charlie's in the right place now," he said. "The doctors will straighten him out."

Faye didn't respond to this. "When did they take him in, Leah?"

"Forty minutes ago, probably."

"Okay. I'm going to check at the desk and see if he's up for a visitor."

In that moment, I saw Faye's life zoomed out. She'd made

other emergency room visits like this. She knew this fear. She knew how this went.

When I got home that afternoon I was surprised by the quiet. My phone was not going to vibrate. Charlie was somewhere else—where, exactly, I wasn't sure. But he wouldn't be calling me or showing up. It was over. I was on my own.

18.

I MADE AN APPOINTMENT AT THE UW STUDENT HEALTH CLINIC
to get tested for HIV and hep C. Before getting my blood drawn,
I met with a nurse practitioner. She asked me if I had any reason
to believe I might have been exposed.

"Not really," I said. "But my ex-boyfriend is an intravenous
drug user. And we weren't using protection."

I thought she was going to lecture me but she didn't. "Do you
know if he shares needles?" she asked.

"I don't know," I said. "I didn't know that he was using needles
until a few days ago."

She nodded, making a note on the computer. "I'm glad you're
coming in to get tested."

My stomach dropped. "You are? So you think I might have
something?"

She shook her head. "No, I don't. But I think it's wise that
you're checking. Even if it's just so you can have peace of mind."
She was leaning forward on her little rolling stool. She was a tall,
graceful woman with short gray hair and dangly earrings. Her
eyes were small and warm and she made good eye contact. Her
scrubs were tie-dye. She didn't seem alarmed or appalled at any-

thing I'd told her so far, and she wasn't speaking to me as if I were a moron, and this made me feel safer than anything she could have possibly said in that moment.

She was one of those rare professionals who I could imagine outside of work, too—tending to a garden, walking her dog. Maybe it was the tie-dye. I wished, suddenly, that she would hug me. I wished that we knew each other in a different context.

"Peace of mind would be good," I said. "I'm kind of freaking out right now."

"It sounds like a huge amount of stress."

"I really didn't know."

She nodded. "I'm so sorry that you're going through this. Are you talking to anyone? A counselor or a therapist?"

I shook my head.

"I could make a referral for you to see someone here at the clinic, if you wanted. Is that something you'd be interested in?"

"That'd be nice," I said, so as not to let her down.

She smiled gently. "Wonderful. I'll put the referral in the system while you're getting your blood drawn."

"Thank you," I said, and my eyes welled up.

Upstairs, in the lab, I watched the vials fill with my blood. I didn't know how I could have been so careless with myself. I felt fragile and horrified, at the thought that my body might be irrevocably contaminated. Maybe this would be the beginning of the end, for me. When I started to really cry, the person drawing my blood—a short, round woman with a thick, long braid down her back—smiled and patted my arm. "It's almost over. You're doing great."

"Thanks," I sputtered out. "When do the results come in?"

"Usually in a few days. I'm guessing Friday, but it could be Monday."

I didn't know what I would do with myself if it was Monday. I would have liked to remain unconscious.

Instead I watched reality TV for two days straight. My classes were done for the week, so I didn't have to leave my bed at all, except to go to the kitchen and the bathroom. I didn't answer any texts or phone calls.

The tests came back that Friday morning, via my student health portal. The results were negative. When I checked, I saw that I also had a message from the Behavioral Mental Health Services inviting me to make an appointment for an initial consultation with a therapist. I never followed up. Already, I felt infinitely better.

The editor from *The New Yorker* wrote back.

> *This is looking really good, Leah. I've gone ahead and marked up the draft with track changes—mostly sentence-level things, although I still think the ending could use some work. I've included a longer note in the draft. Why don't you look through my notes and let me know if you have questions. Send me back another draft when you're ready and hopefully I'll be able to bring that one to the rest of the team to see what they think. Thanks for all your hard work so far.*

Round two. Same deal with the library cell. Other than workshop and the one class I was teaching, all I did every day was work on the story. I gave copies to Vivian and Wilson and they gave me notes. We gathered in Vivian's living room and workshopped the story to death.

We only had three months left until graduation, and I still hadn't gotten any publications. Getting a story in *The New Yorker* would not just be something to put on a cover letter; it would be a massive foot in the door. More than a foot. It would most likely mean calls from agents; talk of book deals; a future secured.

I'd been starting to job search. Adjunct teaching, administrative assistants, nonprofits. Our professors kept telling us: find work that will allow you to write at the same time. I thought about how smug and naïve we'd been at the beginning of the program, thinking that we'd all make it big—write for a living. Now that we were about to graduate, we were coming to terms with the fact that we were going to have to start making money again the normal way.

19.

I GOT A CALL FROM CHARLIE ON HIS HOME PHONE. IT HAD BEEN two weeks since the day Vivian and I had dropped him off at the hospital.

"Leah," he said, his voice level and assured, when I answered. "How are you?" I hadn't heard him sound that way for months—maybe since the first week I'd met him.

"I'm doing okay," I said. "How are you doing?"

"I want to thank you," Charlie said. "I don't say this lightly, but you may have saved my life."

"No," I said. "If anything I was making things worse. I was enabling you—"

"Leah," he cut in. "None of this is your fault. None of it. You're the kindest, sweetest . . . and I took advantage of that. I can't imagine what it was like for you to be with me when I turned into . . . Dr. Jekyll. Or maybe it's Mr. Hyde." He laughed a little. "I always forget which is the fucked-up one."

"The thing is, Charlie, it's not so black-and-white for me. It is kind of like you're two different people—but also, you're still just one person. You're still always Charlie. You have one body, you know? It doesn't just turn on and off, depending on whether I'm with Jekyll or Hyde."

"I get that," Charlie said. "But you deserve to be with someone who's good to you all the time. And I was not. Which is hard for me to think about. To be honest, it kills me to think about. And I have a lot more thinking to do. But I understand that I blew it."

"Maybe we both blew it."

"I think it was me," Charlie said. "And if I could go back and change anything, it would be that I wish I could meet you for the first time right now. Like maybe tomorrow. Run into this pretty girl in the grocery store and ask her out while we're waiting on line. Now that I'm really sober. After I've hit rock-bottom and made all these mistakes. I wish I could be my best self for you."

I lay down on my bed and cradled the phone close to my face. We both didn't say anything for a while.

"I read your story," Charlie said. "The one you emailed to me in December. 'Thirteen.'"

"You did?"

"Yeah. I read it in rehab. I read it every night before I went to bed."

"Really?"

"It's incredible. You're incredible. The way you see the world. It made me laugh, too."

"Thank you for reading it. It's really different now."

"It is?"

"I changed the ending."

"I loved the ending, though."

"The editor didn't like it. She said that the mom leaving felt too dramatic or cliché or something."

"But isn't that what actually happened? In your life? It's not too dramatic. That's just the way life is."

My eyes filled with tears. "Charlie."

"Yeah?"

"I've missed you."

Charlie and I fell back into a relationship. We still didn't go on dates, but we went on walks around the neighborhood or we'd go to the grocery store together or to the corner store on East Johnson. Every once in a while he'd come into a coffee shop with me, but Charlie never wanted to spend money on coffee and he wasn't the type to sit in a café and read or have a conversation over a cappuccino.

I loved going to the store with Charlie. I loved running errands with him, driving around in his car, sitting out in the courtyard while he smoked, holding hands with him while we walked down the street. He teased me sometimes that when we were in the apartment I would follow him around. He'd get up and go to the kitchen, and I'd pad along behind him. Now that Charlie was awake, I couldn't get enough of him.

He'd written me a song in rehab and he played it for me while we sat across from each other on the rug in my living room. He sang differently when he was sober—he was more expressive, and he projected, filling the entire apartment with his voice. Any chance I got, I recorded him playing music. I really did believe that art could save a person. And as much as I wanted to save Charlie, I knew that if anything was going to save him, it would be his music.

One day he asked to read all my stories.

"*All* of them?" I said.

"Yeah. All of them." So we lay on my bed with my computer in his lap and he read out loud every story I had ever written, one after the other. I kept waiting for his attention to wander or for him to take a smoke break, but it went on for hours. He stopped only to laugh at the funny parts and tell me when he liked a sentence. After each story, he talked about the characters like they were real people, like these were things that really happened. I felt so spoiled; like he was finally learning who I was.

At night he would make us dinner. He only knew how to cook a few things: quesadillas, eggs with bacon and corned beef hash, BLTs, steak. For dessert we usually had mugs of hot chocolate.

He wrote something during that time, too. A few pages about our relationship. He gave it to me and asked me to tell him honestly what I thought of it. He said to be ruthless. Truthfully, his writing reminded me of his texts—long-winded and over the top. It wasn't as sharp or honest as the story he'd written back in college. I didn't tell him that, though. I told him that I loved it, that he should keep writing, and that I wanted to read more. That part was true. I did want to read more.

20.

"SO I GOT WORD THAT 'SUPER 8' IS GOING TO BE PUBLISHED,"
was how David put it, his voice uncharacteristically soft. We were
at City Bar at our table. He lowered his eyes in mock humility.
"In their fall issue. The editor of *Harper's* wrote to me yesterday."
Harper's. As if *Harper's*—one of the best magazines there was—
were an afterthought.

His gaze flickered to Vivian.

"Congratulations," Vivian said, along with the others. But she
didn't get up out of her seat or suggest shots.

It was the road trip story from our first semester. I faked happiness for David as we all clinked glasses, but inside I was seething.

He kept looking over at Vivian the rest of the night—like he
was owed something.

I was repulsed by David because I recognized his desperation.
He wanted so badly to be loved, and he thought now it was going
to happen. He thought being admired and being loved were the
same thing—that it all came from the same well.

I checked my email six or seven times right there at the bar—as
if *The New Yorker* were really going to get back to me at ten o'clock
on a Tuesday night.

After that I started checking my email obsessively—dozens, some-times hundreds of times an hour. I didn't do much else those days besides check my email. I was now the only one in my cohort who did not have a publication to my name. Charlie was right—I was hungry for validation. But I just needed this *one*. After this yes, I felt certain, I would be good to go.

Vivian and Rohan hooked up. Vivian told Wilson and me about it on a gray Sunday morning in March. We were sitting at the far end of the communal table at Johnson Public House.

"Rohan and I don't want to make things weird for the cohort," she said, leaning over the table. "So don't tell anyone." JPH during a weekend wasn't the best place to tell secrets, as it was always filled with graduate students, but that day we hadn't seen anyone we knew.

Wilson laughed. "Well, now the only people who don't know are Sam and David."

"David's going to be heartbroken," I said.

"Can I be the one to tell him?" said Wilson.

"No!" Vivian said, grinning. Then she shrugged. "Sure, what-ever. I honestly don't give a shit who knows. We only have a few months left."

"Are you two going to date?" I asked.

"I don't know. This literally happened"—she glanced at her phone—"twelve hours ago. He might come meet us here, actually."

"And we should pretend we have no idea?" I asked. "Also, how was it?"

Vivian smirked. "It was *very* good."

Wilson blushed and busied himself at his computer.

Then Vivian texted me under the table.

Rohan knows what the fuck he's doing!

As if being conjured, Rohan walked in then, the door jangling softly. When he spotted us in the back of the coffee shop, he waved and weaved his way through the crowded tables, pulling his scarf off and unzipping his winter parka with the big fur hood. When he set down his bag on the seat beside Vivian, he was glowing. His hair was still wet from the shower.

"I'm going to grab a coffee," he said. "Anyone want anything? Viv, you want a refill?"

"I'm good," she said. "But thank you."

She was glowing, too.

We all worked diligently for the rest of the morning and then—because there were too many of us there for this not to happen—the afternoon devolved into conversation and gossip, ordering lunch and pastries and more coffee.

I was having a good time. When I finally glanced at my phone several hours later, I saw that Charlie had texted me asking what I was up to.

JPH, come by! I wrote back spontaneously. I didn't expect him to actually come, though, so when ten minutes later he appeared, I was taken aback. We locked eyes across the crowded shop. I watched the anxiety wash over his face when he realized that my friends were there, too.

I felt suddenly that I'd done something bad. Both to Charlie, for not warning him that I wasn't alone, and my friends, by not telling them ahead of time that Charlie would be coming. I hadn't told anyone that I'd been seeing Charlie again. I knew they would disapprove. And I knew that Charlie found my friends stressful to be around. He sensed their disapproval, although he did like Vivian.

Then I felt resentful, that I would need to give anybody a heads-up at all. Vivian and Rohan had been sitting side by side all day—flirting, having fun—and nobody was giving them a hard time about it.

"Charlie's here," I said quietly, as Charlie walked over, and my friends all stopped laughing and returned to their laptops, as if they were schoolchildren and the teacher was coming over to reprimand them.

"Hey, babe," Charlie said.

"Hi," I said, wishing that he hadn't called me "babe" in front of them. "I didn't think you were actually going to come."

He made a face. "Did you not want me to?"

"No, I—"

"Hey, man," Rohan broke in. "Nice to see you again."

"Yeah, you, too," Charlie said. He nodded hello to Wilson and then he smiled at Vivian. "Hey, Vivian. Leah tells me you finished writing your novel. That's great news."

"Thank you, Charlie," she said. "Do you want to sit down? We can pull over a chair."

"I'm okay, thanks." He turned back to me. "I was actually coming in here to see if I could grab your keys and hang out at your place till you're done? I don't want to drive home and then come all the way back here later on. Trying not to blow all my money on gas driving back and forth here all the time."

"Oh," I said, glancing quickly at my friends, who were looking at us. Though I no longer felt scared of Charlie, the thought of giving him my key, even for an hour or so, made me nervous. "I'm actually ready to go," I said. "So I'll come with you now."

"Cool, meet you outside." He tapped his pocket, which was where he kept his cigarettes. "Take it easy," he said to my friends, and then he left.

There was silence as I began to gather my things. Then Rohan spoke. "I thought you guys broke up."

"We're back together, sort of," I said. "He's doing a lot better."

"We're less concerned with how he's doing, and more with how you're doing," said Vivian delicately—the way you'd talk to someone unstable.

"I'm fine."

"I don't really like the way he talks to you," said Rohan.

I looked up, irritated. I wasn't sure exactly what he was referring to, but I knew it would be a mistake to ask. That whatever Rohan would say would inevitably worm its way into my head and lodge itself there. "He's really loving," I said, and I could hear how pathetic this sounded to them. It was all there, reflected back in their faces.

"Why can't you keep hanging out?" Rohan pushed. "Why do you have to go as soon as he gets here?"

Wilson was staring at his computer screen. He hadn't said anything—he seemed intent on not participating in the conversation or even acknowledging that it was going on. I wasn't sure if this made me feel better or worse.

Vivian and Rohan, though—their faces were serious, but underneath it, I knew, they were happy. They were still glowing from last night, from the ease and thrill of sitting beside one another all day; of knowing that pretty soon they'd leave JPH together and go back to one of their cozy, book-filled apartments and have sex again, then fall asleep talking about their bright futures. Whatever it was they had with one another, it was normal.

I was jealous, and right then, I despised them.

What I had with Charlie wasn't normal. I knew that. But who were they to judge? None of them—*nobody*—had ever made me feel as good or loved as Charlie made me feel. The truth was, there were times I felt so happy with Charlie I thought I might break down sobbing. Being with Charlie was the closest I'd ever come to that feeling of all-consuming love I'd craved for so long.

"I'm figuring it out," I said. "I'll see you guys later."

21.

I GOT THE EMAIL WHILE CHARLIE WAS AT WORK. HE'D GOTTEN A new job as a server at a restaurant downtown and was working mostly lunch shifts. I was in the MFA office, having just finished teaching a class, and when I opened the email from the editor on my phone, the words swam in front of me before I was able to string them together. The important ones stuck out, and I understood what the answer was long before I had the wherewithal to absorb the content or the particulars.

Thank you, unfortunately, disappointed, elsewhere, in the future.

I started to cry immediately, the way small children do when they get hurt. Hard and messy, tears mixed with snot. The only one in the office besides me was David.

"Are you okay?" he asked, alarmed.

"They said no."

"Who?" he said, coming over to my desk.

Bawling, I showed him the email on my phone.

"Fuck," he said, and I saw true compassion in David's eyes. This only made me cry harder.

To my surprise, he gave me a hug. "I know you don't see it this way, Leah, but this is a good thing. That you got this close. With

The New Yorker? That's huge. You'll send them another story. And you're going to publish this one somewhere good. This story is really fucking good."

I nodded and pulled on my backpack. "Thanks," I said. "I should go." I walked the two miles home weeping. Every time I calmed, even for a second, a fresh wave would hit me, and I'd start up again. When I stepped into my apartment, I screamed and hurled my backpack across the room. I was no longer crying like a child. I was crying as though someone had died.

When Charlie came over later that night, I hadn't let up. "Let me read the draft," he said.

"No."

But I let him. After reading it, he ranted about how wrong the editor was to have suggested I change the ending. "You should trust your instincts," he said. "The story was perfect how it was originally. Didn't Dot say it was perfect?"

I started to laugh through my tears. "*Bea*," I said.

He frowned. "What?"

"Her name is Bea. Where did you get Dot?" I was laughing and sobbing and wiping my nose on my sleeve.

He smiled. "Okay, Bea. Bea knows what's up. Send the story out to other places. The one with *your* ending. It will get published. The fucking *New Yorker* doesn't know what the hell it's talking about."

"But they do, Charlie," I said, flooded with fresh sorrow. "They're *The New Yorker*."

"Leah, listen." He put both hands on my shoulders. "One day you're going to look back on this and you're going to laugh. I know it doesn't feel that way now. But you're going to be okay.

You're going to keep writing. And this is going to work out for you. I know it. I don't know most things, but I *know* this."

"Okay," I said, believing him. And then I kept crying.

I sulked for three days and then I started writing again. I found a new spot to work in the Wisconsin Historical Society, a beautiful room with cathedral ceilings, gleaming oak tables, green banker's lamps that emitted a soft, buttery glow. I wasn't especially superstitious when it came to writing, but I decided that I was done with the stacks in Memorial Library.

I started something new. I didn't know what it was yet exactly, but I liked working on it—the same way I'd liked working on "Thirteen." I woke up every day, my head already in the scenes, new sentences forming on my walk to campus, details on the tip of my tongue. It was the story of a daughter searching for her mother. What made this story different from my others was that in this one the daughter and mother find one another.

I'd never looked up my mother on the internet. I hadn't google-mapped her address in St. Paul. I'd always been too scared about what might turn up. If Aaron had been able to find out such specific details—*she works at the public library, she teaches a ceramics class*—I didn't know what else might be out there. Perhaps she had remarried. Perhaps she had stepchildren. Or maybe she was alone.

She'd left most things behind—her clothing and her belongings, all her jewelry, including her wedding ring. She'd taken her important documents and, according to my dad, a withdrawal of cash from their shared bank account. She also had some of her own money set away in a separate account from when her parents had died.

She'd left a note for my father. Among other things, she'd written: *Tell the kids I love them. You should bring them to see a therapist.*

My father, when finding the note, had broken down, thinking that it was a suicide note. Aaron and Ben and I had been downstairs in the kitchen when we'd heard a loud and terrible sobbing erupt from their bedroom. Aaron told Ben and me to stay put and he'd run upstairs. Aaron found our father, holding the note in one hand and the phone in the other, about to call the police. When my father showed the note to Aaron, Aaron assured him that the note clearly explained that my mother was leaving us—not killing herself.

We never talk about that night. My father finding the note. Aaron finding my father. And then Ben and I finding Aaron, who was eighteen at the time, weeping in his bedroom. Aaron was the one who explained to us what had happened. Our mother hadn't just left for a weekend this time. She wasn't coming home.

Ben and I slept in Aaron's room. I remember thinking, *At least I have my brothers.* The thought of Aaron going to college in the fall, and then Ben only a few years later, was unbearable for me. Our family split up in all these different places. I hated the idea of being left behind. My brothers assured me that this wouldn't happen—that they would always be there for me, that we would always be there for each other. But something changed that day. After my mother, we all left, one after the other. There was no coming back after that. Home was a memory.

My father had asked us—three teenagers—if we wanted to see a therapist. Ben and I said no. Aaron said yes. I'm sure my mother was right that seeing a therapist would have been a good idea, but the fact that she'd wanted to shirk us off to a shrink had been too insulting.

It took my father a long time to actually get divorced from my mother because she made herself impossible to get in contact with. When she finally started answering his phone calls, she didn't ask for anything from him—alimony, assets, custody. She said she would sign whatever he needed her to sign. She just wanted a clean break.

One afternoon in late March I looked up my mother. It was easier than I thought it would be, typing her name into Google and clicking on the very first link that popped up. It listed the same address in St. Paul, Minnesota, that used to be written on the envelopes she'd send my birthday cards in. I put her address into Google Maps. It was a four-and-a-half-hour drive from Madison.

Part of my hesitation in reaching out to my mother was that I kept hoping she was going to do it first. I was always waiting for her to show up at my doorstep, for birthday cards to start appearing in the mailbox again. An email. A Facebook friend request.

"If I see her," I told Charlie, "I want to know that it's because she really wants to see me and isn't doing it to humor me."

"At this point, hasn't she rejected you enough?" Charlie said. "Does it really matter what she says or does? Who cares if you reach out to her or she reaches out to you? She's proved what kind of mother she is over the last twelve years."

I felt a rush of love for Charlie so intense then that I realized it didn't actually matter to me how things went with my mom. I had Charlie now. "Would you come with me?" I asked.

———

It took a lot of convincing for Faye to let Charlie leave Madison and drive to Minnesota. But finally we were on our way, with promises to check in regularly and to return the following day. Charlie and I had never gone anywhere outside of Madison together, and for the first time I felt like we were a regular couple—our coffees from Starbucks side by side in the cup holders, stopping to get gas and use the bathroom at a service plaza along the highway.

When Charlie took a long time in the men's room I began to get nervous, but then I spotted him across the plaza, standing on line for McDonald's.

"Do you want anything?" he asked, when I joined him.

"We just had breakfast."

He shrugged. "I want to take advantage of my freedom."

We listened to music in the car and for the first two hours of the drive I was relaxed, being out on the road with Charlie. But then interstate signs for Minneapolis became more and more frequent. I imagined knocking on my mother's door and her not recognizing me; having to explain who I was. I pictured the door closing in my face.

When we were kids we'd made multiple trips a year to visit my father's family in New Jersey, but we'd never visited St. Paul. My mother hadn't talked very much about her past. She said that it was too painful.

My mother's mother had died of breast cancer at the age of fifty-two and my mother's father of a stroke four months later. My mother had been a senior in college when her parents died. She and my father had been dating just a few months.

"Your father wasn't like other twenty-two-year-old boys," my mother had told me once. "He wasn't scared off by my grief, and he never made my sadness about himself. He was very patient. I don't think I would have survived that time without him. He became my family, my only real connection in the world. But the truth is, we had no idea what we were doing." My parents got married when they were only twenty-three, and Aaron was born the following year.

When I was younger I thought the way my parents met was romantic, even though their relationship had started and ended in heartache. Being saved from sadness and saving someone from sadness—these weren't just things I yearned for out of the blue. It was something I'd been born into. I didn't know how to separate the feeling of love from the feeling of wanting to escape.

When we got to St. Paul, we drove through quiet side streets without speaking as the GPS told us where to go, and I imagined my grandparents and my mother driving around the same streets as a young family half a century ago. When we turned onto Greenacre, a sleepy suburban cul-de-sac, I told Charlie I needed a bag—I was going to throw up.

He pulled the car over to the side of the road, in front of the house where my mother lived and handed me the empty McDonald's bag. I sat, hunched over the grease-stained bag, dry-heaving for several minutes, with Charlie's hand in my hair. When I heard the spark of his lighter, I looked over at him.

"You're smoking right now?"

He raised an eyebrow. "Should I not?"

"I'm trying not to puke, Charlie."

He put the cigarette out and placed it on the dashboard for safekeeping. "Sorry. This is just sort of stressful."

"Why is it stressful for you?"

"Seeing you stressed out is stressful for me." He looked around, craning his neck, tapping his fingers on the steering wheel. "Also, I haven't been outside Madison in a long time. This is sensory overload."

I was starting to breathe fast and hard. I was terrified that someone was going to walk out of the white house with the purple shutters. My mother—or a man or a child. A teenager. Or that Charlie was going to do something crazy. I wished all of a sudden I was here with Robbie instead, who I knew would be comforting in a moment like this.

"Are you okay, Leah?"

I shook my head no.

"Do you want me to come in with you?"

I glanced at him. He had stopped tapping and was giving me his full attention.

"Okay." I didn't know what he might do if I left him alone for too long.

We walked up to the front door holding hands. There was nothing about the house that would have stood out to me. I could have passed it a million times and never known my mother lived inside. The lawn was covered with old, dirty snow. In the driveway there was a car with Minnesota license plates. The house was much smaller than ours in Brookline; smaller than Charlie's.

I rang the bell. A minute later the heavy purple door opened and a small woman in pajamas stood before us, behind the storm door. It shocked me. I'd remembered her taller—taking up all the air in the house. But there she was, barely five feet. Her long black hair was threaded with silver and it hung over her shoulders. Her eyes were the same. Big, hazel, alert. And she was staring straight at me.

"Leah," she said—my mother's voice—and I felt so much relief, that she'd said my name, that she knew who I was, that I smiled. She smiled, too. Then she opened the storm door. "Oh my God," she said. She hugged me, and all of a sudden I was feeling my mother's hair against my chin—dry and wiry—and smelling what she smelled like—incense and spices and something tangy and sharp, not at all how I remembered her smelling.

Hugging her felt wrong, like trying to embrace something small and sharp, like a tack. I'd remembered parts of her being soft—her stomach and her breasts, the tops of her arms. Now our bodies no longer fit. It felt as though I might crush her or impale myself on her.

She stepped back quickly, ending the hug. I tried to smile, but I was close to tears. How badly I wanted this moment to be simple. I wanted the hug to fix something. I wanted her to be bigger and fatter and softer and stronger than me; for it to be the easiest thing in the world to be hugged by my mother.

I took a step back to feel the familiarity of Charlie behind me. I felt his hand, gentle on my back. "Hi, Mom," I said, and I was aware of the pitch and the tone of my own voice—would I sound different to her? The last time she'd heard me talk I was barely thirteen. "I looked you up," I said, "and I'm living in Wisconsin now, so I—"

"You're living in Wisconsin? Are you in Madison?" She was

smiling, and it shook me to my core to see her smile like that, to hear her voice.

I nodded. "I'm in Madison for graduate school."

She glanced at Charlie. "Is this your husband?"

Tears sprang to my eyes without warning. "No," I said, blinking my eyes dry. "I'm only twenty-five. Charlie's my boyfriend."

My mother held out her hand, and Charlie shook it. "Charlie," she said. "I'm Naomi. It's great to meet you."

My mother smiled at me, and this time it made my insides knot. It was different than the earlier smile. This smile was polite, for a stranger. "How do you like the Midwest?" she asked. "This is where I grew up," she added, as though I might have forgotten this about her.

I shrugged, dizzy. I wished then for Ben and Aaron, who were the only ones in the world who would understand this moment. "It's nice," I said. "I like it."

We were still standing in the doorway of her home, holding open the storm door. The foyer to her house was dark and cluttered with shoes. There were men's shoes, I noticed—a pair of hiking boots, a gigantic orange flip-flop—but I didn't hear any sign of another person inside. I didn't see children's shoes, and I was grateful for that. There was a small table with a basket overflowing with mail, and a hallway with several recycling bins piled high with broken-down cardboard boxes.

"Do you want to come in?" my mother asked. "I'm afraid Todd and I have somewhere we need to be in a few hours, but I'd love to sit down and hear about everything. There's so much to catch up on." She laughed and squeezed my arm. "God, you're beautiful, Leah." She looked at Charlie. "Isn't she beautiful?"

Charlie nodded. "She is."

"Who's Todd?" I asked, nauseated.

"Todd is who I live with," my mother said. "He's an artist. He owns the house." Then she waved us inside, and we followed her to a living room cluttered with cheap, ugly furniture—the kind you'd find in a college dorm room. It was not so different, really, than the furniture I had in my apartment in Madison. The couches were old and sunken and the floor had a scratchy brown rug, speckled with lint. Empty mugs and glasses were everywhere. The room didn't have any overhead lighting, but a lamp that my mother plugged in and turned on. It smelled stale.

"Make yourselves comfortable," she said.

Charlie and I sat down on the futon.

"This is a nice place you have," said Charlie, and I could tell he meant it. Charlie had spent a lot of time in not-nice places. But I hated the room, everything about it. It made me feel shaky and scared. I couldn't understand why my mother lived here and Monica lived in our house.

"Leah," my mother said, sitting down across from us, "what are you studying in school?"

I thought of answering. Of telling her about my graduate program, our workshop, the class I was teaching. But I couldn't bring myself to do that. "This is it?" I said.

Her smile stiffened. "This is what?"

"We're going to talk about what I'm studying in school?"

She crossed her arms over her chest as if to protect herself. Her face had turned hard, and I remembered then the way she could do that. Shut you out. All the earlier happiness and curiosity washed away. "I wish you'd called ahead of time," she said. "I wasn't prepared for this."

"I don't have your fucking phone number."

She winced. Then she glanced at Charlie, like she expected him to intervene. When he didn't, she said to me, "I see you're here for some sort of confrontation. I can sympathize with that. Really. I don't expect you to forgive me. You or your brothers. But now that we're both adults, I'd like to be your friend. And, Leah, you turned out so well. You look—"

"I don't need friends," I cut her off. "I was hoping for something else." I stood, trembling, amazed at my ability to speak so directly. It occurred to me that I was terrified. I looked at Charlie. "Let's go."

"I just want to say one thing," Charlie said, standing also. He looked at my mother. "You've missed out." He seemed to be gaining strength, too. "Your daughter is as good as they come."

And right then, he was perfect to me. Better than any fantasy or daydream.

My mother didn't say anything more as we left the room, but I heard her start to cry, and it took everything I had not to go back and apologize.

I thought she might come running after me as we walked across her yard to the car. To call my name. I couldn't imagine that she would let me go, not for the second time. But when I climbed into the passenger seat and allowed myself to look back at the house, the door was closed.

In the car Charlie drove silently and I closed my eyes and I tried to recall those mornings crawling into her bed. In my memory she was soft and yielding. I'd throw my whole body on top of hers and she'd be so happy to have me there with her.

But maybe it had been just me who'd been happy. Maybe she hadn't wanted me there. It was impossible to know for certain where my feelings ended and hers began. Her face was blurry in my mind. Had she turned me away? Had she hugged me back? I couldn't recall. All I could conjure was the early light in my parents' bedroom, all that warmth under the covers. The softness of my mother's belly as I wrapped my arm around her, holding her tight to me.

After we got settled in the Airbnb, Charlie called Faye to let her know we had arrived safely. I listened to his side of the conversation. I could tell Faye was asking questions about my mother and that Charlie was avoiding giving answers. After he got off the phone we went onto a small porch out front and sat side by side in matching Adirondack chairs. The porch looked out onto a quiet, snowy neighborhood of small family homes, not unlike my mother's street. It was early evening now, and the sky was a deep bruised color, a sliver of moon peeking out between bare tree branches.

"Can I have one of those?" I asked.

"You sure?"

I nodded.

Charlie handed me a cigarette. "I think she's an addict," Charlie said, as he lit the cigarette for me.

"What?"

"Your mom. She was wearing her pajamas in the middle of the day, she said she had somewhere to be. Her place was a mess. She was being sketchy, don't you think?" He lit his own cigarette and inhaled. "She's probably an alcoholic. Did you smell anything when you hugged her?"

"That's not what it is," I said. "I think she just doesn't want anything to do with me."

"I bet those mugs all over the place were filled with booze. And that Todd guy is a drunk, too."

I put the cigarette out in the ashtray and pressed my palms to my eyes.

"Fuck, I'm sorry, Leah."

"I don't think you're right," I said to Charlie. "Stop projecting."

"I wasn't—"

"Just because your dad is an addict doesn't mean my mom is one, too."

"My dad isn't an addict, as far as I know," said Charlie. "Just a dick."

I looked over at him.

"The only other addict in my family is my mom's brother. All I know about my dad is that he's French, which is probably why I'm so hairy."

"Oh."

"I'm sorry," he said. He reached out with his free hand, and I took it. "I don't know anything about your mom."

"That's okay. I don't know about your dad, either. Obviously."

"It's brave what you did today. Standing up for yourself. I hope you don't mind me saying this," he said, "but your mom is a coward."

"I don't mind," I said.

For a second, he looked genuinely angry. "Fuck her."

———

That night in bed Charlie traced a circle with his finger, from the spot where my upper thighs touched to my hipbone, just under my belly button, to my other hipbone, and back around to that original spot, connecting it so that he'd made the circle complete.

"I'm going to kiss you everywhere except inside this circle," he said. And then he did, starting at my neck, moving slowly down to my shoulders. He stretched my arms up above my head and kissed the soft parts of my underarms and along the sides of my breasts. He kissed my ribs and my breasts and my stomach. He kissed the edges of the circle, but he didn't go inside. Then he inched down and kissed my legs, the insides of my thighs, my knees, the tops of my feet, my ankles. By the time he'd moved back up and arrived at the circle, I was so out of my mind—so breathless with anticipation—that I didn't know what to do except lie there and let him keep going.

22.

THE END-OF-THE-YEAR MFA READING HAPPENED A FEW WEEKS
later, on a rainy evening in April in Room 301 of the Madison
Public Library. As more and more people trickled in, the rows
of chairs began to fill up. Soon there was only standing room in
the back. All of our families were there. Vivian's parents were in
from Manhattan—her mother glamorous and talkative. "What a
crowd!" Vivian's dad kept saying, looking around at the packed
room. "What a night!"

Wilson's mother and brother had flown in from Pittsburgh,
and they sat together in the second row, chatting with the people
around them. They seemed even quieter than Wilson, but they
shared his mannerisms—easy smiles, a way of leaning in when
somebody was saying something, and their laughter was identical
to his.

Rohan's parents—his mother in a gold-and-magenta sari and
his father in a suit—were making friends with everybody, particularly Vivian's parents. Sam's mother and his wife, Katie, had arrived just hours earlier from Kansas City after an eight-hour drive.
Sam was seated between them, looking stiff and uncomfortable in
a way I'd never seen him before. David's parents sat silently in the

first row on their phones without speaking to anyone, even each other.

My own family, who took up almost an entire row, were keeping to themselves. They were friendly but they engaged in conversation only when they were approached, not seeking it out.

It seemed arbitrary, the families we were born into. Some things we couldn't change: the parents we had, the childhoods we'd lived. Was it possible to change the way we were in a room?

Then the reading began. As I listened to my cohort read, I was overcome with pride. I'd read all these stories before, many times, but I'd never heard them out loud or in front of an audience. Some of their stories had been edited, but for the most part, they were the same. I thought of us sitting in Helen C. White as a group, workshopping—a funny process, because sometimes the stories were already so good and at a certain point we were splitting hairs, talking more about ourselves than we were about the writing on the page.

There was a time during our first year, before we started thinking about agents and publications and book deals, when it had just been about the stories. It would never be that way again—we were in too deep. But that night it was just about the stories. It felt like we were all at the beginning of something.

When it was my turn I stood and walked to the podium. I glanced up without finding my own family in the crowd. "I'm going to be reading from my story titled 'Thirteen,'" I said.

As I settled into the story, I almost forgot about all the people. I'd worked on it so much by this point that the autobiographical parts were no longer autobiographical. They'd morphed into fiction. The father character was no longer my father but Eli Glass, a man I knew intimately in a way I didn't know my father at all. The story had taken on a life of its own, and that had been the most exciting part of all—when I found myself moving in places I never could have imagined.

When I finished, the crowd applauded, and finally I looked up—first at my father, who was beaming at me. And then at everybody else. There in the back was Charlie. I hadn't invited him to the reading. I wasn't even sure how he'd known about it. He hardly ever went on Facebook. He must have seen the shock on my face, because something came over his own face—uncertainty, or maybe shame. But then he gave me a smile and a thumbs-up. He hurried down one of the side aisles and left.

I turned back to my family, who were clapping and smiling. Ben was the only one who looked distracted. His eyes were on the door where Charlie had just exited the room.

After we all finished reading, we took photos as a group. Then we mingled, talked with one another's families, said hello to our students who had come to hear us read. At one point Ben and I left the room to take a trip to the water fountain down the hall and to get a break from the chaos. As we were rounding the corner near the restrooms, we ran into Charlie.

He had an unlit cigarette in his mouth and was typing on his phone. He was wearing the orange jacket.

"Charlie," I said.

He looked up, his eyes growing wide, his gaze moving from me to Ben. He removed the cigarette from his mouth and put it in his pocket. He blinked at Ben. "You must be Leah's brother."

"One of them. I'm Ben." Ben didn't extend his hand to shake.

"Charlie," Charlie said. Then Charlie looked back at me with apprehension. "You were amazing," he said. "Yours was the best one."

I laughed. "I don't know about that."

"It was. I mean, I didn't stay for Albert Einstein's, so maybe his was better, but I doubt it." Charlie laughed a little, glancing over at Ben, but Ben was stone-faced.

"How are you liking Madison?" Charlie asked Ben.

"Love it," said Ben. "Had some cheese curds. Drank beer by the lake. Leah's been giving us the grand tour."

"Nice," said Charlie, smiling. "You should try and come back in the summer. It's the best time of year. Everyone's out on Memorial Union Terrace."

Charlie was talking to Ben the way he spoke to his stepbrothers— looking for approval while waiting at the same time to be trampled.

"Well, we should get back," I cut in, gesturing back to the room.

"Right," said Charlie. "Congratulations again, Leah."

"It was nice to meet you, Charlie," said Ben.

"Nice to meet you, too. I hope you have a great rest of your visit in Madison." Charlie was already starting to fish in his pocket for his cigarette.

"So," Ben said, after Charlie left, "you're still seeing him."

"Kind of," I said. "It's an on-and-off thing."

Ben raised his eyebrows. "He's not what I was expecting."

"Really?"

He shook his head.

"What were you expecting?"

"I don't know. I was expecting somebody more . . ." He paused. "Not him. He seems like a nice dude."

I knew what Ben wasn't saying. He'd been expecting Charlie to be ugly. Gross. Dirty-looking. I felt proud. That even with that terrible jacket, even with the crushed cigarette hanging out of his mouth, there was *something* about Charlie, and Ben had seen it.

"He is nice," I said then, my voice tough. "He's really nice."

That night, after my father and Monica had gone off to their bed-and-breakfast, I took Ben and Aaron to the Caribou on East John-son where I'd met the cohort on my first night in Madison. We found a few stools near the back and ordered some drinks.

"I need to tell you guys something," I said.

Aaron put down his beer and Ben took a sip of his. My brothers joked around a lot, but they could tell when something was serious.

"I saw Mom. I looked her up and went to her house in St. Paul."

Aaron looked from me to Ben, and back to me. "Holy shit. Are you serious? How? What the hell happened?"

But Ben just sat there clutching his beer. His expression had turned sarcastic. "I bet it went well, didn't it?" When I didn't an-swer, he smirked. "I bet it was a loving reunion."

"No," I said. "It wasn't."

"No." Ben shook his head. "Of course not."

"Dude," Aaron said, slapping his hand on the table. "What *happened*?"

"Well, she still lives at that same Greenacre address. She lives with a guy named Todd, but I don't know if it's her boyfriend. We never saw him. She's the same, though. I mean, she's older, but she's also the same. Her voice and everything."

I described the entire encounter to them, leaving out the parts about Charlie. Aaron was just about falling out of his chair. He appeared almost gleeful.

But Ben wasn't having any of it. Nothing seemed to rile him up. "Who's *we*?" he said.

"What?"

"You said, '*We* never saw him.' Who were you with?"

"Charlie came with me."

Ben and Aaron exchanged a look.

"So Charlie met our mother," said Ben.

I nodded.

"Did she say anything to him?"

"She asked if he was my husband."

"That's odd," said Aaron. "I mean, you're young to be married."

"He had some choice words for her, actually. He told her she'd missed out."

"I'm glad you had someone with you," Ben said resolutely. "That was good of him, to go with you."

"So I take this to mean you two are still in a relationship?" asked Aaron.

"I don't know. Sometimes we are."

"As long as you're being safe," Aaron said. "Even if he's a good guy, I don't want you to be hurt."

"Of course I'm being safe, Aaron."

But I didn't mind it. I liked my brothers best when it was

like this—the three of us, without any boyfriends or girlfriends around.

"Do you guys remember Mom drinking when we were kids?" I asked.

"She drank with dinner sometimes," Aaron said. "She could be kind of cruel, actually, when she drank. But nothing that stood out."

"She was mean all the time," said Ben. "Didn't matter if she was hammered or not."

"So she did get hammered?"

"No," Ben said. "Not in my memory."

"You're wrong, though," Aaron said to Ben. "She wasn't mean all the time. A lot of the time she was sweet. Like, really sweet."

Aaron didn't talk about our mother often, but when he did, I paid attention. He spoke about her with the most distance. He no longer seemed hurt by her.

As we were walking out of the Caribou, Ben said, "So why didn't Charlie come out to dinner with us tonight?"

"I didn't think he'd be welcome."

Ben shrugged, then put his arm around me. "The thing you read tonight was good, Leah. Really fucking good."

I glanced at him. "Yeah?"

"Charlie was right. Yours was the best."

"That's not how it works," I said.

"You're talented," said Ben. "I'm proud of you."

Charlie lost his job. I started noticing bruising up and down his inner arms. It was different, though, this time around. He wasn't falling asleep in the middle of sentences or at the wheel of the car.

And it seemed to happen in spurts, rather than in a spiral—some weeks were better than others. His days now revolved around meeting up with Max. Max, I learned, didn't have a car. Charlie did, which was part of their agreement. In exchange for the use of Charlie's car, Max provided Charlie with drugs.

Charlie was in constant communication with Max throughout the day. He tried to make it seem like it was a friendship. As if he were always doing favors for Max out of the goodness of his heart. I knew that Charlie was lying to me. But instead of prying, I just listened closely to Charlie's side of their cryptic phone conversations. I met Max only once, when he happened to be in the car when Charlie picked me up from class. Max was in the backseat. His girlfriend was there, too. Neither one of them spoke to me, but when I got in the car, Max smiled and raised his eyebrows at me, then glanced at Charlie in the driver's seat and shook his head a little, like he was amused. Max's girlfriend, who looked younger than all of us, didn't even glance up from her phone.

The drive was silent until the end, when Charlie pulled up to the curb in front of Norris Court and he and Max conferenced about the car.

"I'll give you a call when I'm heading to your place," Max said, as Charlie handed him the keys. And it occurred to me that by "your place" Max meant my apartment; that Max had been by here many times before.

Charlie's hygiene and his wardrobe started to suffer. His singing voice sounded different on different days. There were times he could have commanded an entire stadium with his voice. Other times, he was soft and mellow, a little flat—his eyes rolling back in his head. I thought he sounded good no matter what.

Charlie never tried to move in with me again. I think he realized that I wasn't going to break up with him—not tomorrow or the day after anyway—and Charlie was someone who thought mostly in the short term.

And he was right—I wasn't going to. I had surrendered to the relationship. The good parts and the bad. I stopped trying to change him at all—though now I was constantly trying to figure him out.

There were days when he fell asleep in the middle of a TV show and I'd shake him awake. "Charlie," I'd say. "Are you sleeping or what?"

"I'm up," he'd say, forcing his eyes open. "I'm just tired."

"I don't trust you," I'd cry, furious. "I don't know if you're taking a nap or you're high."

"I'm sorry," he'd say. "I'm just tired."

When he went to the bathroom I stood outside listening, trying to glean what was happening on the other side of the door. There were so many times I had one hand on the doorknob, a split second away from opening it, but I was scared I might walk in on him taking a shit. Or maybe I was scared of something else. I scoured the apartment, searching for syringes, elastic bands, dirty-looking spoons. But I never found anything.

I googled *heroin addiction* so often that my internet was convinced I was a heroin addict and advertisements for addiction treatment centers were constantly popping up in the sidebars. *Help is available: speak with a counselor today.* I watched *Panic in Needle Park, Trainspotting,*

Candy. I read *Junkie* by William S. Burroughs and *Jesus' Son* by Denis Johnson. As I watched a 1970s Al Pacino nodding out on the Upper West Side, I realized just how many times I'd watched Charlie nod out, how many times he'd driven me around barely conscious. I watched that movie a lot that spring. It soothed me. This was an old story that had been told before. Also, it was a love story.

One time I found a bright swatch of blood in the toilet bowl and I felt both vindicated and horrified. "Charlie," I said, pulling him in to show him. "What is this?"

"The sub makes me really constipated, babe," he said. "I'd tell you the details but I don't think you'd ever want to have sex with me again."

I never actually knew what he was doing. I was outside his world, even though he was inside of mine. Really, he was my entire world.

He hardly ate anything, but when he did, it was my food. One night I woke up in the middle of the night and heard commotion; light was spilling in from the crack under the door and I found him in my kitchen. He'd emptied an entire pint of vanilla yogurt into a mixing bowl along with the raspberries and blueberries I'd bought from Madison Fresh the previous morning. The green containers that the berries had come in sat empty on the counter.

"Charlie," I said sharply.

When he looked up at me, I felt a sudden urge to hit him.

"Do you know how much those berries cost?"

He didn't say anything.

"I bought those for my breakfast," I said. "You always eat my food."

"I made this for you, babe. I thought you like those yogurt parfaits."

"That's not how I like it."

"It's good," he said. "Try it." He held up the spoon.

"I need to go to bed."

In the morning Charlie said he was going grocery shopping with Max, and did I want anything.

"You and Max go grocery shopping together?"

"Yeah, he has to buy food for his kids."

"He has kids?"

"He sees them on the weekends sometimes. When his ex lets him."

"I'd like berries and some of those Amy's frozen burritos."

"Babe, that frozen stuff is really bad for you."

I raised my eyebrows at him. "Cigarettes aren't great, either."

He texted me one night.

I have a surprise for you. Where are you?

City Bar.

Meet me outside in ten minutes.

I finished my beer and told my friends I was going to take off.

"Already, Kempler? We just got here," Rohan said, even though we'd been there for an hour, at least.

"Sorry," I said. "I told Charlie I'd meet him."

I watched Vivian and Wilson exchange a look that I felt deep in my gut.

"Tell him you'll meet him tomorrow," Rohan said. "It's City Bar night."

"I know," I said. "I'm sorry. I'll see you guys soon." I threw them a smile that I hoped communicated goodwill—*Please don't talk about me after I leave*—and then left, wishing I had just said I wasn't feeling well.

When I found Charlie on State Street his orange coat was un-zipped and drooping off his body like a dirty cape. His hair was slick with oil and a cigarette hung from his lip.

"What's the surprise?" I asked.

"You'll see."

He took my hand and led me down State Street, past the store-fronts and the cafés and the bars, and around the corner past the parking garage on Lake Street, and then into Nam's Noodle & Karaoke Bar on Regent—a combination Asian restaurant and kar-aoke joint.

When we walked in, three undergrad girls were up on the plat-form in the back of the restaurant screeching "Bad Romance" into the microphones. A group of their friends took up several tables in front and were cheering and singing along.

"What are we doing here?" I asked into his ear, glancing around. The place was filled with undergrads and I had the sudden fear that one of my students might be here, might see me with Charlie.

"Sit," he said, pulling me down to one of the vacant tables near the front of the restaurant, on the opposite end of the karaoke stage. I watched Charlie approach the man behind the take-out counter, who also seemed to be organizing the karaoke. Charlie spoke with the guy for a minute, and then stood by, squinting at the stage.

When the girls' song was over, the audience exploded in cheers and the man behind the counter gave Charlie a quick nod and I watched Charlie make his way up to the platform. It did not occur to him to take off his coat.

He held on to the microphone with both hands, as if to steady himself. As the opening chords for "That's Life" by Sinatra boomed over the sound system, he looked in my direction. "This is for the pretty girl in the back," he said into the microphone—his voice emerging a little too loud—and he pointed directly at me. Then he started to sing.

Nobody in the room seemed to be watching or listening to him, except for me and the man who worked there. The drunk undergrads, now that their friends were done singing, were talking and laughing over their noodles and beer. They didn't care about the thirty-one-year-old man in the oversized coat. Charlie seemed oblivious to this. He belted out verse after verse, his voice unwavering. Maybe it was the adrenaline; still, in the ugly neon lighting, with people laughing and yelling over him, for the life of me, I could not tell if he sounded good or bad.

I realized I was sinking lower in my chair. I wondered if I had been getting Charlie wrong this whole time. In the bubble of my apartment—in the silence of the suburbs—he'd sounded magical to me. In the real world, he was high and sweaty and desperately needed a shower. In the real world I was his one faithful listener. But still, he hit every note and his voice, despite the ambient noise, despite all the drunken laughter, filled the entire room.

When the song ended, I clapped, my face warming.

He came over to me. "That was so good," I said. And I kissed him. He tasted like he did when he was using—metallic.

Before we left, I glanced over at the man behind the counter. I wanted him to tell me what he had witnessed. Was that a crazy man up there—or the most beautiful performance he'd heard all night? All year? I would have trusted the man at Nam's to tell me the truth more than I would have trusted anyone else in my life—Vivian or Wilson or Ben or Faye. But the guy was no longer paying attention. He had moved on to the next customer.

23.

I STARTED WRITING A STORY ABOUT A MOTHER WHO WAS A FUNC-
tioning yet unraveling alcoholic. She slept drunk, drove drunk,
helped her kids with their homework drunk. She went to work
drunk; to parent-teacher conferences drunk—to birthday parties
and doctor appointments. She was drunk so much of the time that
her kids didn't know it. They'd seen her sober so few times in their
lives. Then one day, she disappeared.

Halfway through writing the story, I called my father.

"Is something wrong?" he said when he picked up. I almost
never called him.

"Everything's fine," I said. "I have a question for you about
Mom."

"Oh." I heard him stand and walk into another room, so I figured he must have been with Monica. He generally didn't mention
my mother's existence in front of Monica, as though doing so would
be disrespectful.

"Was Mom an alcoholic?"

My father squawked. That's the only word I can think of to
describe the noise he made. "*Alcoholic?*" he said. "No, your mother
wasn't an *alcoholic*. Why would you think that?"

"Well, she must have had *some* issue, right?"

"Leah, I gave up trying to figure your mother out a long time ago."

"Yeah, but . . ."

"She was troubled. Don't spend more time thinking about it." My father had resumed his classroom voice.

"Okay."

"But, Leah. You know it's not your fault she left." He said this last part urgently, as if remembering a line from a parenting book.

"Well, do you know what she did on those weekends she disappeared? Was she seeing someone? Did she have somewhere specific that she went?"

"I don't know what she did. She told me she needed to get away." He sounded surprised. "I'm sorry those weekends had such an effect on you. I should have talked to you three more about what was going on, but the truth is, I didn't know myself. I wasn't sure what to tell you."

"It's okay, Dad." I tried to sound reassuring. "But without answers it's only natural that I start to fill in the gaps myself, you know?"

For several long moments there was quiet.

"Dad?"

"Believe me," he said, finally, "I understand that."

After we hung up, I deleted the half-finished draft of the story from my hard drive.

Teaching was the only time each week when I felt like I was doing something real. Where what I said and how much I'd slept the night before, how well I'd eaten, and how crazy or not crazy I felt had actual consequences.

During class, Charlie's constant texting annoyed me. Sometimes I'd see my phone lighting up in my bag with his barrage of messages, and I'd imagine him in his car somewhere, waiting for me to finish class so we could get back to our bubble-life. But teaching—the shared language and feeling of togetherness that was built over the course of a semester talking about stories—that felt more real to me than my world with Charlie. Conversations with Charlie were like smoke. They disappeared as quickly as they started. He was always there, but he was also somewhere else.

Charlie's friend Danny lived in a part of Madison I'd never been to before—past the university and the two lakes and the coffee shops and all the student housing. His house, a white ranch, the paint faded and peeling, was next to a body shop and across from the highway. There was no car in the driveway, but an assortment of random clutter: an uncovered grill, a lawn chair, a half-inflated baby pool, several trash bins. The house looked dark inside, like no one was home. We were there because Charlie told me he needed to drop something off for Danny on our way to Norris Court from the suburbs.

"I'll be right back," Charlie said, when we pulled into the driveway.

"I'm not coming in with you?"

"It'll only take a few minutes."

He left the car running, and I watched from the passenger seat as he knocked. The door opened and Charlie disappeared inside.

When Charlie finally emerged twenty minutes later, he was followed by a middle-age man. I watched the two of them walk toward the car together, talking and laughing. There was a heaviness to Danny—in his hangdog face, his brow, in the heft of his body. His walk was slow and lumbering. He had a patchy blond beard. His blue-and-white winter jacket was unzipped—beneath it he had on black sweats.

I hadn't been expecting Danny to be middle-age. Next to Danny, Charlie looked adolescent and baby-faced, light on his feet.

"Hey, babe," Charlie said, opening the driver's-side door. "Do you mind climbing in back? We're just going to drop Danny off at work real quick."

Charlie's car only had two doors, and to get in back you had to catapult yourself over. I obeyed, ungracefully tumbling headfirst into the cramped backseat. Then Charlie and Danny got in, continuing their conversation, something about Aaron Rodgers, not pausing for introductions.

I studied the back of Danny's head. His hair was thin and dry, blond with wisps of gray. He was bald on top. He didn't *seem* old, though. He was laughing in the slightly manic, high-pitched way Charlie sometimes did. Not the laugh of a grown adult, but the too-loud sniggering of a hyper teenage boy.

Charlie, who'd been calm and melancholic on the drive over, suddenly was high-strung. He backed out of the driveway and opened the windows so that the frigid outside air filled the car. In the rearview mirror I could see he was smiling maniacally. He pulled out his cigarettes and offered them to Danny.

"All good, man." Danny took out a giant ziplock bag full of

loose tobacco and rolling papers. In his lap, he rolled a cigarette, his fingers moving quickly and expertly.

"Do you put anything else in there?" asked Charlie.

"A little weed. You want one?"

"Sure, man."

I watched Danny repeat the process, and this time I noticed the marijuana he sprinkled in. He handed it to Charlie.

Then Danny glanced back at me. His skin was pale, especially around his eyes, but his neck and his cheeks beneath the scruff of beard were ruddy and rough-looking. "You're really quiet," he announced, not quite making eye contact.

Before I could respond, he turned back around in his seat and laughed. "Why's she so quiet?" he said to Charlie. "Is she scared of me or something?"

Charlie laughed, too. "She's not scared."

There was a minute of silence when nobody spoke and Charlie and Danny smoked their cigarettes and the smell filled the car. I tried desperately to think of something to say.

The truth was, I was scared of him. But also, I was angry. I was angry at Danny, but I was even angrier at Charlie. I didn't like being in the car with them, where I felt somehow both like a small child but also like a parent chaperone. And I hated being told by a stranger that I was quiet. I hated that I cared what Danny thought about me.

"Danny, what do you do?" I said finally.

"What was that?" Danny said, without turning around. "You have to talk louder."

"What do you do for work?"

"I work at Ruby Tuesday."

"That's cool," I said. "How do you like it?"

For several moments he didn't answer. "Today's my first day," he finally said.

Another long stretch of silence. It occurred to me then that these were the exact questions that my family would ask. I could hear Monica's viciously cheerful voice in my head. *And what does Charlie do?* I leaned back and stopped talking.

"Dude," Charlie said, cutting into the quiet. "Remember that evil bitch Carol from Checker's?"

Danny snickered. "Fuck. I haven't thought about her since . . . Jesus, poor lady. When that retarded busboy went psycho on that family? She really lost it. That shit was wild."

Charlie and Danny doubled over laughing.

I looked out the window. The day was sunny but impossibly cold. Sometimes that happened in Wisconsin—winter would return with no warning at all. Temperatures dropped overnight, everything covered in snow and ice again. Today was the kind of cold in which you could see your breath, so that if you went outside with wet hair, it would immediately freeze.

It was three in the afternoon. I felt greasy, like I badly needed to shower. In a matter of hours the sun would set and the day would be over. I'd done nothing that day except wait around for Charlie. Wait for him to wake up, and then wait for him to complete the list of chores that Faye had given him before we were "allowed" to leave the house—shovel the driveway, put away the dishes, tidy up the den. Then wait in the car. And now—sitting in the backseat while we drove across Madison again. Everything felt flat and dull. I could have worked myself up. Gotten pissed at

Charlie for taking up all my time with his bullshit, all that precious writing time down the drain. But I couldn't imagine sitting down and writing anything anyway. If I were at home right now, I'd probably just be in bed watching TV on my computer.

Charlie pulled into the parking lot of a strip mall. "This okay?"

"Yup. Thanks for the ride." Danny glanced back at me and nodded. "Nice to finally meet you, Leah."

Something in my chest hurt. I hadn't realized that he knew my name.

"Yeah," I said. "You, too, Danny."

He got out, stuffing the ziplock back inside his coat pocket, and closed the door.

"You want to come back in front?" Charlie asked me.

I climbed back into the front seat and as Charlie pulled away I watched Danny walk across the lot toward the Ruby Tuesday. He was walking incredibly slowly, one foot in front of the other, as though his shoes were made of lead.

I was having stomach issues. My stomach reacted to everything I ate. Even when I didn't eat, my stomach revolted. Sometimes I'd wake up in the middle of the night with cramps and then get sick for no reason at all.

I went back to the health clinic. I was disappointed when I got a different nurse practitioner than the tie-dye lady. The new woman asked me questions and they did some tests.

"This is most likely anxiety or depression," she told me when all the tests came back normal. "Have you ever considered going on medication?"

"Don't those kinds of meds make you gain weight?"

"Not all of them." She frowned at me. "Are you worried about gaining weight?"

"Yes."

The nurse glanced at my chart and then pointedly at my body. "You're very slim as you are. Are you aware that you've lost eighteen pounds since your physical in the fall?"

I understood by her tone of voice that this was a cause for concern, but inside I swelled with pride and astonishment.

"I didn't know that," I said, furrowing my brow.

"Do you eat proper meals?" she asked. "Breakfast, lunch, and dinner?"

Since I'd been with Charlie my eating had become erratic, like his. Except for when he made us meals, I only ate when I felt myself growing faint with hunger. By the time that feeling hit, I was often too tired to prepare real food for myself, so instead of cooking I would have something quick, like a Luna bar or a frozen burrito or a giant bowl of cereal. "Not always," I said. "I don't have an eating disorder, though."

The nurse typed something on the computer. "Have you ever spoken with a therapist?"

The therapist gave me a handout titled "Ending a Relationship with a Drug Addict." I read through the different pointers—*wait until they are sober, do it in public, follow through*—while she sat and watched me read.

I glanced up. Pamela, that was her name, had a kind face and was wearing a floral perfume that overwhelmed the small room. She had a picture of her three kids, a pudgy-faced husband, and a golden lab in plain view on her desk. This struck me as strange, because I thought therapists were supposed to hide their personal lives from their clients. We were both sitting in red cloth armchairs, facing one another. There were large framed photos of shells on the wall. A card was taped to the back of her door: *Just when the caterpillar thought the world was over, it became a butterfly.*

She asked me who my support network was. I listed the people in my MFA program. Then she asked me what I liked to do for fun.

"I like to read and write."

"That's wonderful, but those are very solitary activities. What are some things you like to do that get you involved with other people? Maybe a sport or a hobby?"

"I like walking," I managed.

"That's great," she said, her face brightening. "So, walks with friends."

I preferred walking alone, but I nodded, smiling back at her.

"What do you think first drew you to Charlie?" she asked.

It seemed perverted to describe to Pamela how good the sex was; how amazing he smelled. I would have liked to describe his face in detail. Better yet, show her a photo. But talking about these things was a conversation stopper. She'd want to go deeper. "His smile," I said. "There's something vulnerable about him. He doesn't hold back in anything he does."

"Something *vulnerable*," she repeated back to me.

I nodded.

"The way you described him earlier, Charlie sounds like a sad young man."

"He's had a hard life."

"What I'm hearing is that you might be a *caretaker*." She smiled coyly when she said *caretaker*, like it was a dirty word.

"Oh?"

"Do you find yourself taking care of Charlie?"

"I think I do take care of him," I said.

"Does he take care of you, too?"

"Yes."

"What about when you get your stomachaches? How does he take care of you when you're in pain?"

Then she asked me about my childhood. When I told her that my parents were divorced and that my mother had left when I was thirteen, she narrowed her eyes, like—*jackpot*.

It went on like this. It was predictable. It was obvious to me that she had an idea of who Charlie was and an idea of who I was. It was clear, in her mind, what should happen next. She was going to try to get me to see how the damage from my childhood had driven me into Charlie's arms. It was all a bit insulting—both to me, and to Charlie. What if it was all much simpler and sweeter than that? What if I loved Charlie simply because he was Charlie?

When the time was up, Pamela asked me if the same time next week was good to meet again.

"Can I check my schedule and get back to you?"

"Absolutely," she said. "Send me a message through the portal."

On my way out I threw the handout she'd given me in the recycling bin.

A few nights later I lay on my bed, doubled over in pain. Charlie had gone to the corner store for ginger ale to settle my stomach. It had been over half an hour since he'd left and the corner store was just at the end of the block. I thought about going to look for him, but that would involve changing out of my pajamas and also maybe taking a shower—I'd just spent almost an hour getting sick in the bathroom.

Finally, I heard the door.

"I'm back, babe," Charlie called. He came into my room with a single can of ginger ale. "Sorry that took so long. I ran into my buddy Jon outside the store."

I didn't know who Jon was. "That's okay," I said, reaching for the can. "Thank you."

"How are you feeling?"

"Not good."

He sat on the edge of the bed and put a hand to my forehead. "Is there anything I can do?"

"Will you stay with me?" I asked. "Don't leave again, okay?"

He squeezed my hand. "I'm just going to go outside and smoke a cigarette and I'll be right back, okay?"

"No, Charlie," I said. "Sit with me." I couldn't get the thing Pamela had said out of my head. *Does he take care of you, too?* "You're always running off."

"I'm not running away, babe. I didn't get a chance to smoke since I ran into Jon and he was talking my ear off. I'll be really quick, I promise."

I pulled my hand from Charlie's. My weepiness had morphed into anger. Or maybe I'd already been angry. "I'm having these stomachaches because of *you*, Charlie. I have anxiety because of this relationship." I pushed the covers down. I was sweating all over. "Can't you just sit here with me?"

"I am going to sit with you, but I just need—"

"I'm always there for you. It isn't fair."

"I *am* there. I just went and got you a—"

"You're not, though. You're so fucking unpredictable." I glared at him.

He stood up. "I think it's best right now if I give you a little space. Just for ten minutes. I don't want to cause you more anxiety and I feel like I'm making things worse. Why don't you drink your ginger ale and rest for a few minutes and then I'm going to come back in and be here with you, okay? Does that sound okay?"

I leaned back on my pillow. I was too tired to keep fighting. "Okay."

Ten minutes went by and Charlie didn't come back. I gave it another ten, and then I called his phone. No answer. I waited more. When an entire hour passed, I got up and brushed my teeth and put on a sweatshirt and shoes. I was light-headed and weak and I was furious. As I looked in the hallway of my building, and then down in the basement, I began to get nervous. I called him again but I got his voice mail. "Charlie, call me back," I said into the phone. "I'm worried." I imagined finding him unconscious, slumped against a wall somewhere, or out in his car, head on the steering wheel. I wondered if I should call Faye.

Outside it had gotten dark. I ran around the Norris Court Apartments, looking for Charlie or his car. Panic was starting to surge, and my stomach was churning—a sign I might have to run to the toilet again. After circling the building twice and no sign of Charlie, I went inside to make sure he hadn't come back in while I'd been out.

As I was about to unlock my door, I heard Charlie's laughter. It was coming from across the hall, from Ariana and Nick's apartment. I froze, listening for more.

At least . . . I thought it had sounded like Charlie's laughter. It was muffled, so it was hard to tell. I walked over and pressed my ear to their door. This made me feel crazy, like a stalker—but I had to know. I heard it again—and this time I was certain. Charlie was inside their apartment.

I knew he wouldn't be honest if I asked him about it, so I waited there for him, on the floor of the hallway between the two apartments.

I sat leaning against the wall for a long time. When he finally opened the door, he emerged in a cloud of marijuana smoke. He was smiling. He didn't notice me.

"What are you doing?" I said, standing.

He looked over, his eyes widening in fear and surprise—like I was some sort of pop-out Halloween horror trick.

I came at him then and shoved him as hard as I could, with both hands. He staggered backward into the wall. Then he began to laugh.

"It's not funny," I said. I was crying.

"You just pushed me," he said, still laughing. "You're so mad."

"What's wrong with you, Charlie? I hate you." I stormed into my apartment, wiping my eyes, but I left the door open for him.

He found me on the living room floor and sat beside me. I could tell by his eyes and the way he smelled that he was high. Pot, though—not heroin.

"I thought something bad happened to you," I said. "I was

looking all over for you. I thought you might be . . . I almost called your mom. And then you made me feel like a crazy person for sitting outside their door listening to see if it was you."

"I'm sorry." Charlie wasn't laughing anymore. "I thought you were going to drink the ginger ale and fall asleep and that it would be a nice break for you to have me out of your hair. I thought I was doing you a favor by giving you some space."

"Don't try to make this into a nice thing you were doing for me, okay? I told you what I wanted. I wanted you to stay with me."

He stared back at me. His eyes were lifeless and bloodshot. It didn't matter what I said, I knew then. He wasn't going to remember it the next day. It wasn't a real conversation.

"I always just want you to stay with me," I repeated, like a broken record.

24.

WE WERE SPENDING MORE EVENINGS AT CHARLIE'S HOUSE. FAYE would make us food and ask me about how my writing was coming along. I loved being around Faye. She was the only person in my life who was happy that Charlie and I were together.

I felt safest being at their house. Like I wasn't the only one looking out for Charlie, and like someone was looking out for me.

I liked how clean their house was; how everything was in order, always in the same spot. Nothing ever ran out—toilet paper, soap, milk. There was ice in the ice trays and there were fresh towels in the bathroom. I liked how every night Faye made dinner at the same time and she always seemed to be in a good mood. I could tell that I made her especially happy, because I loved Charlie, too.

I had fewer stomachaches when I was at their house. It could have been because of Faye's cooking or it could have been because I was just less worried when I was over there.

Faye seemed to love Paul, and even though I didn't like Paul, I liked Faye and Paul together. The way they kissed each other before leaving the house, how they called each other sweetheart and honey. In my family, nobody called each other anything except their given names. For me, *Lee* was the most affectionate it got. We did love each other—of course we did—but we were uncomfortable with each other.

One morning I sat with Faye in the living room while Charlie was out mowing the lawn. She was on the couch, her legs crossed over the cushions, her feet bare.

"How was it," Faye asked, "seeing your mom in St. Paul? Charlie didn't really tell me anything."

"It was hard," I said. "I hadn't seen her for twelve years and she acted like nothing had happened. Like we were just catching up. She said she wanted to be my *friend*."

"That's terrible," said Faye, frowning. "Really terrible."

The truth was, I didn't feel very upset about the visit to St. Paul. The damage from my mother had already been done long ago. I didn't need to dwell on what had happened or try to understand my mother's behavior in order to understand myself. I knew myself remarkably well. I knew what I wanted and what I craved. I understood what made me feel whole and what made me feel empty.

"It was hard," I said to Faye. "But I'm glad that I went. Now I know. Charlie said something. I was waiting all this time for her to reject me again. But by her not showing up all these years—she was already rejecting me. Now I can really move on."

Faye smiled sadly. "You both are so strong."

I smiled and shrugged. I thought Charlie and I were both weak in the same ways, which was part of the reason we were still together. Though of course I didn't say this to Faye.

"You know, I didn't believe in God until everything happened with Charlie these past few years," Faye said. "And then I started accepting that nothing is really in my control. I think things happen the way they're supposed to. If you had told me that one day I'd be living in this beautiful house with the love of my life—I never would have believed you. My life used to be really different."

"Different how?" I asked.

"For a long time it was just me and Charlie. I was working all the time—paycheck-to-paycheck. I've always been happy, even when I didn't have a lot of money. Charlie gets that from me—that *spark*. But I used to feel very alone. I was scared I was always going to feel that way. It was just me and Charlie for years. And I was pretty young."

"What happened with Charlie's father?" I asked.

"We were married briefly. He was much older. He left before Charlie was born. He left when he found out I was pregnant."

"I'm sorry," I said. "That's awful."

She shrugged, like, *Not really.* "Now Charlie has Paul, and Paul loves him like he's his own son."

I nodded, even though this seemed like it couldn't be further from the truth. I glanced out the window to where Charlie was pushing a fancy high-powered lawn mower. He was wearing headphones and bopping his head up and down.

"I was glad that Charlie was with me when I went to see my mom," I said. "He made me feel so loved."

"Charlie's loving. He's the kind of guy who really lets you in," Faye said. "I can see that you're that way, too. You let people in."

I looked at her and waited for her to keep talking.

"I used to be that way, too, when I was younger," Faye said. "It's probably why someone like Charlie's father ended up in my life. Someone would show me a little love and I'd open my arms to them. I trusted it. I learned after a while, though, that there's a lot of bad people out there. It didn't make me less loving, but it made me pickier. At the end of the day, you have to decide what you want to accept in a relationship."

I had fantasies of being with Charlie forever. Part of it was that I knew I could if I wanted; he would never leave me. He and Faye and Paul and their house in the suburbs. They were mine for the taking. But when I imagined a life with Charlie I couldn't picture him at a job or picking kids up from school or driving me to a doctor's appointment when we were old. I couldn't imagine us old at all.

I had applied for and gotten a position teaching writing classes at a community college in Boston. My job would be starting that fall. I decided I would end things with Charlie once I was back on the East Coast. I didn't see any other option. Breaking up in person was too risky. I also didn't think I was capable of doing it.

Charlie knew it was my plan to move back to Boston, but I hadn't told him yet that I'd accepted a job or that I'd bought a one-way ticket back home for August first. We spoke vaguely about having a long-distance relationship and about him eventually moving out to Massachusetts to be with me, but I couldn't imagine he really believed this would happen. His mom had barely let him drive to St. Paul for one night.

I wanted to get married and have children one day. Charlie wasn't allowed to hold his own money. He spent his days driving around Madison with Max. We'd hadn't gone on a proper date since the Weary Traveler last October. Sometimes I thought about these things and it didn't make sense to me why I was still with him. But deep down, I knew.

Charlie had explained to me once what heroin felt like. He said, "Imagine you're in pain—the most excruciating pain of your life. Your skin is on fire and your thoughts are agonizing you and any inch of light or movement makes you nauseous. And you're scared because you don't know when or if it's ever going to end." He was talking about being dope-sick, but I imagined here that he was also talking about the pain of being alive. "But you know that there's a button somewhere, and all you have to do is press that button, and that pain will vanish. It will just disappear." He snapped his fingers. "And you will feel warm and safe and completely protected. That button is heroin."

"Jesus," I said.

"I spend every second of every day convincing myself not to press that button, even though I know exactly where it is and how easy it would be to press it, just one more time."

"It sounds like torture," I said.

Charlie nodded. "For me, heroin is like air."

25.

AT THE END OF MAY THE SIX OF US DRESSED UP IN CAPS AND gowns, walked across the giant stage in the Camp Randall Stadium, and collected our diplomas. It all felt silly—surrounded by masses of nursing and business and veterinary students. All these newly appointed professionals were about to go out into the world and practice law, prepare taxes, deliver babies. Our diplomas meant little. The Word documents we'd edited over and over again, the literary journals we'd sent them to, the hours-long debriefs after workshop—in the huge amphitheater that day, all of it seemed to matter less.

We wrote characters who were doctors and lawyers and social workers. But what did we actually do?

I'd spent so long thinking about how different I was from the rest of my cohort. I was shyer than the rest of them. Depending on the day and my mood: smarter or not as smart; sensitive or not as sensitive. On the day of graduation, surrounded by all the doctors and social workers and lawyers, we were a small pod of six. We were the same. Six people who loved to write, who desperately wanted to write; who had no idea what was coming next.

Sam was the first to leave Madison, since he had a wife and a house waiting for him back in Kansas City.

On Sam's last night, we gathered at Mickey's, a bar and grill on Willy Street. Mickey's felt like somebody's aunt's eccentric house—three big rooms connected by dark, narrow hallways; vintage furniture, like silken couches and settees; walls painted greens and blues with yellow stripes; one room all magenta. Mirrors with ornate frames and chandeliers hung from the walls and ceiling. A pool table in the back, surrounded by couches for lounging and playing board games.

That night we sat outside in the backyard patio, an enclosed space surrounded by a wooden fence, decorated with twinkle lights. It was the first night of June and graduation was one week behind us. Our classes were over; our theses were in. Our students had gone home for the summer. We were drunk and getting nostalgic. We talked about the characters who had populated our stories and novels from the past two years.

We'd all written things that hadn't hit—stories that would probably remain as forgotten, saved drafts on our laptops. But we'd also written characters who had come alive—so much so that they had become a part of us. Some of those stories had made it out into the world, into small journals or on the internet.

The woman and the dentist were part of Vivian, and because we'd read those early drafts—iteration after iteration—they'd become a part of us, too. A year and a half later when her novel would be published by Simon & Schuster, and we would read those characters and scenes for the final time—in print, in a *book*— it would feel like returning home, back to those days in Helen C. White.

"Here's to all our imaginary friends," Rohan said, lifting his glass.

We lifted our glasses.

Summer arrived. After Sam, one by one, my friends left. Wilson had gotten a job teaching high school English in Philly. Vivian and Rohan were headed to New York together. Vivian was going to waitress at the restaurant where she used to work and Rohan would take a copyediting job at a marketing firm. David was the only one who'd landed a fellowship—some boarding school in the South, and he was heading there in September.

Charlie and I spent a lot of our time outside. He was working again, a landscaping job, and going to NA meetings. He wasn't using. He wasn't even smoking very much weed. It was the longest stretch I'd ever seen him sober.

We went on another date, this one to the Memorial Union Terrace. We waited on a long line and Charlie bought us ice cream and then we sat on the docks and watched people out on sailboats and kayaks, groups of undergrads on giant party rafts, their laughter traveling like music across the water. Lake Mendota was a soft pearly blue. It seemed like an entirely different body of water than what it became in the winter when it was practically oceanlike— raw and violent, waves crashing up on the shore—and in the deepest winter, frozen over so completely that small planes could land on its surface.

"Charlie," I said. We were sitting beside one another on one of the far docks, our legs dangling over the quiet water. "Let's get a picture."

We put our arms around each other and I held out my phone in selfie mode and took a few of us together. Then I scooched back and took some of just Charlie. I scrolled through them as he smoked his cigarette. He'd left his ice cream mostly uneaten.

It wasn't often that how I felt aligned with the weather—with how other people around me also seemed to be feeling. I was simply so happy that day.

I moved closer to him again and put my arm around his shoulders. "To tell you the truth, normally a day like this would make me kind of lonely. All these happy people in groups," I said. "I don't do well in groups. But with you I feel like I'm part of something."

He tossed his cigarette butt in the lake. "I think we could be something really special, you and me. I think we could do amazing things together."

"You do?"

"We've already been through so much," he said. "And look how much we love each other. You bring out something different in me. Something I didn't even know I was capable of." He nodded toward my phone. "Just look at those pictures of us. You'll see it. The way we look together. My mom sees it, also. She told me. It's rare, you know. Two people making each other this happy."

I kissed his cheek. I allowed myself to feel it, too. That we were some beautiful love story. "Do you realize how great you are?" I said, laying my head on his shoulder.

Charlie smiled out toward the lake. "Maybe one day I'll get there."

The next morning was July 15. "Charlie, I have to tell you something." I reached over in bed and touched his arm. We were on the pullout couch in the suburbs.

He rolled over, barely awake. I felt, suddenly, that I had been cruel to Charlie. What I was about to do was cruel.

"I got a job," I said. "In Boston. It starts September first."

He sat up, blinking. "Okay. So we have, like, a month and a half?"

"I'm moving back to Boston on August first."

I watched the knowledge sink in. He swallowed. "So we don't have that much time."

"No."

There was panic in his face, but he remained very still. "Why can't you work here?" he said. "There are tons of jobs in Madison."

"My plan has always been to go back to Massachusetts."

"But your family is toxic, Leah. Wouldn't it be better for you to be here? With people who love and support you?"

"I've already accepted the job."

Charlie leaned his head back down on the pillow and closed his eyes.

"Charlie?"

"I don't know what I'm going to do without you," he said flatly. His eyes were still closed and his body—though deeply tanned and muscular now, from working outside in the sun—looked comatose curled up in the sheets.

I wanted to say something back, but I didn't know what.

"Are you breaking up with me?" he asked. His voice was so soft I could barely hear him.

I hadn't heard him ask that question for a long time.

"No."

He opened his eyes then, hopeful. He pulled me close to him. "Okay," he said. "We'll figure it out."

I spent the next week selling my used furniture back to Craigslist and St. Vinny's, packing, shipping my books to Boston, and throwing stuff away. Anytime Charlie came over he didn't mention my upcoming move or the state of my apartment—the bare walls, the emptying kitchen, how depressing it was becoming. Until the two chairs in the living room were gone. When he walked into the big main room with nothing left but the rug, his shoulders dropped.

"It's sad, right?" I said.

"I would have liked to sit in that ugly old chair one last time."

I lay down on the floor. "There's still the rug."

Charlie lay beside me. "My mom said that we could take a trip out to Boston in the fall to come visit you. She's always wanted to go to New England. The foliage and all that." Charlie rolled toward me. "I actually think long-distance could be really good for us. I can focus on my work and my music and you can focus on your writing and then when we see each other it will be this thing that we work up to. The time we have together will be even more meaningful."

I nodded but I didn't say anything.

"Have you ever felt like this with anyone?" he asked. "This connected?"

"No," I said. "I haven't."

"I've been thinking about it and it doesn't really matter that we're going to be apart. When I close my eyes at night and I think about you—the fact that our love exists—to me, that's enough to get by. To get through another day."

"But I can't be the only thing that gets you through the day."

"I know. But life is better with you in it. You make all the shit parts worth it."

"Same, Charlie."

"This is the best relationship I've ever been in."

I didn't respond. It was a delusion. Everything he was saying. But that's what this entire relationship had been. What was the point of being truthful about it now? He was next to me and there was still that hum, and *that* was real. It had never gone away. We held hands and looked up at the ceiling, breathing in the air of the Norris Court apartment. We'd spent a little less than a year together.

While I was going through stacks of papers I found a worksheet of Charlie's from Safe Haven Rehabilitation Center. It was titled "Triggers." His handwriting was small and messy, barely legible in blunt pencil.

NAME A TIME/PLACE/PERSON/SITUATION RECENTLY WHERE YOU HAVE FELT TRIGGERED.

Rohan

HOW DID THIS EVENT/PERSON/SITUATION MAKE YOU FEEL?

Like a loser

SPECIFY WHAT ABOUT THIS EVENT/PERSON/SITUATION WAS TRIGGERING?

Successful, talented, better writer, life on track.

HOW DID THESE EMOTIONS MANIFEST? WHAT DID YOU DO WITH THESE EMOTIONS?

My life is trash, waste of time → addict brain

HOW ARE YOU ABLE TO REFRAME THESE NEGATIVE EMOTIONS?

I can get better at guitar. I can keep pursuing music and continue my own passions.

Rohan is a douchebag.

I don't know Rohan's struggles

My heart swelled, reading Charlie's answers. I folded the paper up into a square and packed it away with my belongings.

On my last night in Madison, Charlie picked me up to bring me back to his house for dinner. When I walked out of my apartment, Charlie was standing in the courtyard smoking. He was wearing a button-down pink shirt, the sleeves rolled up, and slacks. The outfit was too warm for summer and he was sweating through his shirt— but he looked good. Put together, freshly shaven, so handsome I could feel myself pulled toward him, wanting to be close. He tossed his cigarette to the ground and crushed it beneath the toe of his shoe.

"Hey," he said, hugging me quickly.

"Hi."

"I'm really nervous."

"Why?" I tensed, thinking of all the things that might have gone wrong—a fight with Faye, something with his job, or a doctor, or a prescription.

"I bought you something, and I don't know if you're going to like it."

"Really?" I said, brightening. Charlie was not big on presents. His gifts tended to be things like a snack from the gas station or a flower picked from a stranger's garden.

"Yeah," he said, taking my hand. "I want to give it to you over here."

We walked over to Giddings Park, a small grassy area down a hill that overlooked Lake Mendota. There was an old bowed tree on the lake's edge, a bench for sitting and reading. Today we had the spot to ourselves. Charlie and I sat on the hill looking at the water—a deep, still navy, shimmering on the edges with early evening light.

"I thought I had been in love before I met you," Charlie said. "But I know now that it was lust or infatuation or something else. Desperation, maybe." His voice was focused—full of conviction. "Leah, you've seen me at my lowest, but you've also seen me really happy—the happiest I've ever been."

I realized that I was experiencing the moment as if watching us from above. There we were—two young, tall people. We were both sitting with our knees up and ankles crossed, our hands clasped around our knees, our bodies turned slightly toward one another. If it weren't for the intense way we were looking at each other, we could've been siblings. I'd always thought Charlie was so much better-looking than me, but in that moment, I only saw how similar we were. Our faces guileless, our shoulders rounded, our eyes searching.

"I know you're going to Boston," he went on. "And I'm going to be here in Madison, and that's how our lives will be for a while. And that's okay. It's *good*. I still have work to do. Not just for my job and music and stuff—but on my recovery. And, to be honest, I probably got too swept up in our relationship this year. I got distracted from going to meetings and focusing on my sobriety, which is my fault. But what I realized this year—through meeting you, Leah—was that what I want most in this world is to have a family." He paused. His voice had started to shake. "And I want to have that family with you."

He let go of his knees and rearranged himself on the grass so that he was kneeling before me.

I grew hot. My body, my face, my hands. Every molecule inside me.

He pulled a small velvet box out of his back pocket and with trembling hands opened it to reveal a ring. An oval-shaped diamond glistening upon a thin silver band.

"Leah, will you marry me?"

I looked at him.

It was the craziest question anyone had ever asked me. How could he not know that we were about to break up? How could he not understand that this relationship was doomed? That underneath it all this was a *sad*, broken thing, between him and me?

Staring back at me, Charlie's eyes were clear; his pupils huge. He was sober; entirely lucid. His eyelashes were long and graceful. He was blinking rapidly. Behind him was the iridescent lake and the sky, which was softening into evening—the plush colors of Madison in summer. I could see that he was scared, watching my expression for a reaction. Sweat had gathered at his temples and droplets were dotted above his upper lip, and then I felt close to tears. The truth was, I'd never loved a face more than I'd loved Charlie's.

I imagined saying no. But saying no to Charlie frightened me. With Charlie, it was always safer to say yes. As long as we had just one more day, we'd deal with tomorrow another time.

"Okay," I said.

The word was more powerful than I'd anticipated, because once I said it—once I saw the emotion on his face—shock, relief, love, in that order—I, too, felt a wave of emotion. Charlie embraced me wordlessly, and happiness overtook me.

"Can I put it on?" he asked.

"Okay," I said, laughing. Like it was funny. A joke ring, a joke finger.

Charlie took the ring out of the box—his hands were still shaking—and he slid the band on. It was a touch loose, but it just about fit, and it moved me, that he had picked out nearly the right size. "It's beautiful, Charlie," I said. And I stopped myself from asking, *How did you afford it?*

"I know it's not the biggest diamond."

The diamond was the size of a ladybug.

"I don't care."

"I know, but you deserve a rock."

This made me laugh. "The size of the diamond is the least of my concerns."

"Leah," he said, gathering me in his arms. "We're going to have the happiest life together."

And when he said it that time—I felt it. The gravity of the mistake I was making.

On the drive back to his house, Charlie put down the windows and blasted music. The summer air rushed into the car and whipped our hair around. He sang along to the radio—"Get Lucky," "Royals"—tapping the steering wheel with his thumbs, nodding to the beat. He knew every lyric. He sang beautifully. I watched him singing and tried not to break down sobbing. It occurred to me that Charlie didn't know my father's first name. He didn't know who my best friend from childhood was or anything about my four years as an undergrad in college. We'd never spoken about religion or politics or anything that was going on in the news. He'd never taken me out to dinner.

"Charlie," I said, but he didn't hear me over the music.

But then, back at Charlie's house, everyone was there—Faye and Paul and Chad and Tyler—and for the first time ever, the Nelsons' dining room table had been set. All of them were dressed up and they looked nice—especially Faye. When we walked in together, holding hands, Faye stood from the couch in a pink sundress, her hands over her mouth. "Oh my god," she whispered, looking from Charlie to me to Charlie, so I knew Charlie must have told her in advance what he was planning on doing.

Charlie smiled at the floor, deflected the question to me.

I looked back at Charlie's family—all their hope. Not just Faye's hope, but the rest of theirs, too. I saw then how much they cared about Charlie. They were rooting for him. And getting married, to them, meant success. After years of suffering and relapses and rehab, Charlie finding a wife would be something normal—something to celebrate.

"We're getting married," I said, holding out my left hand. And again—the words, the gesture—had more power than I was anticipating. Faye rushed over, wiping her eyes on the back of her hand, and when I hugged her, I started to cry, too. "I love you, honey," she said, kissing me, and when I had the thought, *My mother-in-law,* I no longer knew if I was lying to myself or not.

Chad and Tyler were hugging Charlie, slapping him on the back, and Charlie was grinning, and I found myself glancing over at the portrait of Charlie as a small child. Maybe this really was my husband, I thought, as I watched Charlie laugh with his stepbrothers and then solemnly shake Paul's hand.

"Happy for you, son," Paul said quietly, proudly.

Faye was pulling down a bottle of champagne. "It's not every day that my baby boy gets engaged to the prettiest gal from Massachusetts," she said. "And I love you boys—don't get me wrong—but it's about time we had another girl in the family." And then she popped the cork and everybody cheered and I don't think I'd ever seen Charlie look so at peace.

As Faye passed out glasses, I glanced around at everyone in the living room and thought: *Maybe this is what family is supposed to feel like. Maybe this is where I am supposed to be.*

In the middle of the night I woke up and Charlie wasn't in bed. Instead of getting up to look for him, I reached over to his side and found his phone, which was nestled in the covers. His texts, as of late, were boring—me, Faye, his sponsor. So I opened up his Facebook messages, and saw that he had been messaging back and forth that day with someone named Rafe Thomas. It was a name I'd never heard before. The last message Charlie had sent had been earlier that evening, at 6:33—just minutes before I'd met him outside my apartment and we'd walked down to Giddings Park.

I clicked open the messages.

CHARLIE 6:33PM *hey man you've got any more of that dragon*

RAFE 6:35PM *I'll hit you up tomorrow. Same number?*

CHARLIE 6:36PM *same #*

I felt sick. I put Charlie's phone in the sheets where I'd found it, then got out of bed. I was about to open the door when Charlie came back in. "Hey, babe," he whispered. He put his hands on my shoulders. "Are you okay?"

"Where were you?"

"The bathroom."

"Doing what?"

He tensed in the dark. "Taking a leak." He paused. "What's the matter?"

I took a step closer to him, but he smelled normal. He didn't even smell like a cigarette. And he was still naked.

I turned on the lamp beside the sofa bed. "Who is Rafe Thomas?"

"Damn," Charlie said softly, shielding his eyes from the light. "That's bright."

"Charlie, who is Rafe Thomas?"

"This guy from NA, but don't tell anyone that. It's supposed to be anonymous."

"Why did you ask him if he had more *dragon*? I just saw your Facebook messages."

Charlie sat down on the bed. "Dragon is weed. Rafe is who I get my medicinal marijuana from."

"Don't lie to me," I said, my voice trembling. "I'm not an idiot anymore."

"Look." He rubbed his hands over his face. "I didn't know if you were going to say yes today. I was freaking out. I was basically having a full-blown panic attack. I thought I might line something up as a backup plan, but Leah, you have to understand." He looked at me pleadingly. "I wasn't actually going to follow through. I sent the message just to make myself feel better. Do you ever send a text to a guy you're never actually going to hook up with, but you know he'll text back and just having his text there on your phone makes you feel kind of good? Like it gives you a confidence boost or maybe it gives you the courage to go out and talk to the guy who you *actually* want to be with?"

I didn't say anything.

"That's Rafe Thomas for me. I texted Rafe because I knew he would text me back. He's easy. Rafe is kind of a slut. He'll be there when you want him, any time of day or night. It was an impulse text I sent while I was waiting for you to walk out the door. But you're the one I actually want."

"You called a drug dealer minutes before proposing to me. How the hell am I supposed to go through with this?"

He jerked his head back as though I'd hit him. "Please don't make me feel ashamed, Leah. Please don't do that to me. Getting off this stuff? It's a process. It doesn't happen overnight." His voice had turned low and desperate. "Ask any drug counselor or specialist. In fact, I think it would be really good for you to go to Al-Anon, so you can talk about all this and, like, process it. It's a natural part of recovery, these slipups. But you should have somewhere you can talk about it."

"What happens if we have kids and you relapse?"

Charlie stared back. "That won't happen."

"How can I believe you?"

He took a ragged breath and covered his face with both hands.

"Charlie?"

He walked over to the sliding glass doors. His back was to me, his hands still over his face, his shoulders hunched. I realized, after a moment, that he was crying. "Should I even keep trying?" he said finally.

"What do you mean?"

"Every time I try to be normal, I mess it up." He looked so frail, standing naked by the darkened windows, that my sinuses burned, watching him.

"I don't know if anyone is actually normal, Charlie."

He whipped around to look at me. "But does this mean I don't get what everyone else gets?" His face was swollen, his cheeks gleaming. "I don't get married and I don't have a family?"

I'd seen him cry before, but I'd never seen him cry like this— like something was being stolen from him, ripped away. He looked frantic and terrified, like a little kid.

"Of course not," I said. I went to him quickly and hugged him. "You get all those things, too."

"Because if I don't, I might as well just be a heroin addict." He wept harder, and when he laid his head against my shoulder, he rested his entire body weight against me.

"Come here." I led him back to bed. I pulled the blankets down and we crawled under together. I cradled him close to me, in a way I'd never held anyone before. "You're not and you'll never be *just a heroin addict*," I whispered, as he began to calm in my arms. "You're Charlie and you're a beautiful person. You're a musician and a writer. And I'm in love with you, Charlie. I love you."

In the morning when I woke up, the diamond on my finger sparkled back at me, catching me by surprise. When I turned over, Charlie was already sitting up in bed. We looked at each other without saying anything. We didn't touch.

When I hugged Faye goodbye in the kitchen, she squeezed me and whispered, "See you soon, sweet girl. Miss you already."

We drove back to Norris Court to get my suitcases and so I could hand in my key to the landlord. The only thing left in the apartment was the mattress—which I had bought used and was going to put out on the street for trash pickup. When we walked into the empty apartment, it smelled different without all my stuff in it. It smelled like it did when I had first moved in.

Charlie loaded my bags into his car and then came back inside. I was sitting in the bedroom on the bare mattress, leaning against the wall. All the windows were open and a warm breeze was coming through. When I'd moved into the apartment two summers ago, I'd been twenty-four. Next month I would turn twenty-six. In that time I'd written more than I'd ever written in my entire life. I'd gotten nothing published. And I'd met Charlie.

Charlie came in and sat beside me. He touched my knee, which was poking out from the skirt of my dress. I was wearing the same blue cotton dress I'd been wearing for most of the summer. I'd washed it only a handful of times and I thought of how dirty it was, my summer with Charlie caked into the fabric. When we kissed there on the mattress, it could have been that same kiss we'd had in his den last October. We drew each other close. He let his hand move between my legs, his fingers brushing my underwear, which was already damp.

"Charlie, my bus is in thirty minutes," I said.

"We have to be quick, then."

We undressed and Charlie climbed on top and put on a condom. As he moved inside me, we looked at each other, committing every detail of one another to memory. I couldn't stop thinking about the time, though. We still needed to bring the mattress out to the curb and drop the key off in the landlord's office, and then Charlie had to drive me down to Memorial Union. I had to make my bus; otherwise I'd miss my flight. I knew that Charlie probably didn't care if either of these things went as planned.

"Charlie," I said, propping myself up on my elbows. "We really should go."

"But I want you to come."

"I can't."

He climbed off and I pulled my dress back over my head and he put on his clothing. He threw the condom in the toilet. "You have to visit soon, then," he said, walking back into the bedroom. "At least so we can finish this."

"Can you help me with the mattress?" I asked.

Together we pushed the mattress out the door. It looked sad

and vulgar, covered in mysterious stains, draped on the side of the road next to all the green and black trash and recycling bins.

I ran over and dropped the key off with my landlord and then we got in Charlie's car and drove the five minutes down to Memorial Union—passing Lake Mendota and Vivian's old apartment and all the big old beautiful Colonials along Gorham. We didn't talk on the drive because there was nothing to say. Nothing to make this easier.

Charlie parked across the street from the bus stop. The coach bus was already there and a line of students with their bags had formed. People had begun to board. I hadn't been nervous before, but suddenly I was trembling, my stomach a knot.

We pulled my suitcases from the trunk and walked to the end of the line. As we waited, he didn't say anything about the engagement ring or coming to visit me in the fall. We just stood there quietly, looking at one another. When we got to the front, we hugged goodbye, and when we pulled back, he wiped his eyes. "I love you, Leah," he said.

"I love you, Charlie."

Then I hugged him again, really hard, burying my face in his neck. I knew, somehow, that it would be the last time I would ever see him.

I boarded the bus and sat breathless in one of the first rows as more students got on. A few minutes later, I heard my name and looked up. Charlie was standing there in front of me. My eyes smarted. It was like seeing someone back from the dead. He held up my backpack. "You forgot this."

"Oh my god," I said, laughing. "Thank you."

I took it from him and we hugged one last time, and this time

I watched him walk away from the bus and cross the street, hands in his pockets, back to where his car was parked. He was wearing jeans and an orange T-shirt. He hadn't showered that day or brushed his hair, and his hair was a little wild, blowing around. He looked young and handsome and strong. Before getting into his car, he lit a cigarette. Then he climbed in and drove away.

26.

I BROKE UP WITH CHARLIE A FEW WEEKS LATER, WITH A TEXT. HE fought a little bit, but not as relentlessly as he usually did. He sent his typical long-winded text messages—love notes tinged with threats and accusations—or maybe they were threats speckled with tenderness. But we never spoke on the phone. He asked for the ring back. "I really need the money," he told me in a text.

I moved into an apartment in Medford with a woman ten years older than me—Jade—and I started my job at Bunker Hill Community College. I tried to tell myself that I was doing well, but really, I was more miserable than I'd ever been, even during the worst times with Charlie.

I remembered what Charlie had told me. *I was destined to become addicted to heroin.*

As soon as I met Charlie—the moment he smiled at me in the grocery store, when I realized he wanted to know me, too—I was hooked. It didn't matter who else I met. It didn't matter who tried to talk me out of it. They could have presented me with the most compelling argument in the world as to why I was better off without him. None of it would have made a difference. There was something in me—a part of myself that had been there long before I'd ever met Charlie—that had found something in him that I simply could not let go of.

Jade's apartment on Willard Avenue was fully furnished. She had previously been living there with her ex-fiancé, Fred. Her books were arranged alphabetically on the shelves. The rooms were filled with potted plants, framed art, Oriental rugs laid out on the hardwood floors. The refrigerator was covered with save-the-dates, wedding invitations, and baby announcements.

Jade was an attorney. She must have made a lot of money, because she had a full set of cookware from Le Creuset and the furniture wasn't from IKEA. She was the kind of person who never waited until the next day to do the dishes. She remembered to water her plants and she didn't let mail pile up. The apartment always smelled nice. She was busy all week with work, but then on Friday and Saturday evenings I'd find her sitting on the couch in her pajamas, scrolling on her phone, *SVU* on in the background, cookies baking in the kitchen. She rarely left the house and she never had friends over, despite all the invitations plastered to the refrigerator.

On weekend nights when I barricaded myself in my bedroom, I could hear her around midnight, washing the dishes she'd used to bake. Then I'd listen to her in the bathroom, brushing her teeth and washing her face. She took care of herself. I knew this was what made her depression different from mine. For some reason, hearing her do these things, performing these rituals, filled me with so much sadness that I would start to cry listening to her as I lay like a corpse in the dark.

We started swapping stories about Fred and Charlie. It was the first time I felt like I could tell someone everything.

The more I told Jade about Charlie, the angrier I became. Maybe it was because Jade held back her own opinions about my relationship. She had a lot of feelings about Fred, and she talked about that; it could be that I got wrapped up in her anger. But also, it felt good to talk about Charlie. Jade didn't assume I was looking for advice. When I thanked her for this, she said, "Why would you need advice? You left him."

"After a year."

"It doesn't matter how long. People do things on their own timeline."

Jade had been with Fred for seven years. She'd ended things after she found him taking pills out of her birth control pack. Fred had never been physical with her. He got jealous if she spoke with other men, including her own father. He criticized what she wore, how she spoke, every opinion she had. If she lost weight, he became suspicious that she was attracted to other men. If she gained weight, he commented she wasn't taking care of herself properly. He looked through her phone and email and internet history on a regular basis.

Since she'd broken up with him, he'd sent her texts and voice mails threatening suicide. She'd blocked him on everything, but he made new accounts. He'd come by the apartment and her office uninvited. She'd found notes on her windshield.

Fred wasn't like this at the beginning. When she met him, he was kind, funny, and smart. I met Fred once when he showed up at our door on a Friday night. He was dressed in a nice suit and had a full head of prematurely gray hair. Like Jade, he appeared to be in his mid-to-late thirties. Jade had never described what Fred had looked like before, and I'd been imagining somebody unattractive. Fred looked like someone who had his life together. If I saw him on the street, I'd notice him. He was tall.

"So sorry to bother you this late," he said when I opened the door, even though it was only seven. "Is Jade in?" He had a British accent. She hadn't mentioned this, either.

His apology, his gentle yet disarming presence, his direct eye contact—all of it felt familiar.

"Jade isn't here," I said, even though she was in her bedroom.

"No problem," he said agreeably. "I saw her car, so I thought I'd pop by. I'm sorry to interrupt your Friday evening."

"That's okay."

"Do you think you could tell Jade that I have something I'd like to discuss with her? It has to do with my mother's health. I think she would want to know. I'm Fred, by the way." He smiled apologetically, as if he knew that I might have heard bad things.

"I'll pass on the message," I told him.

When I went to Jade's bedroom to let her know, she pulled her knees to her chest. "He was here? Just now?"

"Yeah."

"Jesus. I'm sorry you had to deal with that."

"What's going on with his mom?"

"She was diagnosed with cancer. He thinks this will be the thing that makes me come back."

"Would you ever get a restraining order?" I asked, since this was what my friends had asked me.

"I'm a divorce attorney," said Jade, her voice sharp. She didn't look scared anymore. "I have a reputation to uphold. I'm defending victims of domestic violence all the time. It's not a good look for me if I have a piece-of-shit stalker for an ex. Also, the courthouse is my place of employment. I work with these people every day. They came to my fucking engagement party."

"They wouldn't understand?"

Fury flashed in her eyes. "He's doing all this crap and *I'm* the one who has to get up in front of my colleagues and talk about it? I've worked too hard to get to where I am in my career."

It was because of Jade that I had the willpower not to answer Charlie's messages, or Faye's. I missed him and I was angry at him and I started to be okay about feeling both these things at the same time.

When I saw on Facebook that Charlie had a new girlfriend only a month after our breakup—a startlingly pretty girl, another grad student, with long dark hair—I cried for weeks. The picture of them on Facebook haunted me. I looked at it dozens of times a day.

Eventually I began to go out with other men. It was the age of Tinder and I'd spend hours swiping, searching for men who looked like Charlie, or ones who looked so different from him that I might be able to forget somehow.

I found myself craving intensity. I asked probing, inappropriate questions on first dates. *Are your parents happy? Do you do drugs? Are you depressed?* The normal people would laugh uncomfortably and try to get back to talking about their favorite TV shows, and the weirdos would get into it. Usually the dates would lead to sex, which was almost always disappointing. Occasionally it would be good, and I'd convince myself that I liked the guy. Then the relationship would run its course in several weeks. It would usually end with a text. Sometimes a guy would ghost me after we slept together, which made me feel worthless, even if I didn't like him.

I was a different kind of sad than I'd been in Madison. With Charlie, I had felt out of control, the way a car accident feels out of control. I wasn't sure which way was up, and every day I felt like something unexpected might happen. I was blindly moving my way through, arms out in the dark, searching desperately for clarity. Now the lights were on and my eyes were open. I was watching it all happen.

Sex made me feel free from myself. Men seemed to communicate better in bed than they did in real life. They said what they wanted, how they felt. Some were sweet and affectionate. They told me how interesting and beautiful I was and how badly they wanted to make me feel good, how happy they were that we'd met. Some of them were crude and rough and said terrible, demeaning things. It was better with the disgusting guys, because with them I could really disappear—get outside my head for a while, surrender to the experience. I always went along. I never said no.

All of it ended in the morning, though. In the morning we were strangers again. It didn't matter what the sex had been like. Then I'd wait all day for them to text me. I hated waiting for texts. I spent so many hours waiting for texts.

Every once in a while I'd get together with Robbie. I'd go over to his apartment—he still lived in the same place in Watertown—the same posters on the wall, the same brown, wrinkled sheets on the bed, the same small blue pipe. He always had Lucky Charms in the cupboard above the sink, a gallon of whole milk in the fridge. He dressed the same; smelled the same; worked the same job at the senior living home. We'd smoke weed and watch TV on his computer and then we'd cuddle. Sometimes we slept together. I always stayed over. In the morning I'd end up telling him about whatever asshole I'd gone out with last and he would frown and get worked up and ask me why I kept "doing this to myself."

"I'm not doing anything, Robbie," I'd say. "This stuff doesn't affect me."

Then one day I texted Robbie and instead of saying, *Come over!* like he usually did, he called me. "I think it's best that we don't hang out anymore," he said over the phone. "I've been thinking about our relationship and I realize that I need to take a step back."

"A step back?"

"Every time we hang out I usually feel bad for the next week," he said. "Our friendship, or whatever it is, is just making me feel pretty shitty. It has for a long time."

The flood of guilt I felt then was so heavy that my whole body swayed beneath it. I was selfish and cruel. And I'd been cruel to the one person who never hurt me. I realized, with a crushing sadness, that there might be no return from this.

"Robbie," I said. "I am so sorry."

"Hey, it's okay," he said kindly. "I just need some space."

"I totally get it."

"I think, to stop myself from reaching out, I'm going to block you. Not to be mean. I don't hate you or anything. I care about you, Leah. But I need to finally move on."

"I understand, Robbie. I'm so sorry that I took advantage—"

"It's okay. I'll talk to you later, okay?"

"Okay, but—"

And then he hung up.

I met Patrick at Aaron and Haley's wedding. He was a grooms-
man, a friend of theirs from Harvard. At the rehearsal dinner, two
fourteen-year-old girls, cousins of Haley's, got up and sang "Eter-
nal Flame," and I started to cry and couldn't stop. I tried to play it
off as tears of happiness. Patrick came up behind me and put his
hand on my back. "Are you okay?" he asked softly.

I knew, at that moment, that we would sleep together.

It didn't happen at the wedding, but he asked for my number,
and we met a week later at a tapas bar in Cambridge. He was dressed
more formally than me and was wearing cologne, was already halfway into a drink when I arrived.

"Of course, I want to get married and have kids and all that
eventually," he said, after we sat down. "But going to my friends'
weddings doesn't put me in any kind of mood."

"That's because you don't have ovaries," I said.

He laughed. "You want kids?"

"The older I get, the less certain I am," I lied. "It's a great way
to ruin a marriage."

Then I changed the subject. I didn't want him to think I wanted
to have children with him. My wish for children was a blurry
want—an emptiness or longing that was more physical than emotional. I felt it in the pit of my stomach, in my breasts.

We got drunk quickly and he suggested going to a different
bar. He paid and ordered an Uber and as we climbed into the backseat of the car, he touched my back, where my shirt met my skin.
"I like this," he said, meaning my top.

The Uber dropped us off in Central Square and he led us up a flight of stairs to a small, dimly lit room. We found two stools a little off to the side, and this time, without a table between us, we leaned in to one another. Our knees touched.

"What do you like?" he asked once our drinks had arrived.

"What do you mean?" I said, though I knew.

"Sexually."

I felt an odd mixture of shyness and boldness. I was entering into something unknown. Some men seemed to know instantly what I wanted from them, and I felt an emotional connection with these men, like they were reading my mind.

"I like the feeling of having no control," I said.

He nodded. He didn't look surprised at all. He reached over and took my hand. "Do you like to be dominated?"

I looked at him and realized there were two of him, overlapping. "Sometimes."

He squeezed my hand. "Let's go back to your place."

I felt sick on the Uber ride to the apartment on Willard. I'd drunk too much on an empty stomach. We were in an Uber pool with two other passengers; two young women on their way home from dinner. They were talking animatedly about their night and their lives, and Patrick and I were quiet. I felt like I knew the women better than I knew Patrick. I wished I could go home with them, instead.

We got dropped off first. When I brought him inside, Jade was there on the couch, but I didn't bother to introduce them. I led Patrick into my room, which I had prepared just for this, earlier that day. Tidied up, washed the sheets.

He took off his clothing first, and then mine, in a fast, impatient way, the way you rip packaging off food when you're hungry. He pushed me onto the bed and told me to turn around.

"Wait," I said. "Let me get a condom."

He was rough and he seemed almost irritated, as he slapped my ass and told me things about my body, as though he were looking for something satisfying and couldn't find it. I felt numb and way too drunk.

I turned around so that I was facing him. Then he started to hit me. It was so surprising—his open palm against my cheek—that I turned my face away from him the way you yank your finger from a hot pan.

Everything was spinning. He continued to hit me. "I don't think I like that," I said.

"Oh," he said, and he immediately lost his erection. We both passed out, side by side, not touching.

An hour later, we woke up, the light in the hallway spilling into the bedroom, our clothes sprawled on the floor, the condom and condom wrapper on the bedsheets between us. Patrick reached over and began to touch me. I asked him to be softer. I thought about how he was at the wedding, when he had put his hand on my back. There was nothing soft about him now.

He climbed on top and forced himself inside me.

"No," I said, realizing it, moments later. "We need to use a condom."

"But it feels so much better."

"I'm not on birth control," I said. I pushed his chest back. "We need to use a condom," I said again. "I'm really not on birth control." I managed to pull myself out from underneath him and stumbled to the other side of the room to get one.

When we started up, he began to hit me, and this time, because I was less drunk, I felt it more. Not just physically, but I saw us from above. Him hitting my face, me wincing. It hurt, but not in the way I wanted it to.

In the morning he got dressed and ordered an Uber. "It'll be here in three minutes," he said. He pulled me onto his lap and kissed my cheek and said, "I'll text you." Then he left. I wandered into the bathroom and saw in the mirror that my breasts were spotted with bruises—yellows and greens, like camo. I couldn't remember how they got there. Then I showered.

In the daylight, my bedroom looked like a tornado had passed through, the blankets bunched on the floor, the sheets twisted on the mattress. I made the bed and climbed on top, clean and naked, and tried to masturbate, but I couldn't. I closed my eyes and pulled the blanket over to cover myself.

27.

Thank you for sending the ring back. I didn't ask for it back to be a jerk. To be honest money is tight right now and I figured you probably weren't getting a lot of use out of it anyway. At the time I also just couldn't believe you'd done that. We'd celebrated with my entire family and it was humiliating to tell them you dumped me like a week later. I understand now why you had to do that, but I don't know why you said yes to begin with. You said in your text you were scared to say no, like SCARED of my reaction, of what I might DO, and that's the part I really have to come to terms with, that the shitty way I behave while I'm using has a lasting impact. I'm a different man now that I'm sober but that doesn't mitigate all my damage and destruction. I really hope you're doing well and at the very least, happier than you were when you were with me. You're an incredible, beautiful, smart and sweet person. I hope you don't waste your time on anyone that doesn't deserve you. I know that I didn't. I wish I'd made all my mistakes that I made with you a few years ago, long before I ever met you. I'm so sorry I hurt you, Leah. I hope one day you forgive me and you can think back on all this and not regret it, or at least not all of it. Love u.

I didn't respond.

The only time I felt in control, like I didn't need anybody, was when I was writing, so I kept writing, mostly in between the Tinder guys. I was still working on the thing I had started during my last semester of grad school, and the seventy pages had turned into almost four hundred. It was a novel now. I didn't know if it was any good. But that's how it always was. You never really knew, but a small part of you—just loud enough—told you it was.

Then I heard back from an online journal saying they wanted to publish "Thirteen." When I got the email, I closed my laptop and took a three-hour walk around the city. My body hadn't felt like that—so alive, pumping with blood and adrenaline—since I'd been in Madison. I wrote the editor back that night and told her the story was still available and I'd be honored.

Several weeks later, when it went up on their site, I posted the story to social media. Ben and Aaron both posted it to their pages, too. As the likes and comments rolled in, along with all the powerful bursts of dopamine, I thought about what Charlie had said about external validation.

Half a year went by. I finished a draft of the novel. Vivian offered to introduce me to her agent over email. I sent Vivian's agent, Sarah, an email with a brief description of the novel. Sarah wrote me back ten minutes later, asking me to send her the first thirty pages.

I started seeing a guy named Theo who worked at a small academic press. I met him at a reading in a bookstore, which was the kind of event where I'd always hoped to meet someone. He was there by himself. His eyes were serious and olive-colored. The rest of his face—his mouth, even his chin—seemed vulnerable. Though he didn't have good posture, I liked the way he held himself—almost as if he'd forgotten he had a body. He appeared deep in thought. I found him handsome, though I wasn't sure everyone would.

He was intense but in a different way than Charlie. He had never smoked a cigarette in his life. He didn't own a smartphone or watch television. He had strong opinions and was deeply committed to the things and people that were important to him, and he seemed to block out almost everything else. His scent was subtle and homey and in no way intoxicating; it reminded me of New England, of old libraries, of fleeces. I often imagined what he might be like as a father. He always showed up on time.

One weekend early on, we drove to Stowe, Vermont, where Theo had grown up. His parents—still married and living in the same house where Theo had spent his childhood—were out of town. It was a beautiful drive, the leaves shimmering like wet acrylic paint in the light—every shade of bronze and gold. As we got closer to the house and the sun dipped behind the mountains, the sky deepened into a Halloween-y plum color. Outside it smelled like clean earth and dying leaves. I felt safe and happy in the car with Theo.

Theo drove an old Toyota Corolla and he played instrumental music on the CD player. Sometimes he pointed things out to me from the window, but mostly he just listened while I talked. And I talked a lot. He already knew about my family and he knew about Charlie. I told him about what I was writing and about every person in my MFA cohort. He didn't always say a lot in return or offer insight the way Vivian did in conversation, but he listened closely. I knew, because he'd refer back to details and stories I'd told him earlier, and he asked good questions.

That night as we fell asleep in Theo's childhood bedroom, in a twin-sized bed under several thick quilts, among all his old books and belongings, I thought that Theo would probably be the man that I would marry. I was blissful, knowing that I'd finally found a good man.

"Am I your girlfriend?" I whispered to him in the dark. We hadn't yet used those words with one another.

He pulled me closer. We were pressed against each other underneath the mounds of blankets, his arm curled around my middle. "I hope so," he whispered back.

I still thought about Charlie then, but not as much. I looked at Charlie's Facebook sometimes. He and his girlfriend had broken up a while ago. Sometimes scents would conjure him—cigarettes, cold weather. I'd never smelled another person who smelled as good as Charlie.

My honeymoon period with Theo was euphoric and brief. We started fighting over trivial things. He thought it was a "character flaw" that I watched *The Bachelor*, and I thought it was a "character flaw" that he was judgmental about the TV I watched. The sex was great, but it wasn't like with Charlie.

His rigidness began to annoy me. He didn't like to gossip. He wouldn't read books that weren't critically acclaimed or books that gained too much popularity. Radio and TV were off-limits because he didn't want to be subjected to the ads.

He felt shame about watching porn, though he did watch it. I knew because I asked him about it explicitly, then pushed him to answer: *Which kinds? What kind of stuff turns you on?* I could tell my questions humiliated him, and also disgusted him. It was tiring being with someone so repressed, someone who was so scared of being like other people. I started saying things to him just to elicit a reaction, just to watch him squirm.

A few months into my relationship with Theo, Charlie sent me another text:

> Hey, I hope it's okay that I'm texting you. I wrote you a
> pretty long message. More like a letter, really. It's
> somewhat intense, but not because it has to do with our
> past, but intense in that I went down this deep rabbit
> hole writing about writing. I wanted to send it to you
> but when you didn't respond to my last text I thought I

might have overstepped a boundary. I wanted to ask
you if you were open to reading my super long message
as I think it might be embarrassing to send out my
vulnerable thoughts about writing into the void and
not get a response. There's only a few people in the
world that I would want to share this with, you being
one of them. Actually you are the only one. But seeing
my name on your phone, or in any context, might be
unwanted, so if you'd rather not receive my long
message, or any message from me at all, that's okay,
too. Either way, just know that I was so happy to see
Thirteen was published, and I miss talking with you.

Later that evening I received a phone call from a Madison, Wisconsin, number that I didn't know. I didn't pick up, but the missed
call prompted me to text Charlie back the following night.

Hi Charlie, I'd like to read your message. Thank you
about my story! It was so exciting. My feelings about
everything (you and me) are complicated. I didn't
really know how to answer your text from before. I'm
glad to hear you've been writing. Also, did you try to
call me last night?

He texted me back immediately and it was the closest we'd
come to *talking* since I'd left Madison.

Not that I know of, he wrote. I don't have any outgoing calls to
you for a long way back.

Oh, I wrote back. **I got a call from Madison last night a little after I got your text. Weird!**

Three days later he responded: **What was the number?**

I never wrote back. And he never sent me the message about writing.

After Theo and I moved in together, it was like a switch had been turned off, and everything about him bothered me. The expression on his face while he read his manuscripts; the sound of his sneezes; the superiority he felt about his flip phone; the fact that he'd never heard of Mary-Kate and Ashley Olsen.

"Are you kidding me?" I said. "*Full House?*"

He shrugged.

"Theo, that's crazy." I googled them on my phone and held up a photo. "You've never seen them?"

"Nope."

"How can that be?"

"*Should* I know these women?" he asked, his voice sharp. "Have they done something important I should be aware of?"

It was a conversation, I was certain, that, if I'd had it with another man—like Charlie or Robbie, for example—would have been funny. We were talking about the Olsen Twins, after all, not a war. It shouldn't have been a point of contention. It dawned on me then that Theo and I never laughed together. We were both too serious to be sharing a home, a life.

Then Sarah, the agent, wrote back. She had liked the first thirty pages and wanted to read the whole manuscript. "Theo," I yelped, and he appeared in the doorway of the bedroom. "Sarah wants to read the whole thing."

He grinned. "Let me see." It was the happiest he'd looked in months.

That night we went out and got drinks at a bar in Inman Square. We talked about the publishing world and I felt for Theo what I had felt for him at the beginning of our relationship. I appreciated his thoughtfulness. How he could focus in on one thing for a long time. He didn't get distracted or bored or turn the conversation to himself. The fact that he didn't have a smartphone was nice. He was never checking it or saying, *Let me google it*. He was the only person other than Vivian and Wilson who had read the draft of my novel, and he'd finished it in less than a week. His notes had been incredibly astute.

Sarah wrote back to me a few weeks later saying that she loved the manuscript. She wanted to help me get the book out into the world. She wrote me a long letter about where she thought the draft needed improvement and I hurled myself into revision, spending all my free time writing. My evenings and weekends were devoted to the novel. Everything else—my job, my relationship, my friendships, my family, my sleep—took a backseat. My novel was the thing that got me out of bed in the morning, the thing that gave everything else meaning. Writing had always been this for me, but now it felt different. I lived in those sentences, more than I lived in my own body. For the first time in my life, I was no longer scared of my loneliness.

Theo didn't seem to mind. He also threw himself into his

work, and we functioned best this way, when we both had projects outside of each other to focus on.

The times we were affectionate with one another became more and more rare. I no longer felt in love with him, and that was starting to weigh on me. But every once in a while I'd get flashes. I'd watch him from across a room or I'd overhear him talking on the phone with one of his colleagues in his *on* voice. There was a certain way his hair fell across his forehead that I really liked, and I'd remember—and those memories would tide me over.

One night we had dinner with my brothers, who were fighting about whether Hillary or Bernie had a better shot at beating Trump in the primaries.

"Hillary isn't the woman to beat him," Ben said. "Don't tell Haley I said that."

"Trump would destroy Bernie," Aaron said, ignoring the comment about Haley. "He would rip him to pieces."

"Everyone's entitled to their opinion," Ben said. "Even when their opinion is wrong."

I glanced at Theo, who seemed not to be listening to the conversation. Theo was mostly silent during dinners with my family. He felt uncomfortable around my brothers—whom he thought were arrogant—and my father, whom he had nothing in common with. He was weary of Monica, bored by Christina and Stephen, annoyed by Haley. I didn't disagree with any of these assessments, but because of this his presence at my family's dinner table never felt especially helpful.

"What about you, Theo?" Ben asked. "Who are you voting for in the primary, if you don't mind me asking?"

Theo, who had a FEEL THE BERN sticker on his laptop and had recently donated twenty dollars to someone campaigning for Bernie out on the street, said, "I'll be voting for Jill Stein." He cut into his chicken.

"Interesting!" Ben said brightly, as I looked at Theo in horror.

"Are you serious?" I said.

Theo nodded.

"What about your sticker?"

"It's a sticker, Leah. It doesn't control me."

"You're throwing away your vote if you—"

"I've actually been considering not voting at all," Theo cut me off. "It's a corrupt system. Especially if it comes down to Hillary and Trump." His neck was turning a hot, indignant pink.

"How can you say that?" I said. "I—"

"There's a simple solution," Ben inserted. "Vote for Bernie!"

Theo didn't respond.

"What about everything going on in our country?" I said to Theo.

It wasn't that I spent much time thinking about our country. It was only when injustice brushed up against my life in a visceral way that I really started paying attention. I was as self-absorbed as I'd ever been. But Theo's self-righteousness repulsed me.

"None of that matters if our planet melts," Theo addressed, deadpan, to his desecrated chicken.

"Do me a favor," Ben said, "and take a look at Bernie's environmental plan."

"Throwing away your vote is selfish," I said to him. "You're not a martyr, Theo. Get over yourself."

"Who are you voting for, Lee?" Ben said quickly.

I turned to my brother. "Not Jill Stein." The truth was, I hadn't made up my mind.

We didn't speak on the car ride home. Every time Theo slowed for a light or a pedestrian, I felt the tension in the car rise. When he almost missed the turn for our exit, fury beat in my chest. It occurred to me that I felt angry at him all the time, though I didn't really know why.

When we parked outside the apartment, he didn't get out of the car. "Was there a reason you were such a bitch to me in front of your family?"

He'd never used that word before—certainly not to describe me. I felt both that I deserved it and also a relief so enormous that he'd said something cruel that I could finally latch onto.

"Don't call me that," I said. "You're an asshole." And then I got out of the car and slammed the door. As I stormed into the apartment, I felt a thudding in my chest—an anxiousness bordering on excitement. I didn't know what was going to happen next.

When he came inside and found me in our bedroom, he looked soft and remorseful. It was disappointing.

"I never should have called you that," he said, standing there in the doorway. "That was so wrong. I felt embarrassed that the conversation happened in front of your brothers, and I felt angry that you didn't have my back. But we're allowed to have different opinions and different politics. Of course we are. I was thinking that we should talk more about the upcoming election. I haven't even told you my thoughts about it."

Nothing sounded worse to me than listening to Theo's thoughts about the upcoming election. I couldn't stand him. It seemed unfair to have such a mean feeling about someone who was generally very decent.

"Theo, I'm sorry, but I don't think I want to be in this relationship anymore," I said. "It's not because of Jill Stein. I think you're a wonderful person. It just isn't working."

He took a step farther into the room. "I think we can work this out."

"I don't think so."

"Leah," he said, and for a second I thought he was going to cry. "I want to make a life with you. That was our plan."

"I know." I looked at him. His earnestness, his soberness. I felt for him, but I didn't want to be with him. "But I'm not happy."

"What are you looking for?" he spit out. Very quickly his sadness had turned to anger. "A relationship isn't supposed to *make you happy*. You find happiness on your own. A partner is there to support you and build with you. It seems as though you're looking for some magic person who's going to solve all your problems, but you have to do that yourself. What we have together is complicated, but it's good and real."

What we have is sad and soulless, I thought of saying. *We never laugh.*

"I'm sorry. I don't feel that way."

"Well," Theo scoffed, "I guess we are pretty different."

I raised an eyebrow.

"It goes back to *The Bachelor*. It's a more significant issue than

you realize. You like that kind of thing. Reality TV, love stories, sentimental propaganda. Even our music taste is drastically
different. I've tried to introduce you to my music, but you never
seem like you're paying attention. You've never really shown that
much curiosity in my interests. You're too involved with yourself."

"I don't think this breakup is happening because we like different music."

"That's not what I'm saying," Theo said. "You're not hearing
me at all."

I moved into a studio apartment in Porter Square. On days that
I didn't teach I woke up early and took long walks along the tree-
lined streets of Cambridge. Old brick apartment buildings, huge
ivy-covered houses with sprawling gardens out front—yard signs
for Hillary and Bernie. I don't think I ever saw a single sign for
Trump on my walks. I'd spend my weekends writing, either in my
apartment or in coffee shops around Porter and Harvard Squares.
It was kind of like my time in Madison, except without workshop—
no group of writer friends, no drunken nights at City Bar.

But there was Sarah in New York City. A woman I'd met only
over the phone and email. Each morning when I opened up my
Word document, I felt as though I were writing to her.

I was never tempted to call Charlie. But sometimes I imagined returning to Madison and running into him by chance. Seeing him
in the corner store on East Johnson or leaning against the Norris
Court Apartments, smoking a cigarette, as if he'd been waiting for
me all this time. I imagined him smiling, us both starting to laugh,

running toward each other. I tried to remember what it felt like to hug him, the feel of his neck and hair against my face.

Sometimes in my imagination it was Faye I ran into, not Charlie, and she'd tell me that Charlie had died. I tried to play out how I would feel, what I would do. I couldn't imagine the feeling, though.

Back to Tinder I went. I was pickier this time around, but found that most men weren't looking for a relationship, even the ones who claimed they were. I switched to Hinge. It was pretty much the same group of men, but everyone was a little more polite with each other at the beginning. One night I went out with a guy who seemed nice in his messages. We had a few drinks at Christopher's in Porter Square. We talked about our jobs and our favorite books. I was better at keeping things light, those days. Our conversation wasn't electrifying, but he had a dry sense of humor and a warm smile. When the bar announced it was closing, he said, "I'm having a great time. I know it's a Wednesday, but would you be up for one more drink across the street?"

We trekked down the block, tipsy. It had started to snow—huge cartoonish flakes that left a shimmering glaze across Mass Ave.

Halfway through our drink at the Abbey, he began to check his phone. He grew quiet. I didn't think much of it until we left the bar and he sprinted off into the night. No hug; not even a goodbye, or *Thanks for coming out*. I never heard from him after that. I wondered what I had done wrong. I went over every single thing I had said that possibly could have made him run away from me.

On a Sunday morning a month later, I saw him walking on

Mass Ave, farther up from where our date had been, hand in hand with a woman. They were laughing and he was holding a little dog on a leash. The woman had a baby strapped to her chest in one of those cloth slings. He looked straight past me, avoiding eye contact with such deliberation that it hit me—he was married.

A lot of them were. Married, in relationships. Some way or another, unavailable.

Once, very late at night, I privately messaged Peter on Facebook. It was three in the morning, and I'd been lying awake in bed since midnight. My heart was beating rapidly, even though I hadn't moved for hours. Over the last few years, there'd been a number of times—usually at night—when I'd start to obsess over how my life might be different if Peter and I had continued to see one another. What if Charlie had been the biggest mistake I'd ever made?

I grasped onto small, movie-clip details, played them over and over in my mind, until it was torturous. Peter holding my foot in his hand in bed. Peter brushing snow off the windshield in the morning. Peter's magnetic yet sane smile. *That was it*, an angry voice would reprimand me in my head—as the images rolled. *You fucked it up.*

I'd grow frantic and sorrowful, certain that I'd missed my only chance. It was so rare that I felt attracted to someone and safe with them at the same time.

To my surprise, Peter responded to my Facebook message immediately.

It's 9am here in Paris, he wrote back.

You're in Paris? I wrote. I wiped my eyes, realizing that I had been crying.

A photo appeared in our chat, of a half-eaten pastry and a tiny cup of espresso. In the background of the photo I could see a tree-lined street, people sitting at small circular tables at an outdoor café. The day looked bright and sunny.

I felt a pang of longing.

It's been a while, he wrote.

Yeah. I tried to think of what I could possibly say next.

How's life? When's the book coming out?

Soon, I wrote.

Great!

A minute went by and neither one of us said anything.

I think about you sometimes. I typed the words slowly, with one finger, and then stared at them. I wondered, on a scale of one to ten, how creepy it would be to say this. I imagined being Peter, sitting at a café in Paris at nine a.m., being on the receiving end of such a message. I pressed enter. Quickly I followed it up with, *sorry if that's weird*.

He wrote back quickly. *Haha, no not too weird, I don't think. What do you think about?*

I sat up in bed, emboldened. *I wish we got to know each other more.* I held my breath, waiting for his response.

Half a minute passed. *Me too. I enjoyed the time we spent together.*

Me too, I wrote.

I waited for two minutes for him to say something else and then I wrote: *Can I come see you in Paris?*

Ellipses appeared immediately. Then went away. Then appeared again. *Haha*, he eventually wrote.

My heart sank.

I'm dying, I wrote. *I have 1 year to live.*

What?? Are you okay?

Kidding. But what if we started living our lives like that, like we were about to die?

When he didn't write anything, I wrote: *I could be there by the end of the day.*

I was fully unhinged, typing the way I used to chat with Smarter-Child on AIM when I was in middle school and home alone with nothing to do—*Fuck you SmarterChild! Want to have sex? I hate you! I'm so lonely I want to die. I love you I love you I love you.*

I should probably run, Peter wrote. *Take care, Leah.*

Ok. Bye.

I met up with Jade in the big Starbucks in Harvard Square, overlooking Mass Ave and Brattle Street. She told me she'd gotten back together with Fred. He'd moved back into the apartment on Willard the previous month. I tried not to let my shock show on my face.

"I'm thirty-six," she said, her voice immediately defensive. "I want to have children."

"I get that," I said.

"Fred wants to be a father more than anything." Then she

shook her head irritably. "I was talking with these infantile mo-
rons on Bumble and half of them could barely get it together to
ask me out on a date. The men my age would rather date girls in
their twenties and I don't want to be with some guy in his forties
who's divorced and already has kids." Suddenly she looked like she
was about to cry. "Freezing your eggs costs thirty grand. Can you
believe that?"

"I didn't know that," I said. "How's it been going with Fred?"

"It's been okay. He's working on his issues with a therapist."

"That's good."

Her face resumed its toughness. "Nobody is happy that I'm
back with him, but it's not their life, right?" She smiled. "Anyway.
How are you doing? How's the book?"

28.

I LEARNED OF CHARLIE'S DEATH OVER FACEBOOK. I CAME HOME
one day from teaching and looked at his page and there were the
posts.

RIP Charlie.

Rest easy, brother.

The struggle is over.

Does anyone know when the funeral is?

And one from Tyler: *Devastated that Charlie is no longer with us.
We'll be posting more details soon. Thank you for the love and support as
our family mourns the sudden loss of my talented brother.*

He had died two days earlier, on February 8, 2017. I waited to
feel something. I was breathing very heavily.

I called Ben. My brother answered: "What's up?"

"Ben?"

"What's wrong, Leah?"

"Charlie died."

"Oh my god." I could tell, by the quality of the sound, that he was in the car and that he'd just pulled over. I heard a click and the phone went from Bluetooth to a normal phone connection. "Oh my god," he repeated.

"I can't believe it," I said. "I just saw on Facebook."

"Leah. Are you okay?"

"I can't imagine what Faye is feeling."

"Who?"

"His mom," I said, and then I gasped and started to cry.

Charlie dying seemed like the cruelest thing that had ever happened.

"Oh, Leah," Ben said softly. "He was a good guy. I could tell that one time I met him. A really sweet guy. This is awful."

"I wish I'd responded to his last message," I said.

"Don't think about that," Ben said. "He knows you loved him, Lee."

Suddenly I was beside myself. "But I wish he knew how much."

After we hung up I looked at Facebook again, to make sure I hadn't made it up. The posts were still there. It had been a year and a half since I'd said goodbye to Charlie at the bus stop outside Memorial Union. There were certain things I remembered about him vividly. And some things—the way he smelled, the way it felt to embrace him, that hum—that I could no longer recall. Those things were gone.

I had his voice saved, though. On the videos on my phone. "Masterfade," "Shelter from the Storm," "Auld Lang Syne." And all those little mistakes. Thank god for those mistakes. I knew them by heart now, from having watched the videos so many times. The mistakes were when the Charlie-ness came out. When he'd turn to the camera and speak directly to me. Those were the moments he'd smile and you could see his different expressions, the way he looked when he had just finished laughing or when I had said something that had made him happy. I had his laugh recorded.

It was obvious to me now that in almost every video I had of him he was high, but I didn't care. I loved those videos. I scrolled through my phone like a madwoman, my heart beating furiously, until I found one. As soon as he started to sing, my eyes welled up with fresh tears. Halfway through the song, a text interrupted the screen. It was Adam, the guy from Hinge whom I'd been sleeping with for the past two weeks.

How's your week going?

Not great, I typed back. I was lying on my bed with the computer on my stomach, open to Charlie's Facebook page. **Yours?**

Oh no! Why not? My week's been good but busy. Work is crazy!

I found out someone close to me died.

I'm so sorry. Are you ok? Do you want company?

Adam was freshly showered, doused with the Abercrombie-type cologne I'd come to associate with him. When he hugged me and leaned in for a kiss, I recoiled at the smell; at the burst of mint that wafted from his mouth. He thought he was there to have sex with me.

But wasn't he? Wasn't that the reason I had asked him to come over?

"I'd just like to sit on my couch and not be alone," I said.

"Sure. Can I get you something? A glass of water? Wine?"

"I don't have any wine, so if you want to drink you'll have to go somewhere else."

He gave me a weird look. "I'll get us some water."

I sat down and he brought over two glasses of water.

"Would it be prying if I asked who passed away?"

Anger rose swiftly inside me, momentarily overwhelming my grief. "Two nights ago, you asked me if we could have anal," I said to him. "You think it's okay for you to ask me that, but that it might not be okay for you to ask me who died?"

Alarmed, he held up his hands in defense. "Whoa. I had no idea if you wanted to talk about it."

"Why would I have invited you over if I didn't want to talk about it?"

"Okay," he said. "Okay. Let's talk."

"His name was Charlie," I said. "We were engaged, but he was sick, so I couldn't be with him, and now I'm stuck with people who . . ." I wiped my nose on my sleeve. "It's sad being with someone who you don't actually like. And I know you don't like me, either. If you did, you wouldn't only text me when you want to have sex. Or come over here tonight because you thought that's what was going to happen."

"Look," Adam said, "I'm really sorry for your loss. You're

clearly going through a lot, and I honestly had no idea. I mean, I didn't even know you'd been engaged. And I'd like to be here to support you. I mean, yeah, we don't know each other really well, but I'm here for you. Clearly sex is not where your head is right now. And I'm fine with that. Seriously, it's cool."

"It's *cool*?"

"Yeah, I get it."

"No," I said, standing up. "You're here. Let's just do it." I took my shirt off and flung it across the room, where it landed on top of the internet router. Then I wandered over to the bed, where my laptop was still open to Charlie's Facebook.

Adam stood, his face filled with discomfort.

"Come on," I said, as I unbuttoned my jeans. I sat down on the edge of the bed and pulled them off.

"I feel like that might not be a good idea."

"I think it will make me feel better."

Adam rubbed the back of his neck.

I slid off my underwear. "You want to, right?"

"I honestly don't think we should."

I unhooked my bra and lay down.

"I think you're very distraught because of the loss you just went through," Adam said. "I don't want to make things worse."

And suddenly, lying there naked, I actually did want to have sex. I wanted to have sex with Charlie so badly that the intensity of the want made me flush. I put my hand over my face—I was so overwhelmed by the memory of being with him that I made a small sound.

"Look," said Adam from across the room, "I think I should go. I don't think I'm the right person to—"

"That's fine," I said. "Just go."

"Are you going to be okay?"

"I'll be okay."

After Adam left, I thought about that first night in the den with Charlie. I thought about those perfect, blurry days in my apartment before Thanksgiving, the night on my living room floor right before Christmas. The time in the Airbnb in Minnesota. The last morning in Madison, on the mattress. I felt guilty when I finally came—I had to be really messed up for being turned on. It felt so good, though, to remember him.

Then I started to cry. At first loud enough for my neighbors to hear—and afterward softly, almost silently, until I fell asleep.

29.

WILSON'S DEBUT COLLECTION OF STORIES HAD COME OUT ON October 1. He was giving a reading in Madison and all of us had decided to go hear him, except for Sam, who had a baby at home. I had kept up the most with Vivian since graduating. She was still in New York City. Her novel, *The Dentist*, had done well, and now she was working on a second. She and Rohan were getting married that winter. When she'd called me up to tell me the news about their engagement, I'd felt a stabbing, full-body jealousy. Far more jealous than when her book had come out.

I did everything I could not to feel this way. I tried to sound happy and excited, the way women were supposed to sound when their other women friends got engaged. I was ashamed of my jealousy. I was ashamed of myself. Of my failed relationships. That I was alone. After we hung up, I crawled into bed and didn't get out for days.

I hadn't told Vivian much about Theo or the other guys I'd gone out with since leaving Madison. When Vivian and I spoke, it was about what we were working on, what we'd heard from the others in our cohort, or we reminisced. Our lives would never overlap in the same way they had in Madison. For those two years, we'd been so invested in one another's relationships—in our successes and failures; in the minutiae of our days, as well as the overarching themes and stories of one another's lives. I understood now that while Vivian had been my closest friend, I'd also been scared about the friendship. What if I lost her?

I knew, in some sense, that I had. When we spoke now, it was friendly, but our conversations didn't have the same fervor of our MFA days. Back then, we never ran out of things to talk about.

It had been eight months since Charlie died when my plane landed in Milwaukee. I'd thought about his death every day, but besides that first night back in February, I hadn't cried. Hardly anybody had known about our relationship, and those who had known about him had disapproved. I didn't know how to mourn Charlie, so I hadn't. When I told my father that my boyfriend from Madison had passed away, he didn't know who I was talking about.

"Charlie," I said. "The one with the drug problem?"

My father frowned. "Overdose?"

I nodded.

"That's a real shame." He shook his head. "Are you okay?" he asked then, as if realizing I might not be.

"I'm sad," I said.

"Of course. These things are tragic."

If there was a funeral for Charlie, I wasn't invited, and an obituary was never posted. There was an article I found online on a local Madison news site that said that on the night of February 8, Charlie Nelson had been discovered dead, alone, in his car in the parking lot of a Chinese restaurant on the east side of Madison.

An autopsy had found that Charlie died from a fentanyl-related overdose.

This information was both precious and torturous. I read the article many times, often late at night. It was impossible not to picture Charlie in his car, in the driver's seat, where I'd sat beside him on so many drives.

I had texted Faye a week after I'd learned of Charlie's death. I had no idea what to say. I knew there was a chance she wouldn't respond, or if she did, that she would be angry with me. I didn't know if she hated me—or, worse, if she blamed me. But she wrote back that same day, and it was as sweet and loving as always.

> **Leah thank you for your message. I'll call you when I'm in better shape. Love you honey.**

She never did call, but I texted her again to let her know that I was going to be in Madison in October and that if she was up for it, I would love to see her.

Of course! she wrote back, with a heart emoji.

It hit me on the bus ride from Milwaukee to Madison. The bus pulled out of the terminal at MKE, and when I looked out the tinted window, I spotted a car with a Wisconsin license plate—the red block letters spelling out WISCONSIN with the orange, green, and red details, and then, *America's Dairyland.* My eyes blurred. I felt his absence then, for the first time. It seemed impossible that Charlie wasn't there.

I took out my phone and found our old texts.

I miss you, I typed.

I pressed send and watched the words move from the outgoing box to our shared thread. I stared at the screen. *Charlie,* I pleaded in my head. *Charlie. Please, say something.* For a minute I really hoped he might. When he didn't, I put my phone away and pressed my face to the window, watching the cars and the cornfields, the billboards, the October sky that was purpling into dusk. My face was hot with tears.

We had to change buses in Janesville, and I wondered with horror if Charlie's father even knew that his son was dead.

When I stepped off the bus to wait for the next one, I was hit again, this time in a new way. The cold in the Midwest was different than the cold on the East Coast. Sharper, less forgiving. On really bad days, it could give you frostbite in less than five minutes. Someone at the bus terminal was smoking, and the mixture of the Wisconsin cold and the smoke was too much to bear. I missed Charlie so badly that I felt like I was being torn apart. I would have done anything to hug him.

By the time we arrived in Madison, it was dark. I could see the capitol up ahead, white, glowing. From the windows, everything looked the same—the wide streets, the grassy sidewalks, the shabby houses with the big porches out front. The couches on the porches. The industrial-looking office buildings, brick and sandstone. The trees planted along East Wash, all the same kind and height. The green street signs were bigger than back home, with a rounder font— INGERSOLL, N BREARLY, N PATERSON, S LIVINGSTON. Being back was like hearing a song I hadn't heard for a long time—but the lyrics and the melody were there—and all of it came rushing back. I knew this place. Rohan had lived on Brearly and David had lived several blocks down on Blount, and if I took a right on Paterson I'd come out on East Johnson and there would be Johnson Public House, and right next door, the cluster of Norris Court Apartments. But Charlie wasn't there.

I was staying at a bed-and-breakfast on Gorham, a block away from my old apartment. My room at the B&B looked out onto Lake Mendota and when I woke up the next day, I opened the window a crack to let in the autumn air. The lake that morning was a soft baby-blue, so close to the color of the sky, it was hard to tell where one blue ended and the other began.

I took a shower and picked out my outfit carefully. A pair of jeans and a turtleneck sweater. I put on a little makeup. I wanted to look nice for Faye. More mature, but still someone she recognized right away.

I called an Uber and entered the Nelsons' address into the destination box. Faye had told me to come around nine-thirty a.m. I didn't know what to expect. If it was just going to be her or all the Nelsons. If she would be different. If she would be crying. I didn't know what to say to a mother who had lost her son.

As I waited for my Uber to arrive, I started to shake. I wasn't prepared for this. I felt, for the first time, filled with a rage with which there was nothing to do. I didn't want a driver I'd never met before to drive me to Charlie's house. I wanted Charlie to pick me up. That's how it had always been. Grief swallowed me whole.

But Jeffrey, my driver, arrived several minutes later in a silver Nissan. He rolled down his window. "Leah?"

I smiled. "Yup." I climbed into the backseat. His car smelled like cheap cologne and bubble gum.

"You're going to Sun Prairie?"

"Yes. Sun Prairie."

"All righty." He waited until I had buckled my seat belt before pulling away from the curb.

We drove through the pretty college town I knew so well—crossing from the east side to the west, right by campus. We passed Memorial Union and the Wisconsin Historical Society and Union South. Then we got onto the highway, in the direction of Sun Prairie. When I started to cry, the driver either didn't notice or pretended not to. It hadn't occurred to me to bring tissues, so I just let the tears fall down my face and chin and into my scarf. As we got off the highway, the city turned to suburbs and the trees thickened. The leaves were ablaze—orange and gold, against a brilliant blue sky. The closer we got to Charlie's house, the harder I cried. Everything ached.

When we pulled up to the house, it looked the same. The perfect lawn, Paul and Faye's matching SUVs in the driveway. Their house didn't look any different from their neighbors'.

"This it?" Jeffrey, the driver, said brightly, as though I hadn't just spent the last thirty minutes sobbing in the backseat of his car.

I nodded, but I couldn't move. I was starting to hyperventilate, seeing the house.

"Miss, you okay back there?" Jeffrey turned around in his seat. He was a middle-age guy with thinning orange hair and pockmarked cheeks. His eyes were kind and watery.

"Sorry," I said. "I once knew somebody . . ." I stopped there.

Faye had appeared in the doorway. In a way, it was like seeing Charlie. My whole heart expanded. "I have to go," I said. "Thank you."

I got out of the car and made my way to her. She was smiling and waving at me and I was weeping.

"Don't cry, sweet girl," she said, as we hugged. "It's okay." But when we pulled back, her eyes were wet. "Come in," she said. "Paul's out on an errand but he should be home soon. I have donuts." She led me inside. "I can't tell you how nice it is to see you, Leah. Charlie would be so happy to know we're doing this."

It was shocking, to hear her say his name, so easy like that. Every time I tried to say something, I couldn't because I started to cry. When we sat down at the dining room table Faye put a tissue box between us. "I know," she said. "I have days . . ."

I nodded and tried to regain my composure. "It's seeing you," I managed. "I haven't been able to talk with someone who knew him. Faye, I . . . I can't imagine what this has been like for you."

She nodded briskly. "At first it was unbearable. I cried for weeks. I don't think I got out of bed for two months. To be honest, I don't remember much of those early days. But Paul was there for me. Paul and Tyler and Chad. My family pulled through; they did. The thing is—now the worst thing has happened. Nothing worse than that can ever happen again."

There was still that warmth about her—that warmth that I loved—but her eyes were bright and hard in a way that was new. I saw, looking at her, that she'd been in hell, and she'd decided at a certain point to leave it. I didn't exactly know where she was now, as I sat with her at the dining table.

Then she told me about it. The night the police had shown up. How the knock had woken her; what it had felt like to open the door and see the officer standing on her doorstep, his hat in his hand. She'd known before he'd even said a word. She told me about seeing Charlie in the casket on the morning they'd buried him. That was the only time that morning she started to cry. When she described how he looked in the suit she'd chosen for him. "He was so handsome," she said, her voice breaking, and her hand moved instinctually toward the tissue box. "My baby boy."

Then she told me that she felt Charlie there with her all the time—when she was getting ready in the morning, in her car, at night before she went to bed. "The hard part is, we can't talk to each other anymore," she said.

But he was *here*, she told me. A song he loved would come on the radio; the sun would come out on a day it was supposed to rain; he appeared in her dreams. At first it sounded crazy to me, but then I realized I did it, too. I looked for proof of him all the time.

Paul never came in. I don't know if he had really been on an errand, or where he was—but it was just Faye and me the whole time. I could have listened to her talk all day. I wanted to know everything about Charlie. What had he been like as a child? Did she have photos of him? I'd only known him for a single year. I didn't ask her any of that, though, and at a certain point she looked up at the clock on the wall and said, "Oh my. That went quickly." She reached over and squeezed my hand. "I'm so glad I got to see you."

I felt a flash of hurt. I didn't want to leave. But of course I stood up. "Thank you for having me. It means a lot to be able to see you."

"Charlie knows, too. He's here, right now."

I nodded, but I didn't believe he was—not in the way she meant it. "I loved him so much," I said.

"He knows you did, sweetheart."

————————

That afternoon I made the walk I used to take all the time, from campus all the way down Gorham, to my old apartment. I hadn't been able to stop crying since I'd left Faye. It was strange crying. Sometimes bursts of sobs I couldn't hold back, followed by quiet tears that felt almost peaceful. A feeling of loss. One that I hadn't felt since my mother had left when I was thirteen.

We never spoke much about it after she was gone. I think it was easier to find solace in people on the outside. For my father: Monica. For Aaron: Haley. Ben and I were more all over the place. Dealing with each other's pain was too much for us—too close, too shameful.

I thought about what Faye had said about her family pulling through. Paul and Chad and Tyler. Did she really think of them as family, in the same way she thought of Charlie?

After Charlie had died, Tyler had changed his profile picture on Facebook to a photo of him and Charlie together as boys. He had captioned it: *Love you forever, bro.* I wondered what Charlie would have thought, seeing that photo. I wished he could see it. I wonder if that would have changed anything for him.

I had reached Norris Court. I sat down on one of the benches in the courtyard, where Charlie and I used to sit all the time. Memory shape-shifts after someone dies. I felt I was looking at him, at myself—those two people clinging to one another for dear life—from a long distance away. I saw the bad and the good. I didn't judge us—any of us.

Wilson was giving his reading in the Madison Public Library, in a different room than the one we'd given our MFA reading in. It was a block away from the capitol, about a ten-minute walk from my bed-and-breakfast. I planned to meet up with Vivian and Rohan beforehand, so we could all walk over together. As they walked toward me on East Johnson, holding hands, it was easy to imagine them together in Manhattan. They both walked quickly, talking—though mostly it was Vivian talking, Rohan laughing at what she was saying. Vivian looked the same, though with short hair now. Rohan hadn't changed much, either, except that his face looked rounder and he now had a full beard instead of scruff. He looked just as happy.

When I saw them, it wasn't jealousy that I felt—but a startling clarity. A jolt. All those Word documents on my computer suddenly seemed meaningless. They weren't real. Nothing was as real as the person beside you.

When Vivian and Rohan reached me, we all hugged and talked about the weirdness of being back, then continued down East Johnson, in the direction of the capitol.

Once we stepped inside the library, we spotted David, who was standing in the foyer next to a table that was stacked with copies of Wilson's book for sale.

David waved us toward him. He still had a mustache, but had shaved the beard, and was wearing a lot of wool and denim.

Then Wilson appeared, looking handsome and anxious in a dress shirt and slacks, and we all surrounded him. Rohan wanted Wilson to sign his book and David wanted to know how the tour was going and I complimented Wilson on his outfit.

"Let's get a photo," Vivian said, her voice rising above the oth-

I COULD LIVE HERE FOREVER

ers'. She handed an undergrad her phone. "Do you mind taking our photo?"

We all gathered together for a picture. Wilson and Vivian stood in the middle. Vivian had her arm looped around Wilson, her other arm more loosely around David. David's eyes were closed for the shot. I was on Wilson's other side, a goofy smile on my face, holding up my copy of his book. Rohan was kneeling in front of all of us, grinning, holding up two copies of Wilson's book in either hand.

"Say cheese," the undergrad said, as he held the phone out in front of us.

I saw the photo several hours later, after it had been uploaded to Facebook and Instagram, liked, loved, tagged, and commented on.

We all migrated into the room where Wilson would be reading. The space was full of people finding seats and mingling in the few minutes we had left before the reading would begin. All the MFA faculty were there, sitting in the front. I hugged Bea Leonard and Carla and was introduced to the current MFAs and the fellows and a new poetry professor. I was having all the standard *hello, how are you* conversations, but every few moments I'd remember that morning with Faye—a pinprick, over and over again in the back of my neck.

Vivian got up and introduced Wilson—a beautiful and personal introduction that spoke not only to Wilson's talents as a writer, but also about Wilson as a friend. "When we were all living here in Madison, Wilson was the one you called when you needed help, because you knew he would always pick up the phone. He was always there for you," Vivian said. I made a mental note to tell her that she, too, had this trait.

I knew that I was not reliable in this way. I was not somebody you could count on to always pick up the phone. I had a habit of disappearing. It was part of the reason I was so lonely, I was sure. My own doing.

Then Wilson walked up to the podium, his book in hand.

"I'm going to read from a story called 'Bad Weather,'" Wilson said into the microphone. He glanced up at us—the cohort. "I wrote the first draft of this story while I was living in Madison, so my friends who are here today know it, but it's pretty different now. Vivian, who just gave that really nice introduction, helped me a lot with it."

The story had changed, but what I loved most about Wilson's writing remained the same. He was funny. The room was laughing, but then out of nowhere there'd be a line or an observation so true and vulnerable, it would take your breath away.

Sitting in a room full of people listening to Wilson read was comforting—not having to talk or interact. Listening to his story made me feel less alone.

He read for about twenty minutes and then he opened it up for questions. People asked him how he came up with his ideas for stories; about his writing process; how autobiographical his work was; and when did he know a story was finished.

After the reading was over, we waited around while Wilson signed books, and then we decided to go to City Bar, for old times' sake.

"Damn," Rohan said, zipping up his coat as we walked toward the bar. "I forgot how cold this place is."

We made our way down State Street, huddled close to one another. We passed by a mass of girls in matching outfits and heels—

some sort of rushing event, and other, smaller groups of undergrads, drunk and rowdy, their nights already underway. As we passed by all the bars and late-night food places, they each gave off a soft, inviting glow. Inside, promises of warmth and beer. Everywhere seemed to be filled with people already having a good time—the very beginning of a Friday night.

I thought of the Nelsons' house in the suburbs and wondered what Faye and Paul were doing right now. If they'd gone out with friends, or stayed in. Had Faye cooked? Were they watching TV? Or had they already started to get ready for bed?

We arrived at City Bar and as we made our way down the staircase, we all began to laugh. It was funny, being back there. It smelled the same—like fried food and beer. And it looked the same. Even our table in the back—the big, high one with the stools—was empty and waiting for us. We rushed toward it, pulled in by the not-so-distant past.

We ordered food and drinks and sat around talking the way we used to, first about Wilson's book, and then about how writing was going for all of us, then more broadly about our lives—jobs, partners, families, varying degrees of feeling settled and not feeling settled. I felt love for my friends, being there with them, and I also felt myself growing quiet. That familiar tug returned; the sense of not quite fitting. A sadness in a moment when you were supposed to feel happy. It was a feeling I associated with being a kid, but it had followed me. Maybe it would be the kind of thing I'd always feel—or maybe one day I'd outgrow it. I was still pretty young.

I kept my phone turned up in my lap, even though I wasn't

expecting a call from anybody. I thought about Jade, how she'd decided to get back together with Fred. I wondered what she'd been able to read on my face that day in Starbucks. I could still recall the look that Vivian and Wilson exchanged, right here at City Bar, when I told them I was heading out early to meet Charlie. That look had hurt more than anything anyone had ever said to me about Charlie.

And right now—if Charlie were to call me up, and say, *Hey, come meet me on State Street in ten minutes, I have a surprise for you*—would I leave my friends? Would I go?

Of course, no call or text came through, and I spent the night with my friends, and had a nice time.

We walked home as a group, but this time, instead of dropping each other off at our old apartments, we dropped David off at the Marriott on the Square, and then Wilson off at his Airbnb on Hancock, and then Vivian and Rohan left me at my bed-and-breakfast on Gorham.

Vivian and I hugged good night and made plans to meet at Marigold's the next morning for brunch, just the two of us, so we could debrief—all the ways that everyone had changed and all the ways we were still the same. I wanted to tell her about my morning with Faye. It was a relief to me that Vivian had met Faye that time in the hospital. That when I would tell her the story, she would understand a little more. I'd never forgotten what she'd said that time about Charlie: *I see why you love him.*

By the time I climbed into bed, I was dizzy with exhaustion. I'd accidentally left my window open and the room was freezing. I yanked it shut, and then pulled the blankets over me—feeling, for the first time since I'd looked out at the lake that morning, peaceful. All day I'd been aching. Missing Charlie. As I was walking around the city, his ghost had been everywhere. Smoking outside of Norris Court, running around State Street in his puffy orange jacket, kneeling before me in front of Lake Mendota.

Now that I was alone, I could finally be with him. I turned off the lamp beside my bed, so the room was dark, and put the volume on my phone to low, in case the walls of the B&B were thin. I pulled up one of the first videos I'd ever taken of him, in my apartment, just days before Christmas. December 23, 2013. In the freeze-frame, Charlie was sitting cross-legged on the blue-and-white rug, leaning against the bad Craigslist chair, guitar in his lap, my computer open in front of him.

I pressed play on the video and Charlie's voice filled the room.

Should auld acquaintance be forgot
And never brought to mind?
Should auld acquaintance be forgot
And days of auld lang syne?

There he was. His fingers alive as ever on the strings of the guitar, the tilt of his head, the way his forehead creased on the high notes, those little lines between his eyebrows.

"This isn't very good," Charlie said at one point, looking up at me. His voice soft and gravelly, his eyes fogged over.

"I love it," came my voice, from behind the camera.

He smiled, then kept on going.

I watched the video, over and over and over.

Acknowledgments

I want to thank Kevin Jiang, who was the first reader of this novel and who gives me the courage to keep writing. Conversations with Andrew Ding about early drafts paved the way. To Lucy Tan, Jackson Tobin, Will Kelly, Piyali Bhattacharya, and Christian Holt—I am thankful for their notes, their insight, their friendship, and for Madison. Mike Broida read a draft with incredible care and thought, and his notes were invaluable.

Allison Lorentzen is a wise and compassionate editor, and I am so lucky to work with her. I am equally lucky to work with Margaret Riley King, who is a brilliant agent and steady support. Thank you to everyone at Viking for their tremendous work in bringing this book out into the world. I especially would like to thank Camille LeBlanc, Kristina Fazzalaro, Bel Banta, and Carolyn Coleburn. I would also like to thank Sophie Cudd at WME.

Thank you to friends who feel like home: Annie Golovcsenko, Deana LaFauci, Kate Woodcome, Laura Olivier, Daniella Lipnick, Lizzy Schule, Evan Jones, Anna Luberoff, Rebecca Luberoff, Rachel Dranoff, Ali Tager, and Jenna Bernstein.

To George, one of the most vibrant people I've ever known.

To Sam, for so much happiness.

Thank you to my parents, who always love and support me, and to my brother, Gabe, and my sister, Sofia, for being the best. Thank you to my grandmother Joan, who has encouraged my writing since the beginning.

Something Wild

A Novel

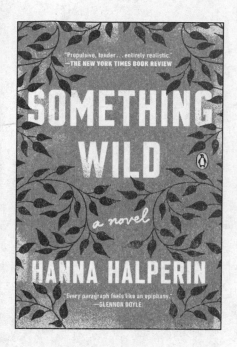

When Tanya and Nessa Bloom travel to the Boston suburbs to help their mother move out of their childhood home, they don't expect the visit to expose a new, horrifying truth: their mother is in a violent relationship. The sisters' differing responses to the abuse bring up their shared secret—a traumatic, unspoken experience that has shaped their lives. In the midst of this family crisis, they have no choice but to reckon with the past and face each other in the present, in the hope that there's a way out of the violence deeply ingrained in the Bloom family.

"Propulsive . . . good books sometimes cut to the bone, and this one feels like a scythe."
—*The New York Times Book Review*

 PENGUIN BOOKS